Angry Macey

Other Books by Jennifer Friess

The Riley Sisters Series

The Wind Could Blow a Bug

When You Least Expect It

Be Careful What You Wish For

Troll Gurl and the Cursed Kingdom

Angry Macey

By Jennifer Friess

Mr. Ugly-Man Entertainment
Adrian, Michigan

Mr. Ugly-Man Entertainment
Adrian, Michigan
First Edition October 2017
Text copyright ©2017 by Jennifer Friess
All Rights Reserved, including the right of reproduction in whole or in part in any form.
To book an event or to purchase additional copies, please visit:
imnotstalkingyou.com

ISBN 9780692946466

To all the Logans of the world who set the quiet girls' hearts afire.

OLD CRUSHES DIE HARD

I thought looking at you
would warm me with desire
like it used to
But instead anger boils inside me
Why her?
Why not me?
She isn't that pretty
She isn't a beauty queen
You could have had me,
any old day
I could have made two sons for you
I could have made you happy

Why are you still wearing
The same clothes you wore in high school?
Does she buy your clothes for you, too?
I would let you be whoever you wanted to be

I have my life
I am happy with it
But you will always be my
"What if"
What if he had asked me out?
...asked me to dance?
...known that I WAS ALIVE.

Your face used to bring me joy.
But now, I just want to punch it
For all the time I wasted pining for you
Stalking you
Loving you in a sick, one-sided way

Go, be with your cute kids
And your wife
And your COMBINED Facebook page
That she keeps the settings all private
and shit
Whatever.

I hate you.
I HATE you.

i love you.
FOREVER.

VAPOR

It doesn't matter.
Nothing matters.
Everything matters.

"Macey, you are late."

And that is how the second part of my life started, with those four little words.

I hadn't slept much the night before, which was par for the course. I was awake much of the night with worst-case scenarios playing out inside my brain. As I finally felt relaxed, my body lifting weightlessly to dreamland, I would be thrown back down to earth with vicious thoughts tearing at my sanity like tiny, pointy-toothed gremlins feasting off my soul. Thoughts of how badly I needed to keep this job that I truly despised assaulted me in the dark and quiet of night, flashing, exploding fireworks that sent my heart into palpitations and caused sweat to bead on my skin. It went on this way all night. The quest for sleep had been useless.

Those words, or just the fear of them, emitting from my boss's mouth would have started me into a giant anxiety cycle in a time as short as a few weeks ago. My stomach would cramp, my chest would tighten, and my brain would jump to a million doomsday scenarios.

But that day, a Tuesday, I could not bring myself to care.

I proceeded to move past her in the tiny, dim back hallway so that I could clock in. I had to push past her to reach my time card. There was actual body contact.

Ick.

It is not like I was here. Not mentally, anyway. The clock thunked, pressing the faded ink onto the manila card. It sounded as enthusiastic as I felt.

Brittany was younger than I by a good ten years. She wasn't quite young enough to be named after the pop singer, so it must have just been an annoying coincidence.

Brittany had ended up on the management track by default. I wondered if in the past employees had been promoted into positions of power because they actually possessed some of the traits a good supervisor should have. Maybe that had been the case back in the good ol' days of the 1950s where the workplace was dominated by men in hats surrounded by a haze of cigarette smoke.

Not Brittany. She had no skills to help in the management of the store except for expertly executing use of her employee discount. But somehow she had become one of several assistant managers merely by working at Cutter's longer than anyone else. She couldn't schedule, she couldn't inspire, she couldn't even be bothered to work weekends. Sure, Brittany was supposed to report to her own higher-up. But he was content to keep the Cutter's ship on the same slow course toward an impending iceberg.

Cutter's was a large chain department store, the name a shortened version of the phrase "cost cutters," but most of the shoppers never realized that or cared. Our store didn't need to be profitable. There were two hundred other locations across the country to absorb our loses.

Usually I enjoyed the lapses Brittany's leadership style afforded me. I was simply a peon as was everyone else who was under her. The difference was I cared about my job performance. I really couldn't help it. It was something that had been ingrained in me all these years. Even though I wasn't compensated enough to care, I did. I got stuck on the cash register a lot, mostly because I didn't resist as much as the other staff. Sometimes it seemed as though I spent half my life straightening credit card receipts with their stupid curly, slippery paper.

I felt like I was Brittany's assistant, taking care of the tasks I knew she didn't want to do and wouldn't do anyway. When corporate called for an urgent count on our slippers and Snuggies the last week before Christmas, she would give that task to me although she would send the numbers I collected in from her email account. And I knew from personal experience that any stock allocated from the head office at this late hour wouldn't arrive in time anyway.

Doing the assistant manager's grunt work gave me a tiny gleam of what I had once had at my previous job that was actually semi-rewarding. I was at the Frontier Central office for fourteen years. I never enjoyed my job, but the people were cool and I got to wear my jeans to work every day. I worked my way up from peon to lead peon to inventory shuffler. I had dreams of becoming a buyer, which was misguided because I had never used any of the outdoor equipment we sold. I made enough there to pay off my student loans, even if I never did put my bachelor's degree to good use. I had gone to work every day and appeared to have a life. But I was an office zombie. I was only going through the motions. I was there over a third of my life and already it seemed like a distant, hazy memory.

I had always been miserable, but at least there I had felt like myself inside. But now, this was a new level of disturbed. It was like when your foot falls asleep, and you begin to doubt if it is even attached to your body any longer. That was my sanity. There was all kinds of other noise happening in my brain, my heart, my soul; so much that I couldn't even think clearly. I would try to concentrate on work, but find out later I screwed up a truly simple task. I couldn't trust myself to do anything right anymore. I would try to leave the house with the stove on or put the wet clothes in the dryer and not even start it.

I hated this new me, this shell I had become. My outside had never been great anyway. The only thing I ever had going for me (or against me) was a little bit of weird splattered like fluorescent paint on the inside. Oh, I didn't know how much longer I could keep up this charade of caring about prices and items and widgets and signs. Didn't anyone else ever want to stop in the middle of the day at their job and just scream and throw things? I'm pretty sure whatever kept our species in line was breaking in me, cracking and crumbling away more each day. Soon my self-control would be gone. I could feel it leaving me now. It might not hold out throughout the day. And when it went, whoever was nearby better watch the fuck out.

What I had actually been seeking over the past several months was someone to advise me to give it up, to quit. And Lexie McCrae, née Marks, my oldest, best, and only friend, was that person. Yet I still stayed because it seemed like the responsible thing. But in the end my inner voice finally screamed loud enough that I heard it and could no longer doubt it. The clock sounded its low, bored thud, snapping me out of my reverie to realize she was still standing there, for no apparent reason.

"Don't you have anything to say for yourself." Brittany's inflection said it wasn't a question.

She was power-tripping me. I didn't have enough respect for her for that to work. She was an adult in age only. She had worked here since she was straight out of college. She didn't understand group dynamics or teamwork or how individuals could still thrive together even in an unhealthy work environment. Brittany only knew this Cutter's bubble and all the ways she had managed to play it to her benefit over the years. She had never been in the real world. She had never had to find a new job after a layoff, then an extended period of unemployment. She had never sat in an interview, knowing she would not be hired because she had too much experience and the employer assumed she would want a higher salary, without ever asking or considering how desperate she might be.

These were some of the significant differences between Brittany and I.

A conversation from last week popped into my head. One I had forgotten even having until now.

"You need to take your job, and the mystery shoppers, seriously."

Mystery, or secret, shoppers were designed to ensure customer quality by spying on the customer service staff without their knowledge. Except, well, sometimes we did know.

I had gotten a low score. I hadn't been a creeper and called them by their name that I was supposed to memorize off of their credit card. If I actually had a photographic memory, I would use it to memorize their credit card number and take myself on an online shopping spree. I also didn't feel it necessary to pester them with the specials for the week. We weren't a fancy restaurant. We sold warm sushi and cold soup, tampons and enemas.

"You know, I used to be the kind of girl to worry myself sick about secret shoppers. Being that girl almost killed me." I was always an honest person. But this was the first occasion I had ever been honest to the point of risking my job. But it felt good.

I didn't mention that the two times I was evaluated prior I had gotten a perfect score. Brittany's loyalties were only as good as your last shopped score.

I considered punching her in the face and dropping her to the floor, right here.

I inhaled in surprise. I had never punched anyone in my life. But I truly believed I was so angry that I could floor her now if I tried. Would probably break my thumb though; I could never remember if it was supposed to go inside or outside when you folded your fingers to make a fist.

"Well?" Her voice was full-on snotty.

That was it. Realization washed over me. I would rather be homeless than come to this den of negativity one more day.

And that thought set me free.

The only sound I could hear was the time clock clicking over to another minute.

"Go to hell."

I didn't even bother to watch the shock register on her face. I simply reached over her shoulder, punched myself back out, and turned and walked away. I disappeared. I was vapor.

PURGATORY

I was free! I was screwed!

I cried in the car all the way home. I had never been homeless. How did they take a shower or do their laundry or get a job with no home address?

The answer to all those things was probably "They don't."

It seemed to be a surprise to both Brittany, by the shocked look on her face, and myself that I had had the guts to walk out.

I was at the beginning of a mental break or mid-life crisis; whatever you want to call it. I would never visit a doctor to get a name for it.

My life went from black and white to static. I went from the desire for happiness in my life to the belief that it would never exist for me. Ever.

The clouds had been shedding their dandruff since dawn. The wind was blowing the powdery dust around. It was collecting in the corner by the front door of my apartment, as it always did. When the sun came out next, the snow would melt and run under my door, wetting my carpet, permeating my living room with a mildew odor. But at this juncture, I wasn't sure I ever believed that the sun would come out for me again. I experienced this every winter when my seasonal affective disorder would hit me in full force, always surprising me with its devastation. It had probably played a part in my sudden departure from work. How big a part, I would never know. I hoped my gut had been the louder voice that day, leading to my questionable action.

I spent a week in bed being depressed. Then another week doing the things I didn't have time to do when I worked, such as taking walks and car rides on country roads. But walking against the biting wind was not pleasant. I did not enjoy driving on the slippery roads with my bald tires and my oil light glowing, mocking me.

Then the next week I got hungry and started applying to jobs. Any job I could find; I could always try to upgrade later.

That is what the voice of reason said in my head. But my heart said I didn't want to end up in the same situation I had just gotten out of. So, I eliminated many potential jobs by not applying. More by not going to all the interview requests I received. If I were on unemployment, I would be required to go to receive my pity money. Because I quit, I didn't qualify. I told myself I wasn't genuinely turning them down by not calling them back. But my anxiety knew different.

* * * * *

It took me forever to fall asleep. The cold had seeped into my bones and no amount of blankets could warm me up again. Sometimes I was shivering so badly I would take my temperature, fearing that I was ill. And it wasn't only happening because it was winter. I had the same problem in June. It was simply another way that I was defective. Add it to the list with all the others: seasonal affective disorder, depression, anxiety, cutting, stomach issues.

I needed to hide. Hide from everything outside that door that made me feel like this. But anxiety didn't work that way. It followed you into your home and into your bed and wouldn't shut up just because you told it to. It might take every bit of remaining sanity you have to contain that while trying to check out at the grocery store while the cashier asks you, "Do you want your candy bar left out?" It is the one millionth time you have been asked that. The answer has always been and forever shall be "no." This poor customer service worker doesn't know that. She is trying to bide her time so that she can head home at the end of the day to let out her crazy.

I understood off-handedly that if I ate something other than garbage food that this feeling may someday go away. But the time for resolutions seemed as though it had already past.

Knowing that everyone quite possibly might feel this way did not help. And how could other people feel this way? I couldn't picture anyone but me heading home at night and melting into a pile of snot and tears.

No, only I.

* * * * *

Even if I manage to have a good experience, it is gone sooo fast. All moments are fleeting; just a tiny specific speck in time. Everything is a memory; some just have not happened yet.

Sometimes I put my earbuds into my ears and turn up the music really loud. Why did I use earbuds when I lived alone, you ask? It seemed to work better to drown out the voices that bitched at me inside my head.

I can only sleep a few hours at a time. And even those few moments of regenerative peace produced by my own body are betrayed by itself, sandwiched between two lengthy episodes of attacks, so strong that it ends up negating the actual episode of sleep altogether. It seems the only way for me to get rest would be to borrow someone else's sane, properly functioning body for a while. Know anyone like that? Cuz I sure as hell don't.

I finally broke down and bought some sleeping pills. Over the counter, harmless unless you gobble a handful.

Not that I would ever think of doing that.

The pills take an hour or more to take effect before they pull you under. It is both a relief and a panic.

I find myself thinking, *What if I never come back?*

The aid for sleep leaves me groggy in the morning. Solve one problem, create another. It seemed like that was how things always went for me. I tried taking a shower & eating some food to rouse me, but that didn't help. In the shower it seemed as though I was washing my legs at a mile a minute. The clock told a different story, laughing at my sluggishly-clumsy, drugged movements. Only caffeine helped. Thank God for energy drinks.

I liked the sleeping pills. I continued to take them, figuring that drugged was good. It took away all my emotions.

Of course, it took away all my motivation as well.

* * * * *

Anxiety.

It is a pain inside; no one can see it, it won't show up on any medical test. It is only me grunting and moaning and crying out in pain as my chest tightens more and more in relation to the increasingly desperate images my brain cooks up.

Anxiety ran in my veins, much like other people had blood flow through theirs. It made me curious to slice open a wrist and see what would come out: bright red, iron-rich blood or doubts and worries and sewage.

I have no real reason for my anxiety. I was never physically abused (mentally, maybe). I was never a soldier. Never kidnapped. Never disfigured with acid because of my religious practices. I am just broken. I wish humans had a warranty. I would totally take my ass back in. As the tears slipped down my cheeks, I realized I must indeed be as weak and hopeless as everyone always thought.

I remembered I had a half-empty (I was a pessimist through and through) bottle of vodka still sitting in the door of my refrigerator since god knows when. I had a can of frozen orange juice in my freezer. If I mixed it with warm water, it might thaw enough that I could make myself a screwdriver. My life already was in shambles. Why not develop a drinking problem as well? That was a goal that Lexie would not approve of.

* * * * *

In the months after I walked off of my only source of income I began to have a reoccurring dream, every few weeks or so.

I was standing at the edge of a jungle, attempting to look up at the sun, but it was so bright it hurt my eyes. It was so painful, they began to tear up. It squeezed my heart. I tried to look away. There seemed to be teal water in front of me, but a big white bar of blindness prevented me from seeing it clearly, a side effect of looking straight at our nearest star. I turned to my right, where there was a guy with brown hair sun-bleached blond wearing shorts and a T-shirt, a button-down short-sleeved shirt open over the top and blowing in the marine wind. But I couldn't see his face either, due to the sun blindness. He was walking toward me with deliberate steps. Was he reaching out for me?

Then I woke up, always, my tears spilling onto the pillow and my heart constricting. Why couldn't I at least get to enjoy the beautiful scenery, including the hunky guy, for even a few minutes in my dreams? It is not like I could ever experience that in the real world. That sure didn't look like the shore of Lake Huron and there was no man in my life right now, except the obese landlord wanting my rent to be paid. If I met him on a beach I might try to drown him in the undertow.

* * * * *

I usually didn't apply for employment to the same establishments a second time. If they didn't think I was good enough the first time around, why would I bother to waste all that energy filling out their online application again? I was excellent at holding grudges. But there were a few businesses within walking distance of my home that I couldn't resist resubmitting to. These included Take Me Home, the video rental store, and Gas & Guzzle, the gas station. Although I had applied to the gas station probably four times over the past three years without receiving any response, I couldn't resist showing up when I saw a sign for open interviews posted on their billboard in big, black plastic letters. Everyone waiting in their best clothes to head into the gloomy back room lined with metal storage shelves stacked with inventory for their interview with the manager. I was standing in a line with kids less than half my age, feeling like cattle headed to slaughter.

That is when one fellow applicant and I struck up a friendly conversation.

"You had to wait so long that you got hungry?" I asked him, eyeing the stick of beef jerky he had purchased a minute ago and was unwrapping.

"Ya. You want half?"

I shook my head in the negative. My unreliable stomach was already starting to churn in anticipation of the interview. I couldn't imagine how irritable that bright red meat stick would make my bowel. I was tempted to buy a candy bar, but I had already had one this morning. It had been a candy bar for breakfast kind of day.

"That was a bad idea," he began a few minutes later. "That jerky had Tabasco on it."

"Now you are going to have to buy a drink."

"That is how they get you."

I chuckled. He was obviously not someone who had had to ever plan out his gastrointestinal interactions.

It turned out the backroom of the Gas & Guzzle was not as exciting as I had imagined. I thought the interview went really well, but I never heard from the manager again. I did learn one thing by attending the open interview: the previous manager didn't like to hire, so he had never looked at any of the online applications. That would have been comforting, except for the fact that this manager had seen my application and talked to me and she still didn't deem me worthy to work there.

I chalked it up to being placed in the "overqualified" box yet again. They saw college degree and assumed I would never stay long. That showed how little they knew. I could be their next manager.

I hated my job at Frontier Central, but I had loyally stayed there for fifteen years. Employees valued each other there. Coworkers had given me nicknames. Lexie often said I talked about the place as others reminisced about college. Sometimes I still flashed back to Frontier, like some kind of echo of past drug use.

I could have been the best damn employee Gas & Guzzle ever had.

Or maybe I would have told off the manager and stormed out one day, as I had at Cutter's. I no longer was in control of my emotions. They ruled me. To think any different was kidding myself.

After I spend time with people, I always have trouble falling asleep because I replay everything I said in my head and think how stupid I was.

I hate this. I hate all of this. I hate feeling like everything I do, every step I take, every dollar I make is a mistake. My head gets hot and throbs. My brain begins to vibrate. The vibration makes me nauseous. I can feel my skull unhinging from itself.

Getting up from my bed, I gave up any hope of sleeping tonight. I went into the kitchen, pouring myself a glass of sweet bliss. On my way home from the interview I had picked up a new bottle of vodka and some Juicy-O, a highly-processed orange juice inspired drink that contained only ten percent juice, to mix with it as Lexie and I had done as teenagers. I assumed it was cheaper than real orange juice. I was too lazy to do the number comparison. If I couldn't get a job, how could I manage to do simple, food-based calculations?

Soon the alcohol provided me a comforting warmth that radiated through my body, like a fireplace on a cold winter's night.

I can't remember what seemed so important.

Ha! I can't remember my own name.

Is that what my laughter sounds like?

When was the last time that I laughed?

* * * * *

Another month passed. I wished Lexie could stop over. Spending time with her was like slipping on a well-worn denim jacket, the soft material caressing my skin. That was Lexie; she soothed my frayed nerves, calming them.

It was cold and rainy outside. I wouldn't blame Lexie for not wanting to leave the house to visit me. The actual reason was that her kids were finishing winter sports and having academic and sports awards nights at school, which seemed to overlap with the spring sports season commencing. It all seemed like a clusterfuck to me. I didn't know how those children did all those activities, could stand all that interaction.

The feeling that most people must get when they walk into a new classroom on the first day of school—unsure where to sit, what classmates might be future friend or foe—that is how I felt all the time. I'm sure for everyone else it goes away. But I could feel the same way after the hundredth time walking through that door: all my nerves tingling; my body on alert, its temperature rising; my blood pressure increasing. It is like a tiny band is playing inside their own hell. No wonder I never liked school.

How could I trust my gut feeling about anything when it was obviously overactive and broken? It tells me there is danger around every corner. If that was true, I might as well just kill myself now.

There were no more walks or resolutions for better health, even though the weather was no longer as cold. Job hunting had become my full-time job; one that didn't pay. In fact, it cost more money to job hunt than to sit at home and do absolutely nothing. I had to buy a new interview shirt. The best I could find on short notice was a shimmery button-down. There was one in a beautiful rose color that reminded me of my favorite hoodie, but of course they did not have one in my very average and popular size. I ended up with a beige one. No wonder I never got called back; I blended into the conference room walls. When I tried to wear it, it gaped between the buttons at my breasts. I was desperate for a job, but not that desperate—yet. So I had to buy some fashion tape to hold it together. I had seen some a month earlier at the dollar store, but it was gone by now. I ended up ordering some online, which of course only came as a two-pack plus shipping. Anyone else would have merely used two-sided Scotch tape, but I was worried it would leave a residue on my clothes, which would be bad as these were my only respectable ones I owned.

There was the cost of printer ink to print resumes and cover letters, postage for those that needed to be mailed, copies, gas to drive to interviews, phone cards for my cell phone so that people could call me, parking garage costs, and dry cleaning for my black blazer that I splattered strawberry yogurt on. I should have known better than to open one of those kid-sized tubes of yogurt with the cartoon characters on the label while wearing it.

I should have known better about everything.

* * * * *

On Friday I had another interview. It was at a temp agency for a factory job. It was a last-ditch effort sort of thing. I had been able to talk myself into it when I had answered the advertisement. It was a bread factory, how bad could it be? They made food, so it couldn't be dirty. On the phone they *had* mentioned it could get very hot. Only overnight shifts were available. When I was in college, I used to stay up all night all the time; it never bothered me. But now it was seventeen years later. If I tried to drive past 10:00PM it was a fight to not to fall asleep.

As I sat up all night Thursday, clicking through infomercials on the television, I could not make the factory scenario work in my head. I had walked through factories before, ones where my dad had worked or famous brand-name food factory tours. But the thought of being abandoned in the middle of all that, an island among noise and machines, frightened me. I knew it was a first world problem. It was probably a job I *could* do, if I could manage to settle my nerves. But I didn't want to do it. By 6:00AM I was in hysterics over it, so I called the only person I had.

"Hello? Why are you calling at this hour? Did you get a job?"

"No. I have an interview today, but I can't," I gasped for air between sobs, "bear to go."

"Why?"

"It is for a factory. A big, scary factory. I am not a factory kind of girl."

"I know. But have you actually seen the place? Is it even that scary?"

"No. But the images in my head are."

"No. No! Jackie, put that down. Brody, please eat your breakfast. And find a shirt." Lexie sighed. "Sorry, I am trying to get them ready for school. But you know I am always here for you, right?"

"Yes. That's why I called. I was up all night. I just can't go. I can't do it."

"What do they make at this factory?"

"Bread."

"You shouldn't be scared of a bread factory."

"I know, but they want me to take drug tests and wear safety glasses and remove my earrings. I am not used to that. That wasn't how it was at Frontier Central."

"Jackie, stop putting cereal in your brother's pants. Brody, Brody! I told you to find a shirt," Lexie scolded. "It may take a while to find a new job like the one you had at Frontier Central."

"I know. I wish they hadn't gone out of business."

"But you hated it there."

"I know, but I was used to it."

"Brody. Brody! Please get your baseball gear together. And for the love of God, find a shirt. I'm not going to tell you again."

"Look, Macey. If it doesn't feel right, don't take it."

That rang with a kernel of truth to me. I had taken the job at Cutter's even though no part of it had matched the criteria I was looking for. At that time I had been looking for full-time work with a short commute. I wanted it to pay at least as much as my unemployment had been. But it had been part time with no promise of ever increasing to full time. I often drove the hour commute, only to be sent home after four hours if it was a slow day. At a smidge above minimum wage, those scant hours barely covered my gas money. See where being conscientious had gotten me?

"The right job will come along for you," she reassured me.

"Jackie, put on your coat. Put on your backpack. Brody, shirt buddy. Please. Sorry Macey, I gotta run."

"No problem, thanks. It was good to talk it out."

" 'Bye."

"Bye."

I held on to the hope of a perfect job as I hung up. I didn't feel any better. I actually believe I was twenty times worse, but now I was resolute that I would not go to that interview. How I felt now, I didn't think I could make it out the door ever again. I had found only one way to calm my nerves of late. I moved to the refrigerator. I took out the bottle of vodka and the Juicy O that were the only items in there and poured them both into a glass. Tipping the glass up, I drank it all down in one gulp. The familiar burn of the citric acid crept down my throat, followed by the uncomfortable warmth of the alcohol.

I didn't leave the house for the rest of the weekend.

* * * * *

Caring hurts too much.

Not caring is easier, because you are simply numb.

But it's hard, because your human heart still yearns to.

Even in sleep, I could not achieve peace. I was plagued by bad dreams within restless nights. The alcohol consumption only made it worse, and it was only exacerbated by the increase in alcohol use and the move into abuse. But it seemed worth the restless nights to relieve some amount of the pain during the daylight hours.

Spiders were crawling inside my skin. I grabbed my arms and dug at them, but all I did was rip the top layer of my epidermis with my neglected fingernails. I didn't even bleed. The wounds began to weep, which only stung the tender injuries as they tried to form a protective barrier against the cruel world but failed. There was nothing that could protect me anymore.

I grabbed the plastic cup I had gotten from a MacRonnell's Kiddie Meal off my nightstand. The kid's meals were cheaper than ones for adults, and sometimes you got new, character-themed household goods as a bonus. Entering the kitchen, I mixed myself more Frooty-Aid drink mix and vodka. All forms of OJ had become too expensive. I drank it down in gulps as big as I could stand. I had learned to like the fuzzy numbness alcohol granted, but never the taste. I went back and sat in front of the television. I no longer cared that I couldn't come up with any questions for Alex Trebek. He had them all in front of him anyway. He didn't need me to help.

Sure, I would possibly feel better if I went outside and got some fresh air once in a while. But it seemed more comfortable to sit on the couch and escape into the worlds presented to me by my magic light box. If I let myself remember what my real life was like, I would have a panic attack. I wanted to distance myself from that for as long as possible. I was trying to avoid those at all costs, even at the expense of not having any feelings at all, even joyful ones.

Other people might wonder how I could be happy watching twenty hours of television every day. But it had always been a comfort to me. The characters' loves and losses kept me from dwelling on my own. When I was young, I had always thought if I found myself not needing to spend time going to work every day that I could easily sit and watch television constantly, probably for up to a year, before I got sick of it. Presently, I was proving myself right.

Why did I keep finding myself watching Disney sitcoms about tweens as they navigated the hallways of school? Why did I put myself through this torture? Did I think by living those years over and over again that I could improve something? My life never looked like the brightly colored ones on the television screen, the characters gliding effortlessly through the tiny obstacle put forth in front of them in each episode.

I woke up at 3:00AM. I instantly ran through a list in my head of all the utilities that were overdue, even before I had opened my eyes to glare at the red digital numbers glowing at me, the eyes of a dragon within the dark. I had a headache. Probably a combination of too much alcohol, too little food, and dehydration. Nothing I could do about the bills, but there was something I could do about the headache. I took two ibuprofen, washing it down with more Frooty-Aid and vodka. I knew it wasn't good to mix the two—pain relievers and alcohol, I mean. But what was the worst that could happen? I would die. That would be a welcome change to this living hell, wouldn't it? I looked at my vodka bottle. It was almost empty. I would have to head to the store tomorrow to get another. I had to leave the house. I had a reason to live. I didn't want to die and rot in the ground. I didn't want to stop having my inner monologues, even if they got low ratings from even me.

So, then I fought to stay awake, fearing death. About 5:00AM I fell asleep once more, only to wake up to Lexie banging on my door.

"Open up. I know you are in there. This is Matthew Perry and I want to make sweet love to you," she was lying as I pulled open the door.

"Shows what you know. I want it hot and dirty with him."

"Ew, I don't ever understand what you find attractive about him. And why are you still asleep at noon? Didn't you get my message? I tried to set up an interview for you today," Lexie rambled. The bright sun shining behind her was distracting, piercing into my sore eyeballs like hot needles.

"It's not noon," I whined.

"11:48AM counts as noon in my book. People who want to be productive adults in the world are awake by now. Even college kids are awake by now, at least to feed."

"Maybe you are thinking of vampires."

"No, they burn in the sun."

"Well, so do I."

"I ran into Mindy, my old manager from the Value Emporium. She said she had an opening for someone to put away stock on third shift. I tried to give her your name, but she wanted you to call her personally. She is only available to interview with today because she departs on a cruise to the Caribbean tomorrow and will be gone for two weeks."

"The Caribbean? At least we know they pay well there."

"No. Her husband is a lawyer. But I thought it could be a start. There wouldn't be many customers there overnight. You could still come home and sleep the day away, if that is your desire."

"Ha, ha. You are so funny."

"It is probably too late to connect with her now."

"That's fine."

"Suit yourself," Lexie proclaimed as she dropped herself down onto my couch. She bounced me when she sat, sinking in where the springs were broken. It was unavoidable, as her rear, always ample, had spread a bit more as each child came along. Somehow, she always wore the extra weight with confidence and sex appeal.

"You have no idea how lucky you are to live alone," she began. I wondered where this could be going.

"The only messes you have to clean up are the ones you create. You are not a slave to three other human beings and two dogs. There is always someone placing demands on me, even Colin. And when the kids are gone to school, I am at work. I never have one moment of peace to myself. Do you have any idea what I would give to live how you do?"

I almost laughed at her, the statement was so bizarre. What did she envy, exactly? My massive debt? My piles of unwashed dishes? The unending loneliness that would overcome me again as soon as she stepped back out the door?

* * * * *

I had had to make one hundred percent of all my decisions myself for so long. Sure, I usually annoyed Lexie by consulting her, but in the end I would do what I needed to do. I won't lie, this kind of aggravated her, especially when the situation played out badly when I went against her advice. But she never said "I told you so" and always provided guidance again the next time a situation arose and I inquired with her. It was so stressful to make all the choices. Especially when it felt like every time I chose wrong. Go with my head and logic and be miserable? Or go with my heart and throw responsibility and common sense out the window? It was a catch-22, one that could drive a person mad. And maybe it indeed had.

Once my only desire had been to make my own decisions, to be in control of my life. But now I was so exhausted. I would give everything for it all to be removed from my weak grasp. I had spent years making plans and budgets and goals and spreadsheets. Now they lay broken behind me like a road of gravel that I never wanted to look back on, jagged pieces stretching out to meet the horizon. And I could no longer move forward, having finally come to the end of the world. Galileo was wrong; the world in front of me was indeed flat. In fact, I was standing on the edge of the cliff to nothingness. One step forward and I would fall into the abyss forever. If I even raised one foot and stood there like that until the one supporting my weight got too tired, it would not even have to be a conscious decision.

Where would I end up? Would my soul cease to exist as I had always suspected? Would Lexie find my body rotting away on my couch? Would the landlord? Would he violate my cold corpse? He seemed like the kind of sicko that would do that. Or would I truly disappear? Is that what happened to all the missing persons mentioned in passing on the nightly news and posted on the bulletin board at the grocery store? Had they also traveled a troubling road, one where they could not come back over their damaged dreams and wrecked lives, where they had no choice but to fall off the cliff? Maybe I was not the only one.

I concentrated on taking solace in this thought, of a community of lost souls, as I drank three more vodka and

Frooty-Aids and then proceeded to sleep away the rest of the annoying daytime hours.

* * * * *

It was truly amazing how fast financial security could be flushed right down the crapper. Two years ago all three of my credit cards were paid off, I had emergency savings, a stellar credit score, and a bad-ass emergency kit. It was stocked with canned food, medical face masks, first-aid supplies, and even a respirator and a hard hat. Lexie used to joke that if disaster hit, she would grab her kids and head straight to my house to take cover. And because she said that, I may have even made sure to have a little extra in case that scenario ever did play out.

I had already gotten behind on bills when I was working part time, instead of full time. Now, being unemployed with no income, I was only getting further behind. The guilt over not being able to meet my obligations was a weight that pressed on my chest every minute of the day. And if I actually let myself dwell on it for an extended period of time, I could not even catch my breath. My body covered itself in a sheen of sweat while my blood pressure rose, dizziness overcoming me. Then I wondered if a panic attack could lead to a heart attack or a stroke. It sure seemed like one. And I was no spring chicken anymore. And my family heart history was pretty appalling.

Heavy breathing ensued, with breaks only long enough for me to chant "Oh God. Oh God. Oh God." Someone eavesdropping outside my window would never know if I was having a panic attack or an orgasm.

I found the liquor could muffle the anxiety, if not completely silence it. I had begun making my Frooty-Aid with stolen sugar packets from fast food restaurants.

Oh, I couldn't afford to eat there. I simply walked in, used the restroom, then went out into the lobby and shoved as many napkins, condiments, and plastic cutlery into my hoodie pockets as I could. I always broke out into a sweat, automatically assuming an employee would confront me on my way back out the door. Sure, these things were set out to be taken... for paying customers. But I never encountered any trouble. I forgot that the employees were pimply-faced kids and grey-haired grandmothers. They couldn't risk breaking a finger before the big game or a hip by confronting an unstable customer. They weren't paid enough to care.

Many nights I considered being the mad woman who holds up the place through the drive-thru, demanding only nuggeted chicken. The fact that I didn't own a gun always stopped me. Maybe I should get one from the toy store and pry off that orange barrel cover. Maybe I could fool someone.

Now I had maxed out all the credit cards to pay my bills, and they were all past due. My savings was only a memory. I gave up having a good credit score and was simply trying to not lose my utilities.

I could sell my car for quick cash. It was paid off. But distances between towns were long and public transportation was non-existent. How would I ever be able to reclaim my life if I wanted to, living out here in rural America with no car?

And if the zombie apocalypse hit tomorrow, I would be very vulnerable. My edible supplies had all been ingested months ago, the flashlight batteries transferred to remote controls and clocks, the trial-sized tubes of toothpaste decremented for everyday use.

* * * * *

The Christmas bell tied precariously to the door jingled as I pushed it open, announcing my arrival. It didn't care that it was out of season. I strolled in, avoiding eye contact with the sales associate milling about behind the counter. I couldn't remember the last time I ate something. My stomach was sloshing. I could no longer avoid it. It was time to come to the store and return empty bottles to buy a candy bar for sustenance.

The little bell rang out again. I wondered if it ever got too tired and wanted to give up. I covertly ducked behind the racks of chocolate and nougat I so desperately craved, suddenly aware I was in my flannel pajama pants and the hoodie with the rotten cuffs that I had stopped wearing outside of the house years ago. I wondered how greasy my hair looked. I hadn't bothered to look in a mirror in a while.

A man in a flannel shirt and a beard entered. I guessed he was a construction worker. I was invisible to him as he grabbed two forty ounce cans of beer, a bag of chips, a package of hot dogs, and a bottle of ketchup. A dinner to be consumed in front of the television, I surmised. It seemed like an exhausted payday Friday kind of meal. I wondered if he would even bother to heat up the dogs. Maybe it wasn't only me. Maybe all single persons' lives revolved around the party store. A sad thought, indeed.

I noticed the setting sun seemed to glint off more cars than usual passing through the traffic light just beyond the door as the bearded stranger left. Yup, definitely a Friday. I suddenly felt even worse about my situation. My days were all the same. They were all a void. Lacking... everything people needed to thrive. I had stopped being "people" a long time ago. I grabbed two candy bars off the rack and sidled up to the register.

"Miss Macey, the usual?" I shook my head in acknowledgement as he turned and removed the bottle of clear liquor from the shelf. His skin was chestnut, making the white of his eyeballs and teeth stand out. They glowed within his head. I had no idea what his name was. I had never asked. He only knew mine off of my credit card. He had such a thick accent that when I first started coming here, I never knew what he was saying to me; I would only nod my head. Now I understood almost every word. How many visits did that equate to? How many bottles of vodka?

On the counter sat a cardboard display of tiny flavored cigars. I had been known to burn through that very same kind when I was in college. I picked out two, adding them to my order.

When I got home I removed the cellophane off of one of the individually wrapped cigars. I held it to my nose and something fluttered in me merely by the smell. I had snuck cigarettes sometimes when I still lived at home. It established smoking in my consciousness as a "forbidden" activity, even when I was emancipated and of legal age. That perception was still ingrained in me. I placed the plastic end in my mouth and held the lighter to the other. I inhaled expectantly. It was an instant rush of nicotine and carcinogens. It improved my mood right away. I alternated my Frooty-Aid and vodka with drags on my cigar.

How pathetic was I that a cigar gave me the dangerous thrill that others got from sky diving or bungee jumping?

* * * * *

Lexie texted me one morning. I don't know which one; they all ran together.

Got some bad news 2 tell u.
I wantd 2 tell u all wk, but didn't want u 2 b mad @me.

A tremor of terror charged down my spinal cord, the effects making my extremities tingle with fear.

Oh no, I thought. This was it. Her husband Colin had wanted to move her to Minnesota, closer to his family, for quite a while now. If Lexie left me, that would surely be it. She was the last thread of the rope I held onto every day to still connect me to this god-forsaken planet. If she cut me loose, I would simply be free-floating out in space, stuck in a rotation that I would have no control over.

We r headed out of town 4 the week.
I hope u can make it that long without me : -(:-)

Good old Lexie. She knew I needed her. She was worried about leaving me for seven days. She would never, ever leave me permanently. She knew that I was too fragile to handle that.

Need me 2 check on the hs while ur gone?

The mere thought of leaving my living room made my breaths quicken at the emotional effort of re-entering the world outside my front door.

Nope. Already got it covered.

I knew I could not reciprocate and be a good friend to Lexie anymore. Part of me didn't even care. I often found myself interrupting her statements with my own, usually not even related to what she was conveying to me, but what apprehension had decided to trot through my head right then. I recognized this bad behavior in myself, but I could not stop it. No wonder we found ourselves talking less and less.

There is a normal anxiety I am guessing everyone else feels when they walk into a job interview. Then there is the kind I used to feel that was at a level that made me be scared of things that were perfectly normal, like ordering food at a bowling alley. Then there was what I felt now; a guitar string being tightened and tightened, any second knowing it could snap into curly metal pieces of uselessness. You might say I felt—high-strung. That same note was being plucked over and over in my head. It really was insufferable. I don't know how much longer I could go on like this without having to find a way to put an end to it. For now I was still dulling it with liquor and television. But that wasn't enough anymore either.

"I don't feel good" I found myself saying each morning to the beige walls of my apartment. Then throughout the mornings. And then all through the day. And it was true. It was not one malady that hurt, like an ankle or finger, but a general malaise that throbbed throughout each part evenly. Just a dull ache you would not think much of until you realized it had been that way for a week and all that minor discomfort had worn down your brain so that you were exhausted, yet cannot sleep. I was feeling suffocated by uncompleted responsibilities, but I had no energy to devote to the tasks. Everything made me want to bust out in tears. The life around me was ugly & gray & should not be mine. It was all wrong.

I hated the beige walls. It was tinged with another, even more horrible color. It was hard to place. Pink, that was it. Beige mixed with a nasty bismuth pink. I had always wanted to repaint them, but never had. I didn't want to do anything to risk losing the return of my security deposit, although I had no plans to move anywhere else. Hell, at this rate my next stop was going to be living in my car. I had wasted five years of my life staring at a color I hated for no justifiable reason. It made me angry. Angry enough to go to the store and buy something bright and cheery and throw it on the wall. Who needed brushes right?

Well, almost angry enough. Anxiety told me it wasn't worth the risk of leaving the house. *Anything* could happen outside that door.

And something else whispered to me.

What is the point of doing? What is the point of trying? Or of being?

* * * * *

SICK

I feel so sick. It is the anxiety sickness, I know this. If I could simply summon a positive thought, it would lessen or go away all together. But that is not happening. Some people think you can just "choose to be happy." Some people have made lucrative careers making books and DVDs about such topics. In my experience, that has never been the case. My stomach is in knots. I feel like I need to throw up. But not the kind where you puke up tainted coleslaw and then you feel better, even as the cabbage bits cling to your bile-soaked lips. No, I feel like if I could actually vomit, my heart is what would come out. Maybe *that* would make me feel better.

My insides were the consistency of greasy chicken noodle soup, boiling with anger and indecision. Someday I would jab a sizeable knife into my gut and quiet it all. Unfortunately, today wasn't the day. I wasn't that desperate just quite yet. But tomorrow looked like severe depression with a chance of bloody.

I know how Kurt Cobain felt. I want to kill myself to end the stomach pain. Or at least stab a hole in my stomach to act as a pressure release valve.

* * * * *

Sober feels as unknown to me as well-rested.

My soul feels like a Michigan winter day, despite the fact spring had actually sprung outside beyond my closed curtains. The gray clouds close in on me. My anxiety & depression form a double-helix of hell that I can't get relief from, especially with sleep.

What if depression is your body's way of telling you that you have been on the wrong path for too long?

There was one good thing about it, I laughed to myself, my voice sounding hollow and haunting. The depression was a refreshing change from the anxiety. While anxiety allowed for at least a degree of occasional happiness, the roller coaster ride had become too much. The fear of even the most basic activities, such as answering the phone or checking the mail could send me spiraling downwards, how others might feel if they were thrown into a pit of snakes. The flight response turning on the adrenaline all the time was like a roommate who wouldn't turn out the overhead light when you were ready for bed. Eventually, it grated on you until you wished you could simply rip the fucking light fixture out of the ceiling with your bare hands, leaving behind a hole with bare wires and a sprinkling of drywall dust. And what reason was there to hold back from doing just that?

Depression was a blanket that laid over you, a heavy weight that even though it pushed you down, it also somehow held you together, from going to pieces.

Organizations always say to "get help" for mental problems—you know, celebrities in public service announcements and the last line of a news article about how some dude shot up a Dairy Twist. But that is only for the super-rich or the super-poor. If you are rich enough, you can pay the deductibles and co-pays, afford the gas to drive to the city where the doctor is, and someone to watch your child so that you don't have to expose them to all your crazy just yet. Or if you are poor enough—like living on the street poor—the government will pay your medical costs. If you are suicidal and living on the street, what the damn fuck motivation do you have for getting well anyway? If you are in the in-between, then there is no help to be found. And in-between is a surprisingly large place as I have been there when I was full-time employed, on unemployment, and now eating away at the dredges of my savings. In another month I will probably be homeless. But what would be the point of getting better then? Maybe there really is no better. Maybe happiness is merely a slick ad campaign from the drug companies.

Health insurance was too hard to understand. At this point in my life, I advocated abolishing all insurance companies and was in favor of health institutions lowering prices so people could actually pay for their health care once again with cash from their paycheck. Banks stole more of your money than they gave you. I was now for using reloadable credit cards and against checking and savings accounts where your money was not actually your own.

I found I could no longer live within the system I had once looked down on others for struggling with.

I had never tried to obtain mental health services. The insurance I used to have didn't list any therapist who would accept it in a fifty-mile radius, and I lived within fifty miles of three major metropolitan areas. Now I don't have any at all. A tax penalty for non-compliance was on my radar of things to worry about, but not high on my list of issues to resolve when my most promising five-year plan involved death.

Worst of all? What if I went and a trained medical professional said there was nothing they could do to help me? I would have put myself into a high anxiety situation that brought about no resolution. I would only find out that I was broken and unfixable, just as I had always known deep down in my gray soul.

* * * * *

I used to be organized. Lexie always teased me about my use of file cabinets and binders, a color-coded system that would give personal organizer Peter Walsh a run for his money.

But I was so out of control now. Information, dates, urgent reminders slipped through my fingers like a box of brand new razor blades. I couldn't catch them all and hold on because they not only slipped through my fingers, but cut them off on the way down as well.

I used to be the kind of person to always take back my library books and rented videos on time. I was currently staring at a DVD in a clear case on my coffee table I had neglected to take back. It had been over two weeks. The rental store kept calling and nagging me about it. But I couldn't bear to answer the phone for them or any of the other bill collectors hounding me.

All would be very good reasons to stop paying my phone bill.

Spiraling depression made it hard to look past tomorrow, which was actually a relief for a chronic planner with no future. A sense of obligation is the only reason I ever got out of bed in the first place. And now that was gone, replaced with empty hopelessness. It takes courage to get out of bed in the morning. I am not that brave.

With every sunrise, another day dawned. Another day of my life slipped away. Each day was excruciating to me, as my future crawled to me slowly on broken limbs. But at the same time, the previous minutes of my life disappeared quickly like water out of a leaky faucet. I can't see how things will ever be any better than this. I have burned every bridge. There is nothing left for me to do now but sit here and rot.

Lexie texted me. I glanced at the preview on my screen.

I love you. I need you to be alive.

Must be my previous text had especially frightened her. I couldn't remember what it had been or how long ago I had sent it.

I wanted to reach out to Lexie, I really did. But what would I say? I couldn't talk about my job or current events or my life because I didn't have one anymore. I could feel her panic when I did talk to her, just as I could from this text. I was beyond help now. I couldn't have a friend because she was too scared of what I might do around her; probably rightfully so.

I am sure that she meant those words from the bottom of her ever-loving heart. But talking to her, even by text, only gave me a chill now. I sensed that she had run out of ways to try to reach me. My sad, hopeless life was too dark for her light to enter any longer. I was losing her. That was worse than all the other losses combined.

We had always been there for each other.

I remembered when she was getting ready for her senior prom. She let me hang out in her room and help her get ready, even though I wasn't going to the great social event of the year.

"I was going to wear my hair down, it is curled so nice, but it is going to rain, I know it. I just know it. Then it will clump up from all the products I put into it." Lexie's hair didn't reach her shoulders when it was wet, and now dry and curled it was shorter still. "It will be a mess, an absolute mess. I could put it up as a plan B. Oh, but it looks so nice right now down. What do you think, Mace?"

I was used to the way Lexie could talk to herself for long periods of time without any input from me. It was actually rather fascinating to watch.

I had her back. I had already brought up the weather website on the computer that sat on her desk, mostly untouched and collecting dust. If I had my own computer, I would find reasons to use it every chance I got.

"I have the Doppler radar right here. Thunderstorms are definitely going to move through in the next several hours. I think you should play it safe."

Lexie let out a long, loathsome sigh, clearly expressing her disgust.

"Fine. Let me find that clip with the rhinestones I bought at the mall last month. You remember the one, right?"

Yes, I remembered that one. I had wanted to buy a matching one so badly, but I resisted. It was something fun and spontaneous girlfriends would do. Although I would be starting college soon and many expenses would be lumped into my college loan tab, I still needed to make rent through the summer.

"Oh, here it is," Lexie said, pulling it out of the shopping bag it had never left since the day she purchased it.

With some swift magic, her curls were now piled on top of her head. Lexie's hair was naturally straight, but I was jealous of how well it would hold a curl when she used the curling iron. Even in elementary school when she had been in the talent show, her mother had given her the perfect head of curls. My hair hung stick straight as I stood behind Lexie and turned over the poster board cards we had both made the night before about global deforestation, I the silent, back-up helper.

"Fabulous," I told her, because I knew that is what she wanted to hear. It was also the truth. But, she always looked put-together. That is not anything anyone would ever say about me.

"I still don't know about going with Ted. I mean, he's nice and all. But he is only a placeholder, a man on my arm."

"More like a boy," I said. She didn't seem to hear me as she continued.

"I mean, I was planning on going with Kevin for like a whole year, and then we broke up, like, out of the blue. And I feel like things are developing with Ron at the Dairy Twist, but he is older and wouldn't want to go to a kid event like prom."

"Ya, Ron is kind of a long shot. No junior in college is going to want to go to a high school prom. He is your manager. Isn't that a conflict of interest or something?"

"Not if we don't tell anyone. And plus, he lets me have free slushies when I close with him."

"I bet that isn't all he is letting you have."

Lexie didn't reply, but she dipped her head quickly to hide the blush that crossed her cheeks, telling me everything I already knew.

"Are you sad you aren't going tonight?" she said, trying to change the subject.

"No. I wouldn't even know what to wear or how to dance anyway."

"You just follow the crowd. Try to fit in."

"Oh, as I do every day? See how well that is working out for me? Plus, no one asked me."

"Well, you didn't advertise that you were on the market either."

"Um, I think I am always on the market. There are simply no buyers." I picked at a hangnail, which reminded me I needed to push down my cuticles more regularly. I started with my right thumb and worked on them, making my way to my pinky. Now was as good a time as any. "Do me a favor. Tell me who Logan Courtney shows up with."

"Gotcha," Lexie replied, winking at me.

Soon after I watched Ted escort Lexie out the door to the gray sedan he borrowed from his father. I bid adieu to Lexie's mom and walked back to my apartment. A small storm cloud ahead of the rest arrived at that moment. My clothes and hair got soaked on the way home. It was a good thing I didn't have any curls to ruin.

If I was going to prom, I would insist on a limo.

* * * * *

I was desperate to find comfort in any way possible. Chocolate would do the trick. Problem was, there was no candy, frosting, or pastries in the house. But desperate times called for desperate measures.

I opened the fridge and removed the plastic bottle of chocolate syrup that had been tilted on its cap to facilitate removal of the last remaining drops. I opened the kitchen drawer, all the silverware giving the familiar jangle as they slid against each other within the confines of the wooden organizer. It was all utensils I rarely used, such as paring knives and serving spoons. All the normal spoons, forks, and knives were on the counter, sitting dirty. Oh, how I had searched for the perfect organizer to fit the dimensions of the drawer. How much had I paid for it? Probably at least twelve king size candy bars worth. That money would be way more valuable to me right now than a chunk of wood processed by an underpaid foreign factory worker. I squeezed some syrup onto the white plastic spoon I had stolen from MacRonnell's and then slowly licked it off, from the outside edges to lastly the center, where the chocolate lake was the deepest.

It was grainy and not creamy. Nougat or peanuts would have helped. But I would have to settle for what I had—as I had done my entire life.

I walked back out to the living room and the television screen was blue, signaling there had been an interruption in service. I abruptly grabbed the remote control and changed the channel. I changed it again. Still blue, all blue. I ran to the window and looked out at the road, but there was no cable truck parked out there.

Sneaky son of a bitch.

He had come and unhooked me in the five minutes I had left the television. It was as though I had left a coma patient unattended and they had coded while I went to grab a cup of coffee.

"AHHHHHHHHHHHHHHHHHHH!" I screamed. My hand went to my head and I pulled at my hair. It hurt, so I stopped. I looked around the living room seething with frustration, looking for something to break. How could I live without my TV? This would mean no more internet either! I didn't leave the house. I couldn't afford to go to movies, or even rent a DVD. I would go insane in this shithole apartment by myself all day, every day.

I used my forearm to sweep all the crap that had accumulated on my coffee table over the past six months and shoved it onto the floor. It made a satisfying clatter as it landed in a pile taller than the table at the end of it. I picked up my shoe and threw it at the screen. It only bounced off, which I was slightly relieved by.

Realizing the remote for the cable box was laying on the couch, I grabbed it up. I tried to fold it in half with my bare hands. When my arm muscles gave a wimpy whine rather than a powerful grunt, I gave up and threw it at the wall. It bounced to the floor, unharmed. Was that shit made out of titanium or what?

"GOD DAMMIT!" I yelled, to no one but myself. Could my life get any worse??? I didn't want to continue like this.

I stomped into the kitchen, grabbed the first utensil I saw and repeatedly jammed it at my arm.

It turned out to be a fork. It hurt like hell, but didn't break the skin. There was a steak knife lying nearby. I guess I wasn't actually ready to end it all, or I would have used that instead.

I sat down on the vinyl floor, my hands touching the crumbs that lay along next to the bottom of the cupboards. This house was disgusting and I was a wreck. I put my head in my hands and cried, waiting for the anxiety madness to pass.

* * * * *

"Ew, this place is messier than the last time I came," Lexie said, surveying the papers, books, and DVDs that littered the living room. "It's a good thing I didn't bring Jackie. I may have lost her in here." Jackie was such a dainty little peanut that the observation was apt.

I really wanted to tell Lexie about the dreams on the beach I had been having, especially the one I had last night.

I had awoken with a start.

My dream was different last night.

There was the same bright sun, the same man with the obscured face. But this time I turned to look behind me. The other way, not far down the beach, sat a little pink shack. My shack. I don't know how I knew that it was mine, but I did. Without moving an inch, I knew what it looked like on the inside, where I slept, where I cooked my dinner.

It was so comfortable there, in that life. I guess I was having a harder time than usual leaving it behind today. Lexie only wanted to prattle on about housekeeping anyway.

"I'll clean it up tomorrow," I replied automatically.

"You told me the same thing last time I was here."

"Oh, ya." I turned my attention from her back to the DVD playing on my television. I had been looking forward to her visit, but not if she was only going to lecture me.

"You know, it might improve your mood, make you feel better, if you picked up around here, swept the dust. You know, had a general walking path from the kitchen to the couch."

I knew she had a point. I could force myself to clean up. And I might feel better for doing it. But I could not hold the monster of hopelessness at bay for long, even if I had the help of Mr. Clean and the scrubbing bubbles.

"You need a mom to take care of you. Heck, we both do."

Lexie's mom had died of cancer while Lexie was still pregnant with Brody. She passed it off as if it never bothered her anymore, but I knew that it still did.

"Macey, what is with this stack of mail on your kitchen counter?" Lexie asked, flipping through them like she had a right to. A few months ago it wouldn't have mattered to me, but now it did.

"Just bills and stuff. I'll sort through them someday, when I have time."

"Mace, some of these are marked *FINAL NOTICE.*"

"Oh, are they?" I responded from the living room, grabbing the movies for Lexie that she had stopped by to borrow.

"This looks like my mail in my care-free twenties."

"Huh. Well, I have always been a late bloomer."

"But you are thirty-seven years old now. You are supposed to become more responsible as you age, not less. I'm worried about you."

"But I spent my youth acting and behaving like a tiny adult. I worried about *everything all the time*. I can't live like that anymore. I used to be a glass is empty with a crack in it kind of person. Now I am a glass is full of alcohol-type person."

"Ya, I'm a little concerned about that too," Lexie paused. "I could call a few places if you like. Try to find someone for you to talk to about all this, other than just me. This isolation-thing you got going on is not healthy," she offered, judgmentally looking around my apartment again. This was a different Lexie than the one who had only months ago dropped down on my couch, comfortable with my declining circumstances as long as they had been invisible to the naked eye.

"It makes me think of our high school counselor. I don't even remember what his name was. Remember, you wanted me to see him too. And I didn't. What would a fifty-year-old man ever understand about the problems of a sixteen-year-old girl who had to balance school, homework, and two part-time jobs. The answer is 'he wouldn't.' So why even try."

"I have to run and pick up Jackie from band practice, but we will talk about this more on Saturday, alright?"

"Why, what the hell is Saturday?" I grumbled, knowing damn well what my friend was referring to.

"The reunion! I know you keep saying you don't want to go, but when the day gets here, Macey Reynolds, you will change your mind."

"I have been saying I will not go for twenty years. I don't think I'm going to be changing my mind anytime soon." In all honesty, every time she had mentioned it to me, I instantly forgot again once she stopped talking about it. It was not a priority to me; nothing was.

"What if I show you this!"

Lexie pulled a red dress out of the large bag she was carrying and presented it to me. I could see it had a large ruffle down the shoulder.

"Oh, that is nice. You will look real good in that come Saturday."

"No, silly. I bought it for you! I bought matching shoes too because I know you don't have any," she said, producing a pair of high heels that I would not be caught dead in.

"Why? I told you I wasn't going."

"Because I know I can change your mind."

"And if I went, I would not be wearing that. You can dress up a mousy-pale nerdy girl, but you aren't going to change who she is. Is that what they call a cocktail dress?"

"You are not mousy, maybe a little paler than usual. I assume we will be having plenty of cocktails."

"Uh-uh. No way."

"Please! You can't make me go alone."

"You won't be alone. You have the dashing Colin to escort you. I don't see why you want to go at all. Those slime didn't treat you any better than they treated me."

"The difference is, I have forgiven them."

"Well, you will have to *forgive me* if I am not there yet."

"You don't even want to go to see Logan Courtney?"

"He might be the only one," I paused, picturing him in high school. Girls in school get sent home due to their clothes being a distraction for boys. Logan Courtney's looks were always terribly distracting to me. "But there is no guarantee that he will be there," I continued.

"I have it on good authority that he will be..."

"Even if he is, it is not like I would talk to him, or he would talk to me. You are the only person I ever want to talk to, and you make house calls."

"Only because you no longer leave. Saturday. You are going with me. No arguments. It's a date."

* * * * *

Logan Courtney was too pretty for a small town. I had always thought so.

He had gone to our school all along, but somehow I never had a class with him until sixth grade. I believe being in his presence rocketed me into puberty. Just the sight of him made me wet in places I didn't know were supposed to have that function. He was the best-looking male I had ever seen in real life, with maybe the exception of the neighbor that lived on the next street over who was a good ten years older than myself who I may have stalked. I have no idea why he had no interest in me. I was a cute fourteen-year-old who looked like an eleven-year-old.

I fell in love with Logan. Every girl has that one boy in school she stares at across the lunch room, that she has dirty fantasies about. For me, that was always Logan. Sure, other girls agreed he was cute. But no one seemed to focus their attention on him like I did.

I only had limited eye contact with him. But when I did, it usually involved me ducking my head and turning away. It wasn't that I was trying to hide the self-conscious flaming red blush that covered my whole face. A smiling Logan was like trying to stare straight at the boiling sun; it was too much. It was an assault on my senses, an overload.

Deep down in my bones I don't feel like anything would have turned out different between us even if I had had the guts to actually exchange words with him on a semi-regular basis.

Don't misunderstand me. I did not actually talk to him or anything. He interacted with me sometimes. But it was such a rare occurrence that I actually drew the scenes into my sketchbook. I logged interactions in the hallways, and even sometimes dreams that I had, especially if they involved us kissing. A sample illustration is the time he playfully bonked me on the head with his silverware in the lunchroom on his way to putting them into the collection bin. Once he chewed on a piece of plastic at an assembly and discarded it. I retrieved it. It has a hole in it shaped like his actual tooth. There is a theme here: objects that his bodily fluid actually came into contact with, touching me, gave me a thrill.

And I missed that. Most days I was compost, the only heat generated from my rotting cells. To feel that warmth again, the innocent lust, the excitement that only comes from not knowing how messy love can actually get. I craved that. And the smell of the cologne he always wore. Lexie had known the name and told me. I always sniffed the bottles at Christmastime every year, when all the gift sets were set up in the aisles at the grocery store. One year I even bought myself a bottle so I could smell him whenever I wanted to. Lexie found it, questioning me, thinking I had a new boyfriend. I felt so stupid and embarrassed that I threw the bottle out. I have regretted it every day since. But I was never desperate enough to replace that bottle. Maybe it would be better if I could forget.

There is no way someone else can understand how fine I find Logan Courtney. The boy's senior picture looked like a headshot for a movie actor. His brown, come-hither eyes drew me in. His lips, the perfect amount of pink, pillowy softness that made me want to suck them, and I have never had the urge to suck anyone else's lips before in my life. His dark eyes twinkled and danced, even in a photo. In real life, it was even more striking.

Photographers retouch all photos they take. That is included in the high prices. Heck, nowadays you can do it yourself on your cell phone with a simple filter.

But Logan's yearbook pic was just above and beyond. I can only come to the conclusion that it was because the subject was so exceptional.

Logan was as close to fulfilling the checklist of qualities of my dream man as I had ever found. The man was gorgeous, even when he was still a boy. Lexie never thought so, but we had never had the same taste in men. He had the perfect hair that did this little swoopy thing in the front, presumably held there by some kind of mousse product, or as I believe, magic. It was probably outdated now, but was perfect for the 90s. He wasn't muscular, but I enjoyed his lean frame more anyway. He had a butt I literally dreamed of squeezing, at night, in my dreams. Then I would have to burn off all those feelings in the morning when I awoke.

My dream man was supposed to be funny. Logan never talked to me enough so that I could make a real determination on this. I mean, I laughed the few times when he did talk to me. But it was more of a coquettish cartoon character laugh. Or, you know, a big dorky, dweeby snort. I would not even be able to recall what he had said minutes later. I guess in reality, I didn't know much about his personality at all. I mean, he was one of the few kids who never attacked me verbally. He seemed nice enough to his friends. He was well-liked by his teachers. I never saw him buying or selling drugs at his locker. He didn't set squirrels on fire afterschool.

As the years passed, the call of his appeal to me quieted, never fully disappearing. And occasionally I did still see him around town. That only served to stoke the old flames of lust within me. As how a sexy man should look, he was my ideal. Every male after that was weighed against him, whether I was aware I was doing it or not. There was a reason none of them had lasted; none could compare to this mythical creature I had built in my mind. Maybe I didn't want them to.

I wanted to believe that Logan and I could still *happen* someday.

* * * * *

There was a knock on the door to my apartment. I ignored it.

It was probably the asshole landlord again, demanding payment for my residence in his structure. I understood where he was coming from, I sincerely did. And I would pay him if I had the money, but I didn't. What I had left wasn't enough for one month, let alone the three I owed him.

My phone chimed, surprising me. I flipped it over. The screen glowed with a new message.

Its me colin at the door. Open up.

I sat stunned, trying to process why he would ever come over without Lexie. I thought for a second maybe he was planning a surprise party for her. That was usually the only reason he ever texted me. But her birthday was still months away.

Anxiety, my steady companion who had left me in the care of Depression for the last several months, landed in the pit of my stomach. She began to gnaw there. Of course Anxiety is a woman. That is why she is so strong, unbreakable. I bowed my head and looked at my stomach then, not realizing why it was acting up. Another round of loud knocking on the door broke into my ruminations. I let my phone drop from my hand onto the couch as a stood up, not giving it another thought.

I opened the door.

There stood Colin McCrae. He was wearing his typical flannel shirt with a white tank top underneath and jeans. He looked like he had come straight from work. His dark eyes didn't meet mine. He seemed to be staring behind me, at something inside my apartment. Maybe the dirty dishes and laundry piled up offended him. The wind tousled his straight, black hair. He awkwardly scratched the back of his head, as if he didn't know what to do with his hands. His hair was longer than it should have been. The stubble on his chin was still meticulous, but his hair had been allowed to grow unhindered. I bet Lexie would get on him about it soon.

He kept looking back at his truck, which he had left running. I watched the white smoke pushing out of the tail pipe and into the atmosphere. I wondered if it had a bad ring. I had had two cars die of that in the past. I had heard that rust was car cancer, but bad rings were much more terminal.

"Look, I only have a minute," he began.

I thought maybe he was waiting for my attention, so I looked at him. But he still did not continue. The arrangement of his features was unfamiliar to me. He looked pissed. I wondered if one of the children had caused a problem. Colin was usually pretty easy going. Still he did not speak. So I stepped in.

"Is it something about Lexie?"

That is when I saw it. He wasn't pissed. He was trying to hold himself together. But as quickly as I saw the sorrow cross his features, I looked away. I resumed watching his exhaust. I could smell it now, the poison irritating my nose and throat.

"She—e." His voice broke.

It was all I could do not to walk over to his tailpipe and wrap my lips around it.

"There was a—"

It would be hot, instantly burning my lips.

"She was turning."

My lungs would try to cough in protest, to expel the poisonous gas; the body's self-preservation reaction kicking in.

"A semi truck."

But I would fight it.

I sensed tears on his face, but I wouldn't look, I wouldn't acknowledge them. I wouldn't acknowledge my own either.

"There was no way to save her."

My head snapped up, finally meeting his face, a mask of grief.

"The kids?"

"No. They—they're fine. They were at school."

"Now?"

"They are with grandma."

"When?" I didn't have to make a coherent sentence as to the occurrence of her burial.

"Um, we are not sure yet. I will call you."

I put my hands up in front of me.

"Texting is fine." I could live the rest of my life without another difficult social interaction such as this one.

"K. I gotta go." He threw his hand awkwardly in the air. I think it was supposed to be a half-assed wave.

He wasted no time retreating from my door. He almost ran back to his truck. He probably resented having to tell me in person. I knew how big his loss was. It was mine as well. I wasn't being naïve, as he shifted into reverse, backing out of the drive uphill to the road. I knew Lexi was his wife. They shared love in a different way than she & I did.

But he still had friends and family. He could lean on them to get through this tragedy. He would always have Brody and Jackie, the biggest pieces of herself Lexie left for the world.

Lexie had been my only friend and only family. I heard Colin gun the engine, the muffler bellowing loudly, as he headed off to make impossible plans. I didn't need to make a plan to cope with this. My body moved on autopilot. I leaned back through my doorway & grabbed my keys off the table, slamming the door behind me. I threw myself into my car, and it automatically drove me to the party store. There the same polite man greeted me, sat my bottle on the counter, and I handed him the last crumpled bill in my pocket.

I went out and got inside my car. It was my cozy cocoon, a safe place. I tried to put my keys in the ignition, but my right hand froze halfway there. I simply stared at my hand. This was bad. The denial was wearing off. I was going into shock. I had to make it home before the full realization washed over me. There was no one to call to come rescue me. That had never been my family, my parents having moved away two decades ago. The person who had always filled that role was now gone.

I pulled my hand back to my body, rubbing it with my left to awaken my nerves. It was ice cold. I knew how to warm it up and how to confuse my body long enough to transport myself back home at the same time. I unscrewed the cap and downed the vodka straight out of the bottle. It was a cold burn to my throat. I coughed and spluttered, some of it running down my chin and wetting my T-shirt. It had no taste and an awful taste all at the same time. I screwed the cap back on and started the car. I threw it in reverse and stepped on the gas. Simultaneously a horn blared behind me, causing me to brake. I had almost backed into another car. I needed to get home in a hurry.

I navigated the few streets back home as tears filled my eyes. In my driveway, I took another swig from my bottle. I could feel the thick mucus forming in my throat, preparing for the big cry. I was positive some backwashed into the bottle. I slapped the lid back on, trying to turn it, feeling it tighten crookedly. By now I had ingested what would have equaled less than two shots. But still, I fell out of the car when I tried to walk. I was not impaired by alcohol, but by an overwhelming sorrow. I stumble-walked across the grass to my front door. I crawled through and tried to quickly slam the door behind me. My shoe got caught in the door and was pulled from my foot. I tried to close the door, but the shoe was in the way.

I pushed harder.

The shoe was still in the way.

"You mother-fucking cock-sucking son of a bitch!" I pushed harder still. This time the shoe gave way, bouncing outside. As the door slammed shut, I couldn't curtail my inertia and my head smacked into the door. I laid there for a second, the pain throbbing. I could feel my heartbeat in my head. At least I still had a heartbeat, unlike Lexie.

I let the grief overtake me then. I put the cold glass bottle to the spot on my head that was on fire as the sobs broke from my throat.

My natural instinct was to go lie on the couch and lose myself in the television. But tonight I couldn't give it the attention it deserved. I walked right by it, even though the DVD I had been watching was still running. It was a gruesome reminder that the world had been a very different place only a half an hour before. I didn't have the energy to turn it off. I headed into the bedroom. I wrenched the cap on my bottle until my hand hurt, trying to remove it. The crookedness made it a more time-consuming task than it needed to be. I took a long swig, and sat it on the bedside table. The cap fell and rolled under the bed. Who the hell needed it anyway? I laid back on the mattress covered with the crumpled sheets. I grabbed a pillow, hugging it to my chest and letting it soak up all my tears.

Just like that, the only person to worry about me was gone from my life. Gone from life itself.

I laid in bed and contemplated that. I imagined the simulated wood grain paneled walls of my bedroom were the sides of a coffin surrounding me. The darkness would turn into nothingness. No sound, no thoughts, just... nothing.

I didn't believe in heaven or hell or resurrection for myself. But Lexie had been a special soul. Always volunteering and donating money, time, or resources, even for people she didn't even like. If there was a heaven, she would surely meet the criteria to make it in.

But I never would. I had to make myself realize that even though I could still hear Lexie inside my head, laughing at my jokes or playing devil's advocate, I would never see my best friend again.

I was all alone.

* * * * *

I prayed for sleep to take me away from this painful reality. But sleep never came. The light peeking around the edges of the curtains and the steady stream of cars driving past outside told me it was a day like any other. But my heart knew better.

My only friend. Died. Up and fucking died. What am I supposed to do with that?

Lexie's last statement to me echoed in my head.

Saturday. You are going with me. No arguments. It's a date.

Famous last words.

Damn stupid fucking life.

No matter how many miles apart the places Lexie and I called home, it seemed like our lives somehow mirrored each other. We were twin souls. We often said we shared a brain, which was actually possible as we were drawn to quite opposite pursuits. Having lost part of my soul was terrifying. I truly had no one now. And I wasn't strong enough to support myself. Speaking emotionally, of course, although it would apply for finances as well.

I realized in that moment that there was no one left to love me.

No parents, no boyfriend, no friends, no dog, no fish.

Everything in the room went out of focus and slanted. I grabbed anything I could and threw it or broke it in a fit of sad-angry rage. And I knew some of it I would miss tomorrow, which only made me feel guiltier, sadder, more depressed now. I wasn't even good enough to hold on to my possessions. Black, nameless emotion ripped through my body. There was so much pain that all my thoughts instantly pulsed toward how to make it stop. That was all I could think of. In the kitchen, there was a knife. In the bathroom, there was the tub, a pink dainty razor, various over-the-counter drugs.

I want to end this now.

I wanted to die.

The thought of the reunion popped into my head. Lexie had been determined to drag me with her. I had been dead set against it. But actual death had now intervened.

Boy, would I be the talk of the reunion if I killed myself.

I'm surprised she didn't off herself years ago.

But just as quickly, another thought entered my head. What if I could silence *them* forever?

To err is human, to forgive divine.

Death was all too human. And I had not a single iota of forgiveness in my body.

But I was bubbling over to the brim with anger.

Isn't it always better to share?

* * * * *

Sleep did come to me, at least for a few hours. Whether it was day or not, I no longer cared.

I dreamed I was walking down the halls, young again, still so vulnerable to my former classmates' comments, stares, laughs that may or may not be aimed at me. I was so naïve that it made my skin hurt, an irritation that only throbbed worse as their words and eyes assaulted me like a steady wind. I was walking, clutching my books to my chest as usual so no one could knock them to the floor, my head curled over just enough so that I could see ahead of me to avoid an embarrassing collision, but not so much that I would actually make eye contact with anyone that could be construed as antagonistic.

The unusual part was that I was wearing my backpack as I walked. Usually I had left it in my locker. It was getting heavier and heavier on my back as I walked. A young Lexie, with her hair shorter as I always pictured her, even now, had been chattering at my side. But now she faded away as I realized all the other students were lining up in a straight line in front of me like some sick game of Red Rover, blocking my path. At this point I didn't recognize any of them. All their faces were just masks of anger. As my straps dug into my shoulders, it hit me what I needed to do.

In a smooth motion more like Bruce Willis in a summer action movie than myself, I swung the backpack off my back, removing a giant machine gun with a rope of bullets hanging from it. All the students fell down like that dog in the video game *Duck Hunt*. Oh wait, the game wouldn't actually let you shoot the damn dog. But I really wanted to because he was always laughing at me. Just like them.

And that was the dream. I woke up being mad at the *Duck Hunt* dog.

And I now knew what I had to do. The message was crystal clear.

Must do what the universe says. Must do what the universe says.

HELL

Nevermind my tears. That is just the crazy leaking out.

The reunion.

It was tempting. Lexie wanted me to go so badly. But could I walk through those doors without her? Face the people I had hated for twenty-six years? She had bought me that ridiculous dress. I couldn't wear that ruffly thing.

Maybe I could do a simulation. I went to my hall closet where I kept my winter coats hiding in the summer. Of course this year they still hung on the coat rack by the door, dust along with stray cooking and garbage smells becoming trapped in the fabric. I had never cared enough to wash them and pack them away, even though the seasons had clearly changed.

Digging around among boxes stacked in the bottom, I found the former copy paper box I knew contained my accumulated collection of crap from school. It was filled with old assignments, newspaper clippings, and yearbooks. I grunted as I picked it up to carry it across the room to my couch and my muscles in my back pulled out a centimeter further than they were supposed to. I would be sore tomorrow.

I gave up making it to the couch. Dropping it on the floor, I plopped down next to it and pulled the top off the box. Piles of notebook paper folded into little triangles lay on top, notes from Lexie. I picked one up, unfolding it and reading it. It said absolutely nothing important to our history, but simply seeing the familiar scrawl of her hand, unchanged since the ninth grade, made my heart clench. I would recognize that writing anywhere.

Some of the pieces of paper had both sides of our conversation on them. Even as I was being tortured daily, there was still hope in my words. Hope that maybe I was wrong, maybe this guy or that one maybe actually liked me and wasn't solely making fun of me. Maybe I had to hold on to that ounce of hope to keep going.

I wanted to go back in time and slap the shit out of that girl.

How could my past self be so stupid? She wanted to always believe the best in people. But humans don't want love and harmony. Inside they only want to kill everyone so that they can be the winner.

I dropped the note on the floor and approached the next layer of my box. I found a couple of old sketchbooks. They were ones I had hidden away from my mother, for privacy. I felt like back then if there was a day that went by that I didn't draw, I would lose my mind. I laughed fiercely at myself. I hadn't created anything of any significance in years. And look where I was now. The insanity had arrived right on time, as I had always suspected it would.

At first there were simply pictures of my neighborhood, the apartment building across the street. Then there were some darker ones, of a little girl in a city holding a teddy bear as she watched the abandoned building she lived in being torn down by a bulldozer. There was another of a girl laying in a graveyard at night, her hair caked with mud (or was it blood?). Deeper into the books, there were some sheets that only had tornadoes of colors on them, violently ground into the paper, most likely destroying the writing instrument used to mark it. Some had words or images mixed into them, such as knives, bleeding wrists, or Logan's name. One page was merely the word "why" in huge letters, the outline filled in with everything I hated about high school, which was everything. There were images representing gym class, lunch, the school bus, loneliness, poverty, and even my favorite band at the time.

Looking through them brought back memories I had repressed, and for good reason. My stomach was knotting up with anxiety, not in the current adult way, but a whole body pain that spared no limb or organ or capillary. Where I had recently only feared making the wrong financial decision and becoming homeless, this was in a more cutting way, like the edge of a knife, sharper, and more direct. It was centered in my stomach the way it always had in high school. It was not the stress of making a mistake with all of the control I possessed as an adult, but a fear that came from being a child and having none at all. I had to attend school—there was no way around it. (In hindsight, it seems as though I could have benefitted from homeschooling during that time.) Once I walked out my front door, I was at the mercy of the world. And the world wasn't very nice, especially their offspring.

Standing at the bus stop in the dark, Michigan winter mornings, the older girls would either bad mouth me, or shun me altogether. I never understood what I did to them to make them hate me so. I pissed them off just by existing was all that I could figure. I wish I could walk back into that memory and tell them they were losers for being seniors and still riding the damn bus. When I was a senior I still rode the bus to school, but I made damn sure I never rode it home one single day that year, even if it meant I had to walk over two miles home. The roar of a school bus passing by still gives me a stomach ache to this day.

It was never anything physical, nothing that left any certifiable proof of damage. It was all mental warfare, breaking me down today so that I would be an easier target tomorrow. At school, most times I could not even get into my locker because other students were blocking it on purpose. I would sometimes go hide in the bathroom until they were gone to avoid confrontation. It worked, but caused me enough tardies to get detention. Walking to classes was a hazard. Close quarters, jammed in with all the other kids and no teachers to witness the cruelty. Books could be dumped, nicknames shouted behind you, a snicker to your right about how your clothes were wrong. It didn't stop in class either. Teachers were blind to it or they just chose to be. I was still called by horrible nicknames. Pencils, sketchbooks, homework were snatched off my desk. Other than the bus, gym and lunch were the worst environments. Girls who judged me harshly with my clothes on could now do to it with them off? There were sports I never knew the rules to and still do not to this day. Some activities I think the gym teacher merely made up for maximum torture. Lunch, where I only had one acquaintance, Dawn, to sit with. Lexie was in another hour because she was in choir. If Dawn was absent, it was only me at the table by myself.

Every time I passed through those double doors I left myself vulnerable to attack. That worry continued to eat at me until graduation day when I would walk out them for the last time and be free of those slimy vermin.

I always heard that it is not good to judge people. But when I look at a sea of people, there is always a dark, dank, black tunnel with cobwebs hanging and puddles of undetermined moisture off to the right. Down the tunnel are my childhood tormenters. I can't find a way to afford them the same niceties as the rest. All but them.

College was easier. No one seemed to care, which wore on me in its own way.

I gave up on the box of memories I didn't want to relive. I would find the yearbooks and look at them later. Or never. I wanted to lose myself in television, but the cable and internet were still off. I had used up all the data on my phone. DVDs it would have to be.

* * * * *

I want to die. I want to die.

It repeated in my head, an incessant recording of my own voice. It was a dead monotone; it made it hard for me to recognize. The actual ceasing of existing and the conclusion of making any new memories or breathing and circulating blood and stuff terrified me to death. It was actually the last thing I wanted—a last resort. But it all hurt so much. It was like being affected by cold outside in wintertime. If you were outdoors long enough, you couldn't stop it from creeping inside your coat, no matter how thick it might be. That was how the depression was.

Maybe I wasn't meant to prosper and thrive. I am a believer in survival of the fittest. It seems kind of obvious when you think about it that you wouldn't want a bunch of panicky, worrying freaks to breed and make more panicky, worrying freaks. Maybe that is the purpose suicide serves. Even though it is seen as such a terrible thing to do and against God's will and blah, blah, blah. But what if it is a natural selection switch— nature— like mama hamsters eating their babies? When you are too old for your mother to eat you, maybe that is when the instinct kicks in to end it yourself. It makes some sense to me. Maybe anything would make sense to me at this point.

Maybe crazy people keep trying to describe their crazy so that other crazy people will realize they are crazy too—and what? Can feel comforted? Unite to form a hostile takeover of the government? Feel less alone?

Fuck that. We are all alone.

With Lexie around, I could pretend that I wasn't. But in reality, she had a whole family network that did not include me. Sure, she said I was like family to her. But she had a sister and a brother, countless aunts and uncles, nieces and nephews. Since my separation from my parents, there had always been only me.

* * * * *

When I was a kid in school, I was the student who always completed my homework. I didn't want to. I probably could have passed the tests without the practice. That is what Lexie did. It was enough to get her by. But I knew it was *expected* of me. That expectation weighed on me. I felt as though if I didn't fulfill it, I would die. Like, God or my teacher or the creepy genie from *Aladdin* would shoot a lightning bolt down and take me out. When I felt so terrible that I wanted to kill myself, I still was not far enough gone to stop doing my homework.

That was anxiety.

Unfounded worry. An extreme and unreasonable reaction to living your life that others do not have. I can name it now. I could not back then.

I believe I can remember the first panic attack I ever had. I was in first grade. My mom always packed my lunch, which I never ate anyway. But one day the cafeteria was having pizza and it always looked so good and all the other kids were always so excited for it that for some reason that day I was going to buy my lunch. I don't know where my bravery came from. Maybe it was naiveté. But they announced over the PA system before lunch that they were substituting hot dogs for pizza.

Number one, the *last* thing I wanted from that cafeteria was their color-changing hot dogs. Literally; I am not exaggerating. They changed from red to green to yellow, like a bruise. I had been a witness to it many times on the trays of other students.

Number two, maybe it is just the years but I can't remember the lunch menu being changed at any other time *ever*. This was not how I had planned the day to go. It was out of my control. And the anxiety built up inside of me. My breathing got all weird and loud. I wanted to stop it. I did, but I didn't know how. The teacher asked me if I had asthma and when I replied no, she told me to stop interrupting the class. When I couldn't stop, she sent me to sit in the hallway. The teacher didn't even care enough to find out why a good student had suddenly started acting out.

What I do remember about that day is how scared I was to walk through that line to collect my hot dog that I would never eat. It was a mystery line, disappearing into the kitchen. Sure, kids came out again. But did they all? Were there secret experiments being conducted on them between the two doors? Were they the source of the never-ending hot dogs? It would be another eight years before I would ever attempt to buy lunch again. That's the thing about anxiety—it doesn't have to be rational or make sense to anyone, not even the person suffering from it. As a rule, it usually doesn't.

Why did no one think this was strange? Why did no one ever try to help me?

I was a kid who always chose suicide as a report topic. I drew pictures of people hanging from nooses for art class that no one questioned. It was always obvious I was bonkers. No one wanted to take the time to fix me. And I don't blame them. Wait, ya, I do.

After that, I fell into a pattern of waking up every day, whether I actually wanted to or not, unready for another day as I asked my brain, "Now what is it I need to worry about today?"

* * * * *

Without any real means of distraction and the loss of the ability to sleep, I found myself taking my old yearbooks out. I didn't even know what I was searching for. I had not looked at these in years. Considering I was only in two clubs and had only one friend, why I had ever spent money on these paper memories in the first place now escaped me.

I flipped to a marked page. There was Logan Courtney's perfect face staring back at me, in prime adolescence, his hormones permeating the picture like a scratch and sniff sticker, waiting to be unlocked from the page. There was a smile on the inside, but it didn't reach my face. Memories of his hotness in the hallways began to warm my heart.

But the book fell open to next page, containing Lexie's image. The vicious pain that had eaten at the pit of my stomach on and off since I had heard the news of her demise reared its ugly head again. I put my hand on my abdomen, but it was useless. I was falling apart from the inside out. No mere mortal hand was going to hold me together.

I did not consciously recall my horrific / difficult / heartbreaking / heinous / awkward / challenging school experiences daily. But they still flickered in the back of my brain, like a gas burner left on low. I guess it probably was slowly heating up my non-stick pan of rage all this time, a cancer spreading hate throughout my body. I hadn't been able to notice it through the dense fog of my broken self-esteem and lack of confidence.

I like to believe that things that happened to me way back then could not happen to students now. Like when they published the phrase "thay it don't spway it" in the school newspaper, an expression I was regularly teased with. They didn't actually use my name. They didn't have to. Everyone knew who it referred to. I'm sure I am the only one who even remembers, because, it was only my feelings that were hurt. It was only my shock that the teacher allowed it to go to print that way.

For the record, I never spit when I talked, even when I still lisped. I had checked in front of a mirror at home. The popular girl next to me in science who had a boyfriend spit when she talked with her braces. I had seen it. No one ever mentioned that. The reading teacher showered the class. *Everyone* talked about that.

I can't remember anyone laying a hand on me. It was always the words.

Sometimes they would switch it up and start using one unfortunate kid's nickname on everyone else they despised that week. Their horrible slurs got repeated over and over again until they had lost all meaning; except for the original target, of course. I still heard their insults whispered to me in my dreams.

* * * * *

Not only was I tormented at school, but at home as well. I had learned that there were a lot of different families, and mine was not one you saw on television. Home was only a safe place if I was there alone. Most of the time I hid out at the local library until such a time that I could go straight to bed when I returned home and no one would think anything of it. It was the best way to avoid engagement of any kind. Everything my parents said to me put down my intelligence and my personality, breaking my spirit.

We had one of those houses where you must eat your dinner or there were consequences. My parents would say I couldn't have any more food until I finished my dinner. But that didn't work on me. Somethings I was just not willing to eat. They would not give me a packed lunch to take to school on those days. I couldn't buy lunch, because of the early hotdog trauma. My parents would hold out until my untouched plate began to grow mold in the fridge. Then they threw it out and we started the dance again.

Luckily there was always junk food available at Lexie's. We simply had to beat her brother to it.

My mom used to buy me clothes she thought were fashionable. And they actually were. I tried wearing them. It didn't work out so well. I began wearing only jeans & t-shirts and sweatshirts—clothes I could try to blend in with. She got mad at me for not wearing the brand names after she spent all that money on them. I figured out soon enough that I could wear exactly the same clothes as the most popular girl at school, but it didn't matter what the clothes were. It mattered who was actually wearing them. That was something I didn't bother to try to explain to my mother. She would never understand. She would say they teased me because they were jealous, that they wished their clothes were as stylish as mine. But I knew better.

I thought if I was perfect, my parents would love me, but that never seemed to be the case. My father wanted me to play sports. I was not good at that. I didn't grow fast enough and my coordination was atrocious. I miserably bombed out in athletics while I was still in elementary school. My mom wanted me to be a social butterfly as she was. I gave up on any group activity within weeks of starting it. I *was* good at art, a solitary, cultural activity, but that was not seen as a saving grace.

Sophomore year my teacher picked out art projects from three students and entered them into a state art competition. I was fortunate enough to win two thousand dollars. I didn't even have time to daydream about all the things I might do with the money, like maybe even put it toward college, before my mother ran off with it. She needed it for one silly thing or another. She implied she would pay it back to me. I got up the nerve to ask about it once. When she began to prattle on about how much it cost them to raise me, I knew I would never see it again.

When I was fifteen, I got a job against my parents' wishes bagging at the grocery store. It was almost as if I was getting paid to avoid her. Actually, I started working for Lexie's mom under the table acting as an assistant at her candle parties a year earlier. My dream was my very own place. I could keep my things how I wanted. I could eat what I wanted when I wanted. I could make my own decisions without criticism or judgment. But that dream seemed like it was far, far away from ever being fulfilled, as dreams often are. I don't know what made this one different than my others, that I actually believed it could possibly maybe come true.

Then I read an article on the internet about a child actress in Hollywood who was emancipating from her mother. I figured it was only possible because the actress was rich and famous and lived in Los Angeles. But the reasons listed were that her mother was controlling, misusing her money, and used violence against her. All those same things could be said about my mother and father. I lied to them about how much I made at the grocery store, because they wanted my whole check for room and board. I was taking a chance that they would never bother to check how much minimum wage was these days.

It paid off. I needed to build up my savings to be able to prove to the court that I had the means to live on my own and support myself. My mother thought she was so smart. She wanted me to have my check electronically deposited directly into *her* bank account. But I was one step ahead of her. I told her the grocery store was so old school that they issued paper checks. And that I had checked, and the bank would only let me cash them since mine was the only name on them. Good thing she never checked up on the pile of bull I fed her. Actually, I was having it direct-deposited into my own checking account.

Then I withdrew the amount I had to pay her. Lexie's mom had come with me when I opened the account. She was an adult to my childishness, no one ever asked if she was related to me. She never even had to sign anything.

I studied up on emancipation from my outpost at the library. I had to find a lawyer in town to do it pro-bono, but such a gracious creature did exist. I knew my parents would go nuclear when they got served the summons to appear in court. My mother said this would make her look like a bad parent.

Duh.

Luckily I had a plan in place for this situation. I slept on the floor in Lexie's bedroom for three months while the court proceedings took place. Oh, it didn't take a full ninety days for the proceedings. It only took three days, spread out over that time. Lexie didn't understand why I was doing all this, why I didn't just wait two more years until I was eighteen to leave. She wanted me to stay with her family, for her mom to be my mom. But as accommodating as her mother was, she made it clear that this arrangement was merely temporary. Lexie's mom put up with me because she considered me a good influence on wild Lexie. But she already had three kids, she didn't want a fourth. And I understood where she was coming from. That would be a lot to ask of anyone. Therefore I never did. Although I'm sure that Lexie hounded her.

The day the court granted me my freedom was liberating... and scary as hell. I truly had no one to fall back on if I failed. I would be hungry and homeless. But, actually, that had always been the case. But living with your family, you could fool yourself into believing things were different than they in fact were.

I lived in the cheapest apartment I could find closest to high school and my job, as I had no car. The place was a shithole, but it was *my* shithole. My only furniture was a red bean bag chair and a mattress on the floor, but it was all I needed. My grades instantly improved. I got a second job during the summers, and socked away any extra pennies for emergencies.

I got into a college nearby. The cost was covered by scholarships and student loans. I kept my savings in cash and never reported it the school. I had learned a thing or two from my mother, such as "Never let the U.S. Government know for sure how much money you have." Little did she know I had used that same tactic against her.

I lived in the dorms at college, so I could once again avoid the cost of a car, insurance, repairs, and gas. Don't get me wrong, I would have fuckin' loved a car. My life would have been much easier and fuller. But, you have to make due. Being emancipated, I had no parents to fall back on in an emergency. It made me more responsible than the other students I was surrounded by. It only added to the things we didn't have in common. I wasn't interested in making friends or getting drunk. On school breaks I crashed in Lexie's room, even if she wasn't always there. I made myself as scarce as possible so as not to wear out my welcome.

I had to prioritize, as I did my whole life thereafter. I always wanted a dog, but at first I couldn't have afforded one—the food, the shots, the flea, tick, heartworm prevention. (Yes, I researched it all and priced it out and it never worked in my budget spreadsheet. Hell, I could never get food to work in my budget spreadsheet, even after I was working forty hours a week at a real, grown-up job.) Later, I found any place I could afford to live would never allow one.

I became a business major, because it was practical, taking art classes where I could for electives. My degree turned out to be pretty useless. I only used it to shake my head at the big mistakes the businesses I worked for as an employee were making. I was never in any position of power to exact change. I was from the "everyone should go to college" generation, which only created a gluttony of job seekers in the market. There were people in my graduating class who worked at MacRonnell's, and not as managers. They were slinging the meat right next to the high school kids.

Survival always came first. Follow the logical career to keep the bills paid. Push art into a closet in the back of your mind where you won't hear it scream or see the bright colors flashing in protest.

One day blends into another. Years seem to pass in a blink, all while you begin to petrify in your adjustable office chair.

You begin to adapt to this unnatural life where durable carpet tiles replace the feel of soft grass under your feet and the glow from fluorescent lights replaces the sun. You ignore your body when it tries to tell you that you get up too early and spend too much time sitting down. If you ignore it long enough, it all blends into a bland sense of hopelessness you dismiss as exhaustion.

First you grow roots into the ground, then you harden to a fossil.

I am thirty-seven years old. I thought I would be married by now. Doesn't everyone? It is not like no one ever asked me. Actually, it is exactly like that. I had never been that fond of children, but I figured I would have some of those by now as well. I could be dropping them off at school every morning in a minivan. I obviously hadn't been close to my family in years, but maybe I could have been with my in-laws. I could have taken a dish to pass to a large Thanksgiving feast, and hosted Christmas filled with gifts and a robust tree shedding more needles than the family Labrador Retriever sheds hair.

It brought tears to my eyes to think about. My heart ached at the realization that I had no idea what a life filled with that much love must be like. And I never would.

I always wanted to travel: Canada, London, Australia—anywhere that speaks English. But I didn't. Because I thought I couldn't afford it. Ha. I was one of the most responsible people I knew. I had thousands of dollars saved up when I got laid off, and more laying around in my 401k. What did I use it for?

Groceries and shampoo and toilet paper and garbage bags.

Why didn't I take the risk and just *go somewhere*?

ANYWHERE! ANY-FUCKIN'-WHERE?

What was the worst that could happen? I could get all my utilities shut off and lose my house and be homeless? Well, hell, I was facing all that anyway. The extra funds had only served to delay it a few more months.

I could feel my face, my whole body getting hot as I thought about it. I could feel the blood pumping more violently through the arteries in my neck. My heart did a samba beat inside of my chest. Thinking about all this made me so furious. I had wasted half my life. And don't argue with me because my hereditary family health history is not good. Longevity is not in my future. Which only made me angrier, that I only had a small time left to accomplish everything and no means to do it with.

What would I do first, if I could, to remedy any of this? Dye my hair pink. Get a tattoo. I've waited so long, I would have to make it a big one to make up for lost time. Or maybe many small ones over the course of a week? And a piercing. Maybe my nose or my eyebrow.

I had always wanted to do such things, but I never did. I had worried if I got laid off, they would impede me from getting hired at a new job. So, instead I fought my natural eccentric urges. I buried who I yearned to be deep down inside. I put on a big fake act for interviews, and still didn't get hired. The real me churned and fought to get out, but I buried it still deeper, where it turned darker, but did not die. It became tainted, unable to experience happiness any longer.

And who is to blame? There must be someone, and not me, because I have spent my life doing everything right. Could be my parents and their lack of emotional and financial support and general parenting skills. Or it's God's fault for not sending me more money or a good boyfriend or a job I could love, even though I am still unaware of what that would be. Or it could be all those assholes in school that stripped me bare of any self-confidence long before I even knew I had any to be robbed of, before I knew it was a precious commodity that I must protect.

I could list them, their nasty little teenage faces imbedded in my mind permanently, no matter how hard I tried to rip them out. Their crimes, not huge atrocities but small ones, tiny to them even, added up for someone who was never taught to be strong.

Cody Micucci: Got the laughs by making jokes at everyone else's expense. Best way to avoid being a target was not to sit by him. Stupid assigned seats; I always got the bad roll of the dice. And he had such a stupid name that it would have been easy to make fun of. But I wouldn't find out until college that "coochie" was slang for a woman's crotch.

Sidney Perenboom: Another stupid name. Usually she ignored me or gave me snotty looks, which I was fine with. But on one particular day, she decided to pick on my makeup. And that is when I quit wearing it. Forever. But the joke is actually on her, because I have had a lot of extra cash over the years by not purchasing any, and there is no amount of makeup that can cure my kind of ugly anyway. I hope she is out there somewhere now, a starving cosmetics consultant. It's a universal law: what you put out in the world comes back to you three-fold.

Berit Gorman: She had all the adults fooled that she was sweet and good, but she sure threw nasty remarks my way. She was petite for her age and had hair that was too short and straight for the fashion of the time. She was like a nasty little Chihuahua. She pointed at me so that no one would look at her. Another person with a stupid name.

Russell Dunn & Chris Hughes: I don't know how they even managed to pick on anyone, they were so stupid. But they did. And that included me, often with lewd questions I wouldn't dignify with a response—because back then I didn't even know what they were referring to. At least I would have the satisfaction of knowing that Russell wouldn't make it back to the reunion. He had died in an industrial accident five years ago. Did I ever mention that I did a happy dance when I found that out? I should not speak ill of the dead. But he spoke ill of me the whole time he was alive, so turnabout seemed like fair play.

Troy Janz, Greg Toller. Disgusting human beings.

Christie Lang, Robin Smith, Chelsea Abraham, etc.: All the popular kids who participated by omission. They didn't necessarily add to the taunting, but they made no move to discourage it either.

There were others who also fell into that category, but they were at the bottom rungs of the high school social ladder, like I was. In such situations we would just make eye contact and know that there was nothing we could do to help. Multiple bottom feeders made no match to a shark. The best we could do was swim deeper, and hope the teeth didn't choose to sink into us today.

How much blood had I shed over the cruelty they used to bury me alive? I first learned that cutting existed from a teen girl magazine. It was the kind of article meant to deter, but I only gobbled up each word, praying that this may indeed be my salvation. A way to injure, but not kill myself? A way to let the pain of their words escape from the dark places they lived inside of me?

Sign me up!

It was almost a year before I realized it wasn't helping a darn thing. Not that I think it would actually help anyone. But it didn't even make me *feel* better. It wasn't providing mental relief. It was only making it harder for me to wear short-sleeved shirts.

Just thinking about all of them made my blood boil. All those years and there was nothing I could do about it. Nowadays schools tried to claim kids would get in trouble for bullying. As if. It is always one kid's word against another. And the one with all the perceived power is going to use that advantage to make threats to discourage such a confrontation with authority figures from arriving.

How about the notion that you can text the school when you are being bullied? Do you like your phone in one piece? Then I probably would not recommend that either.

And Lexie actually thought she could drag me back there, to relive my own personal hell with all those real-life devils? With only the promise of the sight of Logan Courtney as a reward?

She must have been dreaming. Sure, Logan gave me the hot pants every time I saw him, but he was all old and married now anyway, like the lot of 'em. Happy, content, loved.

And I wasn't that much different than I had been back in school. Inside me still beat the heart of a fourteen-year-old girl, pushing blood through the clogged arteries of a seventy-year-old man. I contented myself with buying Stitch T-shirts and Hello Kitty phone cases because they momentarily lit up my otherwise sad life. But I could never find a way to take real action to achieve happiness.

I believed the strength to live another day, move, survive, lay in the tiny objects I spent my limited income on willingly, albeit with a guilt chaser. But they were only hunks of molded plastic. The life force to prosper had always only been inside myself. But I had to pull it out. Accessing it oft times was painful to the core. But it did exist. It was often clouded by my doubts, and more recently alcohol, but it was there. Tears streamed down at this realization.

If I had saved up all the five dollars I had paid on each occasion for tchotchkes and multiplied it by all those years, I probably could have had a tidy sum; perhaps enough to get me halfway to Hawaii. But I felt as though I was deprived of so much, by myself or the fates, that I couldn't go on without an incentive. I needed to allow myself these tiny rewards at regular intervals so that I could find the will to push on. It was the only way I could keep going.

Or maybe that is merely what anxiety told me.

Maybe happiness just wasn't meant for me. Ever.

* * * * *

I never told my mother about my bullying at school. Hell, I didn't even know to call it that. I just thought of it as "teasing", and no one has ever been hurt by teasing, right? It was only names, a minor invasion of privacy now and then, and a general attitude of cruelty and exclusion. But none of that ever left any physical marks. Except the ones I made myself.

Words aren't powerful. They simply leave someone's mouth and float off into the air. They don't stick to you like dirt and make you feel like less of a person, so much so that you can't possibly believe that anyone will love you ever. Sure, there are little moments where you forget. But after midnight or before the sun rises and the birds sing, you remember. It hurts. It hurts worse than a knife stabbing you physically. Mental pain has no limits. And you pray for death to end it, even though you don't believe in a god, so it is a hopeless waste of time anyway.

I didn't tell my mom or the teachers. The teachers saw and didn't deem it worth their time. My mom may have caused a stink because she enjoyed doing that. I would never have wanted to give her that satisfaction. She would have lost interest in that cause before long anyway. She would have only seen it as *my* shortcoming.

Somehow before I had always found a way to power through the crap in my life and to emerge out the other side, more or less, intact. Even when I was struggling through high school and emancipating myself from my parents, I made it through.

Creating art had once gotten me through the tough times.

Watching television had once gotten me through.

Listening to music had once been enough to make it.

But as I kept losing utilities, nothing was cutting it anymore. My natural gas was turned off, which meant no cooking, no baking, no hot water, no drying laundry.

Now my power was out too. There was not anything to do but sit in the dark and think about all I had missed out on.

I kept looking at the yearbook by flashlight. I now know the meaning of white, hot rage. It was when light streaked across your vision, filling it up so that you were blinded by the white, angry emotion and nothing else mattered as your body trembled with rage.

Hiding my true emotions all these years had left me exhausted. I just wanted to lie down and let the torment eat me alive. What would I become when my anxiety and depression took over in the void where common sense and responsibility had left me? This must be what a slow descent into madness feels like. I was officially giving up.

Alcohol had numbed my way through the obstacle of each day.

But now it wasn't enough. I wanted the storm of emotions to end. I was too far down the rabbit hole this time to see a way back out of it again.

It wasn't like today was any worse than the rest. They all sucked. It was like I had reached my last straw and suicide seemed like the only answer. I thought of it every day. My life situation, emotions *always* felt like *too much*. Suicide was a comforting thought. It was an actual plan to cope. There were so many things in my life out of my control, especially other people's lives or deaths. If you have physical pain, you take an aspirin or get cortisone injections or surgery. Mental pain was not that easy to fix.

I threw the yearbook down on the floor. Why bother putting anything away? I had an inkling of a plan brewing and if I were to follow through, this whole joint would be ransacked by the police as a crime scene anyway.

My feet were cold. I looked down at my naked feet and couldn't recall when I had taken my socks off. Maybe before my shower? And when had that been? The day before Lexie died?

I got up and walked across the room. I pulled open my sock drawer, the wood squeaking as it rubbed against itself, the varnished orange shining even in the fading sunlight. It had never been attractive, but it was functional. My sock supply was depleted. The only ones left were the ones that hurt my toes that I refused to ever wear. I should have emptied them into the trash with the rest of my life a long time ago. I couldn't even bear to think about when I would do laundry again. I could feel my blood pressure rising, making my body feel like a ticking time bomb. I could barely manage to not jab a knife into my heart every second. Details such as laundry and showering and dishes were massively overwhelming to me right now. The papers I kept tucked along the side of the drawer were now falling over, impeding my sock search. I tried pushing the papers back up, only to watch them fall again. Then I spotted it.

Lexie's birthday card.

Her birthday wasn't for another five months. But I always bought her card early. She was easy to shop for. I knew what she would love, because it is what I would love. I always put it in this special spot in my drawer... then usually forgot about it until the day of. Some years I bought another card, forgetting I already had one and she received two. I had no one else to buy for besides her kids, so it didn't matter. And now there was no one. I thought of Brody and Jackie as my niece and nephew. But Lexie had always been the link. With her gone, Colin would probably move them back to Minnesota to be closer to his own family.

This little card, sitting in my hands, would never achieve the purpose it had been created for. And it really was the perfect sentiment too. A tear dropped onto the colorful, glossy picture. Or was that snot?

"How could you leave me!" I screamed at her ghost, ripping up the card into four jagged pieces.

I instantly regretted it. Her birthday would come around again. And I would still need something to commemorate it—commemorate her. For her grave. I gathered up the pieces and put them back in the drawer again, pounding it closed.

* * * * *

Lexie had framed the composite picture of our graduating class and hung it up on her bedroom wall where it remained for many years after. I never had any idea how she could look at those people's faces day after day and not see that they were wolves in sheep's clothing. Every time I looked at it, it was like one of those holographic Halloween decorations: a face of a cherubic youngster in a faux antique frame that with a movement of six inches to either side would transform it into a gruesome zombie. She seemed blind to it. Was I the only one who resented all of them so much?

My "classmates" (I use that term derogatively) seemed to instinctively know that if Lexie was by my side, she would stand up for me. Due to this unspoken factoid she never had to because the wolves knew to always strike when she was not around. That way they could verbally abuse me to their heart's content.

I tried very hard to push most of it out of my mind over the ensuing years.

But it wouldn't all go away...

"Hey, can I borrow a pencil?" Russell Dunn, the nasty red-headed boy in my assigned group asked me from where he sat to my right. It was time for group work, so we were allowed to talk.

"No," I replied, not meeting his eyes.

I hated this classroom. It didn't used to be a classroom. It had been converted from a storage room because there was a shortage of space. Therefore, all the windows were up near the ceiling. You could see the light outside, but not any actual trees or grass or birds. It was reminiscent of a mental hospital. Or prison.

"C'mon. Give me a pencil."

Not even a please.

"No, I don't have one," I said, still not giving in to his hungry stare. I could feel my body temperature rising. The only reason Russell ever talked to me was to harass me and my body knew

that. I wanted to flee, but that wasn't an option available to me at this moment.

"C'mon. I know you have one..."

I inhaled, knowing what was coming next.

"Mathey."

I knew he would use that mutilated version of my name. He was not original. He never deviated from being the jerk everyone expected. After all, he had been one of the original adapters of "Mathey." But even after hours of contemplating ways to beat him at his own game, I never came up with one. My brain wasn't sadistic like his. I hoped it never would be. I had no clue why he targeted me. I was less popular than him. I wasn't in any activities where I was a threat. I was nothing. Why even bother with me?

"C'mon. You not going to talk to me? Mathey?"

My cheeks blazing, I tried to concentrate on my book as much as I could. My eyes scanned the same paragraph over and over because I could not process it with him pestering me. There were other students sitting across from us, more witnesses to my humiliation.

"Thomething wrong?" he egged me on, imitating Daffy Duck. "Cat got your tongue?"

There was no way I was saying one word to him. While my mother's imposed speech therapy had all but eradicated my lisp years ago, I still had trouble controlling it when I was nervous. I hadn't publically spoken in front of the class in five years. While I *was a meticulous student, I had always feigned not completing my work to get out of it. I hated lying to my teachers.*

I hated being made fun of more.

I absolutely hated that it acted up out of anxiety at the exact time people teased me about it. It was the perfect storm. I couldn't speak up for myself because I would lisp, only giving them more of the weakness they were already oppressing me for.

"Mathey, Mathey. Not gonna talk to me?" he sang.

I continued my failed attempt at ignoring him. His head outsized his body. Should I take a chance and speak up and point that out to him?

"Leave her alone, Russ."

I looked up, surprised at the sound of Isaac Sadler's voice. He had never been one to prey on me, but I also had never known him to stick up for me either. He usually laughed at whatever came out of Russell's giant, ugly mouth, as did everyone else within spitting distance. Isaac didn't look at me, continuing to write his assignment. Maybe the teasing in such a small group was too intimate for him. I was sure no one had ever teased Isaac about anything a day in his life. He was popular. He sat on the throne on which that role afforded him.

"Aw. I'm just playin'. Right, Mathey?"

Russell was an idiot. He didn't care if he repeated himself all day long. It had the desired effect for years. He made others laugh and I just continued to get more upset.

"I'm trying to work." I managed to push out through clenched teeth, avoiding my trigger sounds.

"So, go ahead and work. Woth stopping you?" He laughed at his own statement.

I turned the page. I couldn't focus on the words, but it was something I could do with my hands. I didn't want to look at him. I really needed this time in class to study. I would not have time to finish this after I got home from work tonight. Not if I wanted sleep, anyway.

"Why do you let him talk to you like that?" Isaac said, almost meeting my eyes despite his mop of blond curls hanging over his forehead.

I was surprised, as Isaac never talked to me. And I occasionally thought he was good looking.

'Let him?' I thought. Was there any way to make him stop? Because I would love to know the secret. Trying to be myself obviously didn't work. Neither had talking back. I tried ignoring him, like The More You Know public service announcement bull-shit would recommend, but that seemed to only allow it to go on and on, a never-ending river of shit.

"I bet you have a pencil at home. What do you do with it, huh?"

Isaac stood, picking up his book and notebook. I watched his tall, thin frame retreat to the library. It seemed like an easy escape, for me to follow him and go there too. But I knew Cody Micucci and Chris Hughes were already down there. Cody and

Chris were like brothers from a different mother. I hated them both. The only thing worse than either one of them was both of them together. The gruesome twosome.

I didn't know where this line of questioning was going, but I sure wished he would follow Isaac down to the library. Adrian Whelan still sat at the table, but he was dutifully working, his pen scratching obsessively against the paper in his notebook like a man driven. He seemed disinterested in my desperate plight, although being as he was within two feet of us, he couldn't have missed a single word.

"What do you do with a pencil, huh? Do you put it between your legs?"

Oh, God. He was going there. Isaac had probably foreseen it. Why couldn't I have the power to fry Russell with the hate burning within my laser eyes?

The words "shut up" were on the edge of my tongue, but I denied them exit from my mouth. The lisp would have surely kicked in. What happened after that would not be pretty.

"Do you put it in and out? Does it feel good?" he said, making a motion with his hands that I was ignoring.

He didn't need me to answer. He was already working an image in his mind that made me sick to contemplate. Some people may have run off at this point, gone to hide in the bathroom. But I wouldn't. It could be construed as what he was saying was true, which it was not. Running was always a sign of weakness that would be used against me on the next occasion. That could conceivably be as soon as next period.

"Just lay off."

I stared at the top of Adrian's dark hair as he continued to work, but we had both heard him clearly. He had taken a stand for me. By the sound of it, he was getting exasperated with Russell's drivel as well. Maybe Adrian could feel how powerless I was in this situation. The stench of my weakness permeated the air.

"Aw, don't you want to know? Don't you want to know what Mathey does with her pencils at home? Do you go 'uh-uh'?"

I hated that he formed everything as a question. As if he expected me to answer him.

Russell was trying to wear me down to my breaking point. I was getting closer with every tick of the clock. I looked up at the high windows, already knowing that they provided no escape. Why couldn't this class be over already?

"Are you going to go home and cry to Mommy? Oh wait, you can't." He had no shame. It didn't bother him the least bit to leverage my own family drama against me.

Adrian closed his book, gathering his things. His clothes and hair were always immaculate. I noticed it again today as he left for the library.

And then I was alone. I had ten more minutes left in this circle of hell, before I proceeded under my own willpower to the next.

* * * * *

Lexie was the positive force, the only sun in my life. I rotated around her. Now she was gone.

I missed the artificial scents of flowers and fruits that followed her everywhere she went. She had started wearing the body sprays and lotions as a way to cover up the smell of the cigarettes she smoked, even though it hadn't worked. I never told her that though. If she thought she didn't smell like a genetically-engineered watermelon that had resided next to a tobacco patch hit by lightning, she was fooling herself.

She had stopped smoking briefly when she was pregnant with Brody, and with Jackie permanently. But she kept wearing the girly products anyway. I didn't buy such things. Sometimes the scent was so strong it burned my nostrils and gave me a stuffy head. But I would give anything for her to sashay into my house right now, leaving behind a trail of Lexie.

Her life was always more full than mine was. Lexie had her family of course. But she was always going out somewhere. Back in the day she was involved in activities that I wasn't a part of, such as church events, choir, and flag corps. Then, of course, our freshman year in college she had begun to date Colin. It was much harder to gain or keep her attention after that. They had periods where they were broken up before once again "making up," but he seemed to captivate her attention more when they were apart. I couldn't win.

I wanted her life. I always knew that.

But I didn't begin to realize how infected I was with every little detail of her life until I began to look through my box of mementos from school. Nothing in there was mine. It was clippings from the newspaper with her picture. There was a program from the senior party night I declined attending that Lexie had brought me. It listed her as most likely to adopt too many homeless dogs. I was never sure if that was a testament to her caring spirit or people imagined her living in a house coated in dog hair and urine. There were poems she had written when she broke up with previous boyfriends. There were drawings I had made... of said boyfriends being impaled by arrows and swords and swordfish and such. I had done them to make her laugh. She hadn't even cared enough to keep them. They were all in my possession.

I knew her school schedule, then later her work schedule at Value Emporium. I not only memorized Lexie's schedule, but also that of her children & husband. If she deviated from it, I felt betrayed. I tried to analyze her every thought, everything she said. I took it as a praise or an insult. I cared more about her life than I did my own. I talked to her every day. Sometimes only texts or emails, but *every day*. Up until the last few months, anyway.

That was over now. How could it be? How would I go on? Our lives were entwined, always had been since fourth grade. Without her, it didn't seem possible that I was still sitting here, in this world, while she was no longer of it. She was prettier, outgoing. I followed her everywhere, like a little puppy. She was my leader. If she said I needed to change my shirt so that I could look cooler to get into a night club, I did it, even if I wasn't thrilled about it. I never would have chanced being rejected by her. It would have been a cut too deep to bear.

I had lived my life all this time through Lexie. And I thought my life sucked before. To realize that it wasn't even my life was somehow achingly worse.

I thought I had loved Lexie as a sister. But what if I hadn't actually felt real love in my entire life? I didn't feel love toward my parents. They had been there, but not in the way I needed. I had never had a romantic relationship of any consequence. And there was always Logan. Lord knows my obsession over him was pure lust, no matter how much I had tried to deny it to myself over the years. The pain of unrequited love, burned into my empty heart, blossoming into an obsession, reignited every time I had to pass him in the hallway or watch him run in gym class. I wanted so badly for Logan to notice me. But I was equally terrified that he would, and begin to treat me just as the others did, people he sat at the same table with at lunch. Maybe it was through the fear of that situation that I manifested his silence. If so, it was self-torture.

Maybe I didn't know how to love. Maybe the empty warmth of obsession was all I knew. Maybe it is all I had to try to fill the hole inside of me.

Maybe I was truly broken; beyond any hope.

And now, to have the only thing I ever thought was truly real in my life be cut from me? It was like losing an umbilical cord, the life force that kept me going. I had been neutered of the one thing I cared about most, more than my own well-being. It hurt. I felt as though she had betrayed me. She was going to force me to attend the reunion. I was loathing the idea. But I knew she would have made me.

I knew it.

But, she was gone. My future was suddenly, irrevocably changed. It didn't feel like she had died in a freak accident. She had left me. On purpose. Broken up with me. Abandoned me for greener pastures and pearly gates.

I knew she wouldn't do that in real life.

I *knew* that.

Granted, she had been by less lately. I knew she was losing the battle to reach me.

I took another drink, feeling it burn my throat. I coughed.

I didn't want to be, but I couldn't help it. I was mad at Lexie. She was a traitor. She had left me. Left me with all the pieces of my life to pick up. And I couldn't. It was like the pieces were Stonehenge. There was no way I could lift that on my own.

The sketchbooks had to remind me why I never wanted to see these people again in my life. I had no use for them. They were history and that is where they should stay…

And there was only one way to bury them all. I took out my senior yearbook, the shiny gold 98 embossed on the cover. I flipped through it and reminded myself who should be top on my hit list.

Now I was left on a beach, with no one. Not even the man of my dreams was there to rescue me. And a storm was rolling in. A big, nasty, dark, killer storm. And the villagers could try to take cover, but it wasn't going to work. Not with what this storm had planned. They were all right in the destructive path.

VENGENCE

Guns don't kill people. People kill people.
People kill people. Guns kill people faster.

It was so intimidating to walk into the gun store. Sorry, hunting supply. I was on a mission and only had my mind on one goal: metal in my hands. I was a woman walking into a man's lair. Women were traditionally the gathers while men were the hunters. And I had liked it that way. Up until now, when I had something that I needed to hunt.

I had no idea what criteria I should be considering for a successful gun purchase. If I still had internet service at home, I could have researched it. I was praying I would get a good salesman for once who was more concerned with servicing the customer than making a big fat commission.

Ha, pray. Pretty sure that ain't the appropriate course of action right now. I was about to purchase my own weapon of mass destruction to take down ninety-eight victims. God wasn't listening to me. I was going to hell.

I was pretty sure a handgun wouldn't hold that many bullets. As I pulled open the front door, I barely heard the door buzzer as I entered and wondered idly how fast I would be able to reload.

Both men behind the counter were busy with other customers, so I took a minute to calm myself and get the lay of the land.

I needed something small, easy to conceal.

I didn't see any hand guns, but there were rifles in racks hanging on the walls. I took one off, fumbling it like an idiot, but caught it at the last moment before it crashed to the floor. I held it up like I imagined a hunter might, looking down the barrel at my imaginary prey. I believed the back of the gun was called the butt. I laid it on top of my shoulder, imagining how bad ass I looked.

"That's not quite the right position," a young man said. He had materialized out of thin air, or possibly the door to the back room. "Here, let me assist you."

The man was young and I wondered if he was a second or third generation employee. He attempted to show me how it worked, more than simply putting the bullets in it. But it was beyond my understanding. All I knew was that after I loaded it, it worked as if by some kind of fairy magic.

When I let him know I was actually interested in a hand gun, he led me up to the front counter where I had seen the other customers when I entered. It turned out the counter was a glass case containing all the smaller weapons.

I tied up his time for quite a while until I picked out a model that I thought I could handle. "Is there a waiting period?"

"No, but you have to go down to the police station and pay a fee before purchase," he said.

"Just sounds like a cash grab."

"Maybe, but it's the law."

"So, I can run down there now?"

"You could, but if I were you I would drive."

I smiled in spite of myself at his juvenile joke. I was positive he wouldn't be so friendly to me if he had any inkling of my true nefarious intentions. The gun I purchased today would get traced back to their store. Sure, they would be able to prove I had bought it legally. But another crazy misusing firearms was the last thing they needed.

Or was it? Wasn't it always that after such a tragic event the politicians threatened to make stricter gun laws, and then gun enthusiasts went out and bought a few more in protest? Maybe something good could come out of my planned tragedy. I could help sales for lowly small town gun store owners across the country.

I quickly exited the store and hopped into my car. I started it, but did not pull out of the parking spot right away. It occurred to me that sizing up firearms with a salesman was one thing, but having my name on file at the police station was quite another. Sure, I could pass the background check no sweat. I had never been arrested (yet) and my crazy had never been documented for anyone to find. But after the act, it would provide damning evidence of premeditation. What would I do after my heinous act? Would suicide be the best option? Or living out my days with malcontents behind bars in questionable hygiene conditions?

I shuddered. I wouldn't make such a decision now. I would have to wait until the heat of the moment to decide. Maybe there would be a way to escape afterwards, in the chaos that was sure to ensue. Maybe I could run off into the woods...

And what? I was no Bear Grylls. I could barely survive a night in a tent in a well-lit campground with a newly-renovated bathroom. Did I really think I could piss in the woods and sleep in dead leaves, all while keeping myself concealed from the authorities? That seemed unlikely.

My course was set. I backed out of my parking spot and pulled onto the road. I drove the short distance to the state police post. I managed to clear my mind of images of prison as I instead concentrated on the terrified faces of my former classmates. I tried to imagine how the years would have aged each of their faces, robbed them of hair. Would wrinkles add more joy to my endeavor or make them all seem more pathetic as they ran away from me like scared bunnies?

It was harder to keep the murderous images in the forefront of my brain as I was inside the police station. A man at a window handed me a couple of forms and pointed me to a chair with a desk attached to it. It was a school desk—how ironic—except sized-up for adults. I remembered taking my written driver's license test in one like it. Maybe it was a hand-me-down. Government agencies were always complaining that they lacked funding. Such recycling must happen.

Sliding into the desk only strengthened my resolve. It was all I could do to not doodle pictures of bleeding alumni and my hit list onto the margins of the background check paperwork. I smiled. I knew who the first names on my list would be. Chris Hughes for me, Cody Micucci for Lexie. And there wasn't a single list. In fact, there were three lists. A list of people to definitely kill. Then there was the second string→I wouldn't seek them out, but would definitely shoot them if they got into my sights. The third list was people I didn't really want to shoot, such as spouses attending that I had never even met. But if they married those assholes they were either just as bad as them or deserved to be put out of their misery. But, oh hell, I wasn't going to try to avoid anyone.

I only had two hours to try and get some practice. That was bound to cause me to be so sore as to make the actual dirty deed difficult to execute. My muscles had begun to atrophy while I laid on the couch for months, barely going outside to see the light of day. I was approaching forty years old. I anticipated needing a healthy dose of ibuprofen for pain and a large energy drink. Maybe two of them. Especially at seven o'clock at night. Hopefully they wouldn't have a bad reaction and kill me first. I guess that would be God's chance to take me out of the equation tonight and save some lives.

I contemplated all this for the forty-five minutes it took for them to run my background check and make change for my fifty dollar bill I used to pay the twenty-five dollar fee. All I had left to buy the gun was the fifties I had stashed away as the last of my savings.

But one person kept showing up in my mind.

Logan.

What list would I put him on?

I hated him so badly that I wanted him dead; he would even make a beautiful corpse.

But a crazy part of me (Wait, what part *wasn't* at this point?) wanted him to live. I knew he wouldn't ever be mine. But shooting him would remove all possibility with certain definitiveness.

Maybe I should go with Door Number 3: use my gun to my advantage, take him hostage and force him to have sex with me.

I was so enamored by option three that I almost rear-ended the car in front of me on the way back to the gun store. I walked in with my permit, spent the last of my life savings, and walked out with a 9mm pistol, ammunition, and two clips.

I headed to the firing range to see how bad I was. I was a horrible shot. After two hours, I could only manage to hit the very far edges of the target half the time. And that was after half the guys there had tried to give me pointers. I even tried to imagine the bullseye was the face of Chris, but it didn't help my aim any. Maybe I should start the shooting after everyone had partaken in the buffet. Maybe the extra calories would slow them down enough to allow me to hit them.

I packed up my gear, snapping the lid shut on the case I bought for truly this one time use. I had already put a Hello Kitty sticker on its plain black plastic shell—just to make people wonder. I had always been an oddity. Why not embrace it now, when I had protection against everyone else's opinion: 9mm of protection. Plus, the sticker would look cute sitting on the shelf in the police evidence room.

"Keep it up, honey. A little more practice and you will get there."

Number one, didn't this guy know he should never call a woman with a gun at her fingertips "honey?" And number two, he didn't know that this is my only *shot* to improve my accuracy. I had used up most of my daylight hours driving around the county trying to find this state-run shooting range.

Returning home, I unlocked my apartment door, and flipped the light switch. There was no response. I flipped it back and forth a few more times like a dummy, then proceeded into the living room. Old habits were hard to break. Luckily it was still light enough to not yet require lights to see where I was going. I had lost utilities left and right this week. Not that it would matter much longer. I started stripping off clothes right there in the living room, not bothering to make it to the bedroom first where the unbelievably feminine red dress Lexie had bought was waiting for me. As I made it down to my bra & panties, I decided to take the gun out of the case to admire it again. It was power, raw and ready to be molded in my hands for any purpose that I chose.

I should have been scared to buy a gun. But every move I had made since I found out Lexie had died was as though someone was showing me the road I needed to travel. My overactive gut did not fret about these decisions. A warm glow had begun to reside there. I went to an unfamiliar store and purchased a gun. I had to go talk to a policeman. I went to a place teeming with strangers and shot off my gun.

I was revived as if I had been awakened from a coma. I had motivation running through my veins for the first time in as long as I could remember. I had a sense of purpose, a reason to be alive even if just for a little while.

I was reborn as an assassin.

It felt good.

It felt right.

"You're home. Now pay me my money before I change the locks next time you leave."

He startled me and bothered me and depressed me all at the same time. The landlord figured since I had not locked the door behind me, he could stroll right in. Which, since I was delinquent on my rent, I suppose he legally could.

It was a reflex. I held up my gun as I had been practicing all afternoon, cradling the grip between my palms, overflowing my tiny toddler hands. My right index finger was on the trigger, the safety was off.

His eyes got wide as he took in the sight of me standing there in my bra and panties, training a gun on his fat stomach. Even as bad a shot as I was, the odds were in my favor to hit something that large. He lifted up his hands and backed out of the door slowly. But when he was out of the sight, I heard him mumble "crazy bitch."

He had no idea how right he was.

As much as I hated to lay it down, I placed the gun on the table. It was already beginning to feel like an extension of my hand. I closed and locked my front door, then proceeded to shower and put on the too fancy dress that had been Lexie's final gift to me.

It was fortuitous that she had picked red. Of course, she was probably rolling over in her embalming fluid if she had any idea what I was about to do.

Ugh, that was a nasty image.

I wouldn't be about to mow down my classmates in cold blood if she were still here. If she were still here, I would have some bright spot in my future.

But she was gone. Now there was nothing. How could God turn my life from just regular shitty to monumental shitty so quickly? Two years ago I had had a full-time job, a best friend.

Utilities. It all began to crush my soul again, so I reached into the fridge and downed some strawberry-flavored vodka. It tasted like crap, but it took the edge off and gave me a buzz. I hoped it wouldn't impair my aim any more than it already was. I took three ibuprofen and chased it with the vodka.

I hated carrying a purse, especially when I was already too girly in the fancy dress and heels. There had already been a chill creeping into the air when I had returned home. So I grabbed an ancient jean jacket and put the gun and extra clip into the roomy inside pocket. I had watched Lexie once sneak a whole bottle of vodka out of her parent's liquor cabinet in her black version of the same coat. It was over twenty years old, what better attire to sport to the reunion?

Should I lisp out "That's all, folks" before I gunned them down in a hail of bullets? Or was that being too dramatic?

* * * * *

Closing my car door, I walked between the vehicles in the half full parking lot as I headed into the American Legion. The event was due to start at 7:00PM. It was 7:15PM . I wondered how many more would wander in tardy. The sign by the road proclaimed "Welcome Class of 1998" in black, plastic letters. I pulled open the door without hesitation and strutted in. My confidence was met with another "Class of '98" sign, this one made from poster board and pre-cut paper letters like teachers' use on their bulletin boards. How many of these lamos had become teachers? Bullies molding the minds of the next generation—nice. There was a line at a table next to me of people collecting their name tags. I didn't have time for such bullshit. I moved past and headed right into the banquet hall.

Crepe paper streamers were strung from one side of the room to the other in our school colors of yellow and blue, sporting facial tissue flowers where they were attached. Somebody went all out on these decorations—not. Maybe all the money had gone into the food. I walked past one side of the long buffet table. A few people were filling their plates already. Most people were still standing and talking among the round tables, little candles in the center of each one. What was this, Valentine's Day? The overhead lights were bright so that we could all see who the hell each other was. I resolved that the candles were stupid as I dove into a gap in the sparse food line, forgoing the tongs and plucking a chicken tender from the warmer with my bare hand. A woman gave me a dirty look. I didn't recognize her off-hand. A wife, maybe? I smiled sweetly to her, with a mouthful of chicken. I strutted past a table someone had claimed with purses and jackets. I grabbed up a pair of tickets that had been left there. I assumed they were drink tickets.

I did a quick survey of the room. Some of the faces were instantly recognizable. Some were harder. Some were strangers. But my heart still burned with hate for them all.

Oh, this was going to be fun.

"Hey, Macey."

I didn't recognize the voice. Having skipped the check-in table, I wasn't wearing a name tag. The only ones who seemed to know my face were those most heavily invested in my torment back in the day, so I prepared myself before I turned around. It was Troy Janz. He had been one of the guys who would act out in class, getting in trouble. I had no idea why he would want to talk to me.

"How are you doing?" he continued.

That was a weird way to start.

"Oh, not so good since my best friend died on Wednesday."

"I heard about that. Must be tough."

"Yes. Attending her funeral tomorrow is sure to be difficult," I quipped.

He hesitated for a minute before he began again. I swear to God if he called me "Mathey" I was going to smack the butt of my gun into his skull so hard that he would drop before anyone would even know what happened. I could rub any blood off on my red dress and say it was wine. I think I was born for this violence thing.

"I wanted to apologize. I have thought a lot about you over the years. I'm sorry for how I treated you. I was a bully."

What? It was surreal.

"My little daughter is in school. Now I am dealing with it from her point of view. It had me thinking about you a lot."

First, ew. I never wanted him thinking of me. Ever. Second, I never wanted an apology out of any of them.

I was almost touched for a moment. Until I remembered all the times my name had rolled off his tongue as "Mathey." All the times he had told me to "thay it don't spway it," as if it was nothing more than a catchphrase he got off the latest sitcom. As if it didn't hurt me every time someone set it free into the atmosphere.

My hate would not go away that fast. It had been stoked for too many years for someone to just pour a pail of water on it and think the light of the orange insanity embers would die out. I would rather have revenge. Maybe he was trying to make himself feel better. I didn't want him to feel better. I wanted him to suffer.

Sometimes I thought that I had blown the bullying I received out of proportion in my head over the years. I am aware that can happen. That is why human beings are the worst witnesses in a court of law; our minds corrupt our own memories. It wasn't merely how I remembered things now. Someone else was corroborating my misery. *Someone who had been on the other side.* He had no reason to remember at all. Troy seemed to remember the wrath of evil he had thrust on me better than I did. He obviously thought it was pretty severe to come and apologize. And he was one of the tormentors. And he wasn't the worst. He wasn't even in the Top 5.

He was still standing there, waiting for some kind of response. I had many, many to give him. But the ultimate one I was saving for later. I could let anything fall out of my mouth now, and it would be totally inconsequential anyway.

So then why couldn't I think of something?

"Too bad it took you so long to realize all that." It didn't come out with the bite I had intended, but I think maybe he got the message. I didn't stay to find out. I turned and walked away. As you would suspect, that was not my last encounter where I was required to socialize. I really hadn't thought this reunion thing through.

"We are so sorry about Alexis."

No you aren't. You didn't even know her. No one called her Alexis. You will all be very sorry real damn soon.

I kept hearing those same five sentences over and over again. I lost track of which ones were coming from outside my mind and which ones weren't. They grew louder and louder until it was a roar pushing me through the crowd.

Until I had to stop because I could no longer move.

I was glued to the floor. While the image of young Logan Courtney in my old yearbook had left me breathless, the real flesh and blood human being was almost more than I could bear. My blood pressure, already way too high, skyrocketed and for a second the room went sideways before I grabbed onto the back of a chair nearby to steady myself.

I knew I sounded like a cliché from a smutty romance book at the grocery store. But no one knew what he had meant to me during those torturous years. I would never have found the energy to drag myself to school every morning amid all the taunts and teasing if not for the chance to see Logan.

Lexie knew me better than anyone and had used it against me to get me among *these* people once again tonight. And this would be the last time. It is a good thing Lexie wasn't here to witness what I was about to do. She would have to settle for rolling over in her grave. Or, well, the casket at the funeral home. I wondered if that would cause it to fall off the little stand they set them on and her body to tumble out. I shivered at the image.

I was sad to see Logan's face had thinned with maturity, his boyish features chiseled into manhood. But the new characteristics of his appearance were more than adequate upgrades. Black stubble now covered his chin. The fact that the dark brown hair on his head used to be a lighter shade when school started in the fall from his long days in the summer sun was just a memory. His burnt almond eyes danced as he talked to old acquaintances; I had forgotten how impressive that could be in person. He wore his hair shorter, close to his head now, gone were his youthful curls. He had aged well, better than the rest of these damn hicks. He still had all his hair. He didn't have wrinkles around those warm eyes yet, but I could already tell they would look perfect when they did settle onto the landscape of his face. He was now more cautious with his smile—he didn't give it away as often and freely as he had during our school days. It used to pop out all the time, an impish grin that kept me going during unending, insufferable days, not that it was ever for me.

He reminded me of Kevin Costner in *Field of Dreams*. With well-polished looks, Logan had it all together. He was a little world-weary, experienced, and wore it well.

Of course one thing had changed. There was a female making her way through the crowd next to him. I assumed she was his wife. He didn't have his arm around her and they were not holding hands, although he did gesture to her during introductions. Maybe they were not as happy behind their white picket fence in their big house as they would have the world believe. This inner monologue made me realize I still held out the tiniest hope to be with him one day.

Stupid girl.

My anger flared a bit, setting the tips of my ears on fire.

The woman had dark hair, a deep molasses. It looked fake. She probably colored it to hide the gray. She didn't actually look old enough to have gray hair yet. Had he married a younger woman? I didn't know much about Logan, but I always pictured him a little dim, needing a woman to hold his hand and help him through life. She wore a dress covered in midnight blue sequins, landing a few inches above her knees. It looked fancier than the occasion called for, but then heck, so did mine. She wasn't as thin as I would have pictured, but the shine of the decorations disguised her extra pounds well. I guess she had a nice face. But all I could picture was the word "bitch" written all over it. And maybe a target. I had her in my sights. And soon I could have her in the sight of my gun.

I wanted to move out of Logan's anticipated path, right by me, but I couldn't. Maybe it was morbid curiosity, to know what his final words ever to me might be.

He was walking away from the person he had been talking with, so he was close to me by the time he turned his head and his eyes met mine. He was taller than I remembered, a good six inches taller than me. My heart squeezed at that realization, his sexual appeal to me increasing more when I didn't believe that could ever be possible.

The only emotion in his eyes was the residual good cheer from the last person he had conversed with. No recognition. I could have just been another spouse he had never seen before, not someone he had spent hundreds of hours in the same classroom with.

In that moment I hated him.

Obviously he had not thought of me since school let out, as I had him. Not that I actually expected that he had. But even the slightest flicker of recognition would have given me hope, hope enough to spare him.

"Oh, Macey, right?" he smiled and pointed at me.

Oh ya, wonder boy was going down with the rest of these dirty dogs. I waited a beat more, to hear the obligatory "We are so sorry about Alexis." But it never came. He had to know we were close in school, always walking together in the hallway. I was far from popular, but it was a small class. And he lived local, he had to have seen us now and then at a community event or our picture in the newspaper. He had to know that we were still close. The talk of the whole reunion was her sudden death. He couldn't plead ignorance to current events. Or maybe he could. What was that saying? God doesn't give with both hands? Maybe he was "pretty" dumb.

I turned my body, literally giving him the cold shoulder, and marched away. I may never see Logan Courtney alive again, and I was good with that.

"What's her problem" I heard his wife mutter under her breath.

God, if only she knew. Her life had probably gone totally as she had planned it from girlhood: meet cute guy, trick cute guy into marrying her, move into his family's already paid off house, get knocked up to trap him into the marriage for the long haul, throw in another kid, just to have a spare. Ya, I bet the she-devil's itinerary had progressed something like that.

I wanted to turn around and slam my fist into her face. But with my luck I would hurt my hand and then not be able to pull the trigger, which would be the real tragedy. My arm was sore enough from shooting earlier, even with the help of the painkillers.

I walked around the room, not knowing how to mingle and not wanting to. I was watching for my moment. It would have to be after all those arriving fashionably late showed up, but before the early bedtime people began to filter out. And if I waited until most of them had pickled themselves in booze, it might make things go easier—slower reaction times and all. Actually, liquor didn't sound like a half bad idea. The vodka shots I'd had at home anxiety had burned off. So I used the tickets I stole and ordered two drinks and poured them down my throat. They went down smooth. It had been forever since I had had a properly mixed drink. A year ago, that would have had me on the bathroom floor, vomiting and falling asleep. But in that time I had built up my tolerance. I was pretty sure that wasn't a good thing, as Lexie often took to informing me. It wouldn't matter soon. Nothing would. Everything would.

* * * * *

I HATED THEM.

There should be a stronger word, but there wasn't.

But, I know I hated myself just as much for not standing up to them, for what I was about to do. But most of all, I hated myself because I truly believe that what they said is in me must have been there all along. I deserved their taunts, but I still hated them. I wanted to give them a taste of their own medicine.

My body pulsed. Any second I might burst into a million pieces & explode. It would at least put a stop to feeling like this. The energy built up inside of my flesh bag finally being released. Then the sweet peace I craved. Even if the quiet could only come from death, I would take it.

I was going to do this. I looked into the streaky mirror in front of me. I did not recognize the person staring back at me. Her hair had air-dried. It hung in perfect waves in the style I had wanted all my life. Her blue eyes were hollow, with dark circles under them. Her red-painted lips curled up in a sneer disguised as a smile. She was wearing a dress—a dress, for God's sake. I didn't know her. But soon the media for a hundred miles around would know her. The local news would no doubt cover it. Maybe even the national networks. I should update my profile pic before I sprayed lead. Somehow, over the years, I always sensed in a madman shooting scenario I would be the one with a gun. Maybe I should have done it years ago and gotten it over with.

The woman in the reflection was obviously a being ruled by her emotions. They burned just below her skin. If I squinted, I could see steam bubbling and escaping out of her pours. She smiled again. I put my hand into my pocket, cradling the weight of the gun in my hand. There was only one thing left for me to do.

You have always been a little pussy. You let them say any shit they wanted about you. You never stood up for yourself. They made you think you didn't deserve their respect.

"It is time to show them."

The sideways looks.

The whispers.

The fear of being myself, walking down the hallway, what clothes to wear, what notebook or backpack to buy, to even open my mouth.

It would all end now. This was a brilliant idea. Why had no one done this before? There was no way to heal the mental wounds that they had inflicted upon me. So why not take them all down with me? Poetic justice.

I took a deep breath and walked out into the hallway.

I was going to do this.

I placed my hand on the steel and plastic in my jacket pocket, warm from being beside my body.

There were a few people around me, they would see.

They would give warning screams, tipping off the others in the main room. It wasn't ideal, but I wanted this over and done with. I was tired of this calling in my gut. I never thought I would feel compelled by my inner voice to commit murder, but that is exactly what I had been experiencing for the past twenty-four hours. All my demons I had fought against my entire life were now going to eat me alive if I didn't let them out this instant.

I pulled it out of my pocket and made three deliberate steps toward the rec hall. There were two female gasps. Nothing was going to stop me. Then Logan was there as my first target, right in front of me, talking in his beautiful voice, sounding like a broken calliope of angels.

"Jesus Christ, what are you doing with a gun?"

And I raised it, pointing it at him. I aimed it right at his heart, at point blank range. At the heart I had wished would love me all these years. The two women nearby ran off. Probably to call the cops. My last seconds of freedom and life were ticking off quickly. I wanted to kill him in that instant, I did. I wanted to stop all the pain of longing after so many years. But I met his beautiful nut-brown eyes and knew I couldn't. The longing would still be there, and then it would be joined by regret at ending his life. The two would be at odds and possibly tear me apart if given the opportunity of a long, uninterrupted rumination on the subject, such as in an orange jumpsuit in prison.

There was no explanation with all my premeditation why I didn't actually pull the trigger.

He must have witnessed the doubt and indecision pass across my face. Lightning quick he grabbed my wrist and wrenched the gun away from me, dragging me to the fire exit and pulling me through it. We were out in the cool night. Together. Alone. My cheeks were on fire. I touched one and realized it was wet with tears. I didn't even know why they were falling anymore. I realized Logan was still holding my right hand in his left, and the gun in his right. His lips were moving, but I couldn't hear him. I could only hear a loud roar, like a waterfall in my ears. I don't know how long I stood there staring at his beautiful face, changed with age, different, but still how it should be, how I could have predicted it would look at thirty eight years old when I was in sixth grade and first felt the warmth between my legs that he caused. Then he pulled me so hard that my right red heel broke and my boob almost popped out of the top of my dress.

"Ow," I protested. I was now within the cloud of his all-too-familiar cologne. It always smelled like a sweet pine tree to me. How many nights had I fallen asleep recalling this smell? It was almost enough to make me forget the dilemma we found ourselves in.

I was empty, drained, but in a good way. Actually, the best way. In that brief moment, I breathed easy. I felt a sense of accomplishment, as if I had completed my intended mission. The sight of Logan had stopped me at the last minute, but it still felt good. There was no longer a weight on my chest. The past and present were clean slates, no bad vibes and no good expectations. There was just little me, standing in front of Logan in a ridiculously fancy red dress. I couldn't even remember how I had gotten there.

"The cops are coming. Don't you hear them?"

And now I could hear a siren approaching. It sounded like only one car.

"Here's the plan. We'll tell them you were joking. And I knew it. No one else was supposed to see and get scared. You'll have to lose the bullets though." He proceeded to dump the ammunition out into a nearby bush.

"Will I get into trouble?"

"This is the local police. I should be able to smooth it over with them. They have known me since before I was born."

I had lived here since I was born. But I had no such perks. No one knew me.

"But I was going to kill people."

"For Christ sake, don't tell the cop that!"

I was grateful that he was taking me seriously. If he had thought it was all only a joke, I would have been shattered.

I hadn't realized it, but I had begun to watch the scene play out between us like I was watching a movie.

"Why are you talking to me?" It was like I was trying to talk to a script writer through my television. This was all surreal. This was supposed to be the last scenario to ever have a possibility of happening tonight, or ever.

"What do you mean? I'm trying to get you out of trouble."

"Why does it matter to you, one way or the other?"

"What?"

"Why help me?"

"Because you are a fellow human being?"

"You don't know me from Adam."

"I know you as well as anyone else in there."

"Bullshit."

"Bullshit?"

"You chummed around with all those popular people in school. I was invisible to all of you. And when I wasn't, I was the butt of all the jokes."

"I never teased you."

"That might be true. But you also didn't stop them. Or give me the time of day."

"You were shy."

My face instantly contorted in disgust. It was all I could do not to spit. I swung my head down, then back up again.

"There is no such thing as shy. It is merely yet another label people use to group others into easily-manageable categories, like ADHD and autism. We used to deal with all three on the same spectrum of normal. Now everyone has to have their own ray diverging off the line that used to be normal. There is keeping quiet because you have nothing to say or because you are afraid of getting picked on if you do open your mouth. That is all."

"You keep blaming us for your life. But it is your life. We didn't choose your college or pick your job or car. If you are unhappy, it is your own fault."

I had always seen school as a living hell, but I got up every morning and attended anyway. It was my "sense of duty" that always compelled me to attend, against the better judgement of my guts.

"But don't you see? It was you, all of you, who robbed me of my self-esteem, made me feel like shit. Made me want to die. The fear of death coming for me is my number one cause of panic attacks. But I was in so much pain I was ready to welcome it with open arms and end it all, because your criticism, your cruelty, terrified me more. It hurt so much that I just wanted to escape it any way that I could."

"I don't know what you expect us to do about it now."

"I want you to pay. But I don't want to go to prison."

"Macey—"

My wry laugh interrupted his statement. "I have waited so long for my name to come off of your lips. That is now the second time tonight. But I can't believe it is under these circumstances."

"Macey, no matter where you are at now, you can start over."

"I never got to dye my hair pink. I never got a tattoo. I always kept my appearance respectable, in case of unexpected lay off and job search. But, somehow, I missed out on life. I lived behind balanced checkbooks and a spotless credit report. But I have never traveled the U.S. I have never been on a plane. I just woke up one day and realized that my life was a lie I told myself.

"I did everything I was supposed to for fifteen years. Scrimping, saving, eating Velveeta singles melted over saltine crackers three times a day—and where did that get me? Where the fuck did that get me?"

"There are people who worked harder, longer—fifty years even. Maybe you haven't earned it yet. Didja ever think of that?" Logan was blunt, but he wasn't angry at me. He seemed as though he was trying to understand me.

"I couldn't live like that *one more day*. I've... I've always felt that I wasn't wired right. Maybe this is my proof."

"You have to quit being mad at others for the things the world didn't give you."

"I'm not mad at the world. I'm mad at you!" I screamed it at his face. I saw my spittle fly in the dim glow of the parking lot lights that crept around the corner of the building.

"Why?"

"Because I had a crush on you. I was in love with you, in that obsessive way only a sixth grade girl can be. If you had looked at me back then, maybe I would have felt like I was something. I felt like no one ever loved me."

"That is your problem. I have nothing to do with that."

"But you could have."

"But I didn't. And I never will."

His statement hit me as hard as a slap in the face. I watched him reset his jaw, obviously not meaning it quite so harshly. He began again. "You are not the only one who suffers. Some of us just do it silently." He paused. I could see his thoughts scrolling behind his eyes. "I'm bisexual."

"You are?"

He affirmed his statement with a nod of his head. I wondered if he had the bravery to repeat it.

"But you've been married to a woman for like ten years?"

"Yes. But I'm attracted to guys. I think I would rather be with one now. But I wasn't miserable with my wife all those years. I love her too. And our kids, the life we built together. I haven't been living a lie. I just haven't fully fit into my life so far."

"Why admit it now, after all these years?"

"Because I just had a gun pointed at me. And I don't think you were joking with your finger squarely on that trigger. I saw my life flash before my eyes. And I didn't like how it ended up."

All the hate and anger drained from me. But something else did too. All the animosity, resentment, feelings of inadequacy as a result of years of belittling by my peers blew off into the wind, past Logan's head and out toward the baseball field. I blinked quickly, thinking I was imagining the sight of them flying off, multi-hued psychedelic butterflies. Maybe I had.

He hugged me as I broke down. I cried for many reasons. The two most prominent were in regard to him. I was devastated to admit that my lust for him would never be reciprocated. I had to let that die now, or it would continue to fuel my angry fire and destroy me. But I also cried tears of joy.

This thing we had now, this budding friendship, had the potential to be more satisfying, fulfilling than a high school roll in the hay would have been. His arms held the pieces of me together from breaking. It was wonderful.

"What would you do right now... If you could do anything you wanted?" he asked me. I couldn't look anywhere but into the deep pools of his brown eyes.

"You... joking. I know we are past that now."

"Funny. Tell me. Like if you won the lottery."

"Probably move to a shack in Hawaii & paint."

"Then do it! Go!"

"Are you insane? I can't go to Hawaii? I have no money. I am practically homeless here. To some degree, my problems would follow me wherever I go."

"Then what do you have to lose? Go be homeless in Hawaii. At least maybe you would be happier. And it would be warmer. Heck, maybe I could even come with you."

"What?"

"Wouldn't you be less miserable there? With me? Unless you don't want me."

"Of course I would want you. That sounds like a dream. But you barely even know me."

"Once you get talking, you are kind of an open book."

"But you have a wife and kids. How could you just leave them?"

"Trust me, I am not being spontaneous. This is something I have thought about for a long time."

"Wow. So I'm not the only one so lost?"

"Not at all. Everyone is in their own way. Apparently your filter for hiding it got broken along the way."

"Yes. I can tell you the exact day and time; January 16, 2018 9:23AM." There was a moment of silence. It seemed Logan didn't have a response for that. So, I decided to demand some clarification. "So you just want to go live in Hawaii & be homeless? Like Chris Pratt did?"

"Oh, he's hot."

"OK. I don't think I will *ever* get used to you saying stuff like that." I shook my head and continued. "I've never even had a long-term boyfriend."

"Oh God, please tell me you are not still a virgin."

"Nooo. And thank you so much for the vote of confidence. There were guys and experiences along the way, but none that ever stuck around."

"Thank God for that."

A stranger quickly came around the side of the building, discovering us. I jumped, startled because I was lost in this fog of our own little world Logan and I had created. Logan put his hand on my back to settle me. I realized the man wore a uniform. Maybe Logan was trying to prevent me from running. But I had been through so many emotions in the last—how long had we been out here? I realized my legs were cold below the short dress. I didn't know how I was still standing. There is no way I could think of running, especially with a broken shoe.

"Why, there you are Logan." He looked down at the small wire-bound notebook he had used to inquire about me all night and read slowly from his own scrawled handwriting. "And is this Massey Reinhart?" the cop said, butchering my name.

"Yes, this is Macey. What brings you by tonight, Burt?"

Burt was so thin he might blow away in a stiff wind. He looked at us, puzzled, his black mustache at an unnatural angle. He must dye it because the dude had to be close to retirement age. He had been old when he had come and spoken to our kindergarten class about stranger danger. We were at a reunion that proved that was a long damn time ago.

"Well, I got a couple calls that this little lady pulled a gun on you. Is that right?"

I laughed, nervous and hysterical. To myself, I sounded like a hyena.

"Well, yes she did. It's a little joke we play with each other."

I wondered how Logan managed to keep his voice so calm.

"Ya, all the time," I chimed in. I had almost forgotten the cover story we had manufactured so long ago.

"I pull one on her, the next time she pulls one on me—"

"I didn't know you had a gun, Logan?" Burt looked mystified.

"Well, I don't. But the boys have toy guns."

"Can I see the gun used tonight?" The officer held out his hand expectantly.

I instinctively shrunk back toward Logan. As had become the norm in our short and strange interactions of this night, he took the lead, reaching behind him to pull the gun out from behind his back where it had been tucked into the waistband of his jeans.

Officer Burt took it from him and studied it, weighing it in his palm. "But this is a real gun. A real beauty too."

"Ya, she really got me good tonight. Man, I never expected her to pull a real gun on me. Macey pulled out all the stops for the reunion."

I wished Logan hadn't reminded him what my correct name was.

Burt removed the clip then pushed the slide to look inside. "No bullets, that's good. Needs a good cleaning though. So you didn't intend to do any harm around here tonight?"

Logan jabbed his elbow so hard into my ribs that I almost fell off my one remaining heel.

"No sir."

"You do realize I could arrest you right now."

"But no harm was done," Logan said. I noted a hint of agitation in his voice. Logan thought his family history afforded him ownership of a part of this town. He wouldn't like it if the officer disagreed with how he saw things should go down.

"It is posted on the door that no weapons are allowed."

"Oh God, I totally should have seen that!" I gushed.

"You totally should have," Logan agreed. We sounded like we were reading from a bad sitcom script. And we hadn't rehearsed enough.

"If you go run and lock it up in your car now, I won't make any more fuss about it. I asked around, and everyone said you were a good, upstanding kid in school. They told me how shy you were, not the type to be lugging a weapon around with you. And any friend of Logan's must be a good egg."

Burt gave a parting wave and walked back around the corner of the brick wall, out of sight. He didn't even hang around to see if I would actually put away the gun.

I laughed out loud then, and Logan's charming voice joined in with mine. I stumbled on my broken shoe again, and Logan caught me.

I so wanted to tell that man that he was full of misinformation. They couldn't even begin to know the real me, then or now. I was not, in fact shy, and I wasn't a friend of Logan, until maybe a half hour ago.

"I almost lost it when he said the shy ones weren't the type to carry a gun. Doesn't he watch the news? It is *always* the quiet ones that turn out to be mass shooters!" He gave a big belly laugh.

"Are you calling me mentally unstable?" I struck a serious tone.

"Haven't you spent all night convincing me that you were?" He was befuddled.

"Yes, you are right."

And we smiled at each other. Real, genuine smiles.

"So, I guess you had better be putting that gun into the car."

"I think I'll probably head home. Packing to do and all. If I am really going to move, that is." I looked at him questioningly.

"Ya. I was serious. I just need a couple days to get my affairs in order. Rip apart my family and all that."

"You don't have to, If you are having second thoughts, you can change your mind. I mean, I won't..."

"No. I want to. I need a change as much as you do. Let me give you my cell number."

"So we can have our mid-life crisis together?"

"Sure. That sounds lovely."

He smiled at me, his eyes twinkling in the light. He leaned down and kissed my cheek, and at that moment I felt like the luckiest girl in the world.

* * * * *

I arrived home to find Mr. Bloated the Landlord had dumped all my possessions on the front lawn. It made it a more pressing issue to pack promptly. Thankfully, my elderly neighbor Betty gave me a flashlight so that I could find my suitcase and duffle bag. I proceeded to load them up with all the clothes and earthly possessions I could carry. I put the luggage in my trunk, then tossed my pillow and favorite purple

Woolrich blanket into the backseat. I drove to the nearest twenty-four-hour superstore and parked.

I knew my worried brain would not let me forget that my debts and obligations which had overwhelmed me here would follow me to Hawaii. I had to give a Social Security number to get an apartment, a job. The creditors would triangulate my position quickly, and with interest. But the reality is, I had no home and no friends here. In Hawaii I would have a roof over my head and Logan next to me in his bed. That is more than I could have ever hoped for in my entire pathetic life.

Crawling into the backseat, I covered myself and went to sleep. There was no struggle tonight; sleep came willingly.

* * * * *

I woke up in my car. The sun's glow was beginning to announce its impending appearance over the horizon. There were already tears in my eyes when I opened them. They were left over from my dream. I had always had very vivid dreams. It was both a blessing and curse.

In this one Colin came to my door to tell me Lexie was dead, much as he had in real life. But now as he told me Brody and Jackie stood behind him. I watched them maturing into adults before my eyes, watched Colin graying. I turned and looked at the mirror behind my front door. I already looked sixty. Colin's voice faded away on the wind. When I turned back, they were all gone. My door was open for no one. A wave of loneliness swept over me more intensely than I had ever known. Then I woke up.

As much as I hoped she was still alive, my current homeless circumstances only illuminated to me that yes, indeed, all the agonizing events of the last three days had indeed happened. Lexie would never allow me to sleep in my car as long as she had a floor and a blanket in her home.

I rubbed the tears away with the back of my hand, new ones ready to take their place. I wiped my nose on my T-shirt. I wished I could have a shower before attending the funeral, but it looked as though that was not in the cards. I checked to see that my phone had fully charged with my car adapter overnight. I texted Logan. He was already up, having had a trying night himself. We agreed to meet for breakfast. I threw a denim jacket over the rotten T-shirt and sweatpants that served as my pajamas, climbed into the driver's seat, and headed for the MacRonnell's in my hometown.

"You still want to go with me to Lexie's funeral?"

"Well, 'want' is not the best word to use, but I know you need my support." Logan looked at me sideways. "Are you sure you are up for seeing many of the same people from the reunion again so soon? Do you, like, have your anger under control?"

"I think so. I'll be an emotional mess today, but it won't be on account of them. I have to pay my respects. I owe Lexie that much. And I will leave my gun in the car." I made what was supposed to be a cute, mocking face at him. I was pretty sure it only accentuated my ginormous nose and my thick eyebrows. Add in the red-rimmed eyes, I'm sure I beamed heinousness all through the restaurant this horrible funeral morning.

"What's say we pawn that for flight money before we go, eh? Just to be safe?"

"Did you get any sleep at all last night?"

I felt bad for him. He didn't look like he had gotten a wink.

"Ronni and I were up until 5:00AM talking. Then when I went into the guest room to sleep, the kids came in and woke me up."

"At least you had a bed to sleep in."

"Why? What happened?"

"No, no. I shouldn't have brought it up. I want to be here for you right now."

He raised an eyebrow and shook his head. "This is a two-way street. Besides, today is the funeral of your best friend."

"I got kicked out of my apartment. I slept in my car last night."

"Oh my God."

"It wasn't so bad. How did it go with Veronica?"

He rubbed his hands across his face and made an indistinguishable grumbling noise. "As good as could be expected, I guess."

I had noticed the dark shadows under his eyes when he walked in, but now I saw the untamed growth of black stubble on his face. The former me, Logan Lustatron 3000, had a sexy little tingle in my loins over his disheveled appearance. New me promptly bitch-slapped that thought out of former me's head.

I knew that it made no sense to begin a platonic friendship with someone I had lusted over for decades. But, somehow, it felt right. I had always wanted to give myself over completely to him. And that is what we had now. Well, minus one thing. But I had proved through the years that I could survive without that.

"She claimed she knew, that she had suspected something for years, but I couldn't tell. It may have only been a cover to keep her pride." He stared down at his hands clasped together on the table as he spoke. "She seemed mostly upset about having primary custody of the kids. I thought she would be happy about that. I wanted to divide up assets last night—ya know, thinking ahead to the cost of a plane ticket and rent in my near future." He looked up now, his eyes meeting mine. For the first time today, I saw his old twinkle in there. "And of course needing to float your ass for a couple of months." I saw him suppress a smile from his lips. "But she wants to have lawyers work it out between us." He shook his head. "The children will be lucky if they have any college fund left after all the legal fees."

"Maybe she will come around about that. You did kind of spring it on her suddenly. You tried to broker an entire divorce proceeding in one night, a very *guy* thing to do." I smiled at him.

"Huh. That makes pretty good sense."

We both began to eat our fast food breakfast now, even though our meals had taken a turn for the cold and congealed.

"So, when are we off? I'm all packed." I chuckled at the ludicrousness of my situation.

"Did you get all your stuff?"

"Everything I really need. It would be too expensive to ship everything out there. I left what didn't fit inside my suitcase on my front lawn."

"But you got your art supplies?"

"I don't have any art supplies."

"You told me you were going to be a painter in Hawaii..."

"Well, that's what I want to do. But I haven't made anything in years."

"What? You haven't made *anything*?"

"I mean, I doodled in my notebooks during meetings at work. I may have constructed the odd craft project here and there. But I haven't bought any paint or pencils or anything in years."

"What kind of paints do you prefer?"

"Acrylic. I don't want to keep making changes to the same barn or sky over and over. I want to paint it once and be done. Unless I muck it up. Then I can paint over it without the wait."

"And you are confident you still have your skills?"

"Hey, you asked me what I *wanted* to do, not what I was good at."

"Oh Lord, what have I gotten myself into."

"Mid-life crisis, times two." I smiled at him, and was relieved when he returned it.

"Next we should probably book plane tickets and look for a place to stay when we get there. Oh, but we can't go to your place."

"Because mine has four wheels. And we can't go to your place—"

"Because my angry wife will be there."

"Did you tell her you are leaving her for men, but are moving away with a woman."

"No," Logan sighed. "I left you out, for now."

"Probably for the best," I added. "You let her walk all over you. Your kids' names even all start with the same letter, which happens to also be the same letter of her name. Seems unfair, right?"

"How do you know my kids names?"

"I did a fair amount of stalking you back in the day." My mind flipped a new page. "You know, I don't have any money for a ticket."

"I told you that you could sell your gun."

"I'm not sure I can. I enjoy the power too much."

"Exactly why you probably should sell it."

I whipped my head up, expecting to see Lexie in front of me. It sounded exactly like something she would say.

"How often are you supposed to clean a gun, anyway?" I asked, remembering Burt's comment from the night before.

"Only when you use it. Which will hopefully be never again." Logan finished his breakfast sandwich and wiped his mouth. I could hear the abrasiveness of his stubble against the napkin. He picked up his cell, unlocking it. "Let me check my phone. Real estate. There must be an app for that."

"Sounds like a plan, Stan."

"Please tell me I am not about to leave my wholly reasonable wife to live with Dr. Seuss?"

"Oh, I think you already know the answer to that."

* * * * *

Two plane tickets to Hawaii later and an unsuccessful search through hundreds of pictures online, Logan and I hit the town to see what items we could unload for quick cash. Our flight was set to depart in the morning. Since the reunion it had only become crystal clear to both of us that there was no place left for us here.

With an online ad and a low price I sold my car in a few hours. Before that I drove it to cash in any jewelry I had of value. I only allowed myself to keep one diamond ring of my grandma's. Truth be told, it only had a diamond chip in it and little value. I could always sell it later for food, if I needed to.

Logan drove me to a pawn shop where we sold my gun for slightly more than I had paid for it. I felt a longing to keep it, for it was the talisman that had brought Logan and I together on this course. I still couldn't bring myself to believe this would all follow through to our desired conclusion.

I rummaged through my bags that were now in the back of Logan's SUV, looking for the black dress I imagined was in there. After what Logan informed me had been fifteen minutes—he may have exaggerated for effect or it may have been the truth, it wasn't the type of day to tell—I remembered I didn't own such a garment. I could have probably bought something earlier with my pawn shop earnings, but the thought never occurred to me. I wouldn't be comfortable in a dress anyway. I found a black short-sleeved shirt that didn't look too casual and black pants that I used to wear to Cutter's. I changed into them in Logan's vehicle in a parking lot as he stood guard outside. Once I had them on together, it was evident that the pants had been washed one time too many—or twenty. They were considerably more faded than the shirt that it was supposed to match. Logan said it didn't matter. I was inclined to trust his gay-man innate fashion sense, but I more expected that he was humoring me in my already fragile state. I was fine with that too.

Logan drove us to the funeral home. It all seemed unreal. I spotted Colin's pickup in the parking lot. I instinctively looked for Lexie's cute little blue sedan too.

Someone must have driven it here, right?

Logan was holding one of the heavy glass double doors open for me before my slow brain clicked. The familiar car had gone the way of Lexie; probably in a junk yard by now. I had mourned her, but the loss of an object that held so many of our shared memories also deserved our respect. She had bought that car brand new twelve years ago. It hadn't had a wash and wax in years, but the memories it held had still shined brightly. I could no longer count the number of times we had driven it to the mall or the two hours to her grandmother's house. She had driven me home from the hospital in that car when I had had my appendix removed. Hell, Jackie had been born in that car. Colin had to spend the next week cleaning the seats and floors. I wondered how many more inanimate objects linked to her would disappear from my world, adding to the void she had created by being at that intersection at the wrong time.

Logan put his hand on my back as the tears streamed down my face. If he knew the real reason I was crying he would know I was crazy. He would have me committed.

It was a closed coffin. While everyone knew they only had closed coffins following the most disfiguring incidents, I was grateful. I didn't want to see her dead. I wanted to remember her lively personality and her boisterous laugh and the color in her cheeks when a cute guy passed by. I wanted to remember her at fourteen standing at the bus stop, not afraid to board the bus full of hooligans as I was.

Lexie was my super hero.

Many of said hooligans were here today. Many were out-of-towners. They only made an appearance because they were already here for the reunion. I did my best to ignore them. It was easier with Logan on my arm. That gathered its fair share of stares. If anyone asked him about the unusual coupling, I was too distracted to hear it. I don't think he would have told them the truth anyway. It wasn't any of their business.

My eyes caught sight of Brody and Lexie at the same time they spotted me. Brody managed a half smile at my arrival. His dirty-blond shaggy hair had been tied back in a ponytail. Jackie looked like a devastated pixie, her short-cropped black hair stopping above her blue eyes as large as saucers, holding more pain than an eight-year-old should be asked to bear. Strangers in public often mistook them for the opposite of their actual genders. I believe Lexie loved it, a kind of fuck you to established norms.

Lexie was my super hero.

As her kids ran up and hugged me, those words were what kept echoing in my head. Maybe that is what would get me through this day. I glanced at the stuffy old family members sitting in the chairs. They stared at me as if I might as well have been from Mars. Who did they think they were? I bet they didn't know her half as well as I did. Hell, I spent every holiday at her house and I had never seen any of them there. They were probably only in it for the free church meal afterwards.

The thought of food made my stomach turn. Colin came up to hug me, his children still on my hips. A new batch of tears released from my ducts.

Lexie is my super hero.

Logan and I had gotten there only minutes before the service. The religious dude presiding over everything was from their church. I had met him before when Lexie had drug me to church functions to keep her company. At least that is what she said. It seemed more likely that she was trying to help me through my misery. But she never had. In the end *she* had been the one to bring me to my breaking point, through no fault of her own.

She is my super hero.

The pastor greeted me and asked me if I wanted to say any words.

Ha! A funeral was miserable enough, but adding the horror which is public speaking to it as well? No way, José. I had avoided it for twenty-five years. I wasn't going to start now. Although, if I would do it for anyone, it would be Lexie. But I didn't trust myself to say pleasant words today, and I believe she would understand that, wherever she was.

And she wasn't in that body in the maple box up front.

She is my hero.

* * * * *

After the service, Logan drove me to the cemetery, but I couldn't seem to get out of the car for the graveside service. So we sat and watched from the car, him holding my hand the whole time. I couldn't hear what was being said, but it didn't matter anyway.

After all the other cars had gone, Logan drove me past her grave, unmarked, still a hole being filled in by the groundskeepers. In a morbid way, I wished I was staying in town to see what her grave stone would look like. It was the only thing that made me hesitate for a second about leaving. But I knew staying where everything reminded me of Lexie every day would be a grave error. I supposed Colin could send me a picture of the stone once it was placed.

Logan went to the bank and withdrew a large sum. He admitted to me that his wife would not be happy about that, but he wasn't leaving her penniless or anything.

"It must be nice to be well-to-do," the snarky comment escaped my lips.

We sat in one of the small, sit-down restaurants in town. It was a place to kill some time until our departure. We were nomads now; individuals with no home.

"It's not. There is always one more thing we need to buy to keep up with our friends or the kids need to keep up with theirs. There is always a new bill for a new service. The house always needs fixing. It is that pressure that beats you down each morning when the alarm clock rings. It was fortunate I was able to hold on to the nest egg that my father left me over the years."

"Now imagine all that, plus you are all alone, the only wage earner, with no savings, and your car dies. You can't get to work. That is my own little hell."

"So what did you do?"

"Begged the dealership to fix it now and let me pay them on payday."

"And that worked?"

"Yes. But that was a number of years ago. And the head of service knew I was a regular customer who had gone there for years."

"Don't you know dealerships overcharge you?"

"Don't you know dealerships usually fix the problem the first time, instead of misdiagnosing it or putting a Band-Aid on it the first couple times?"

"You sound attached to the place."

"Only to the service manager," I replied honestly.

"Did you two have a thing?"

"Ew, no! He was, well. I always thought of him like a pseudo dad to me."

"Did he know that?"

"Of course not. You don't go around telling total strangers that inside your messed up head they are your family. Even I know that would freak people out."

"You really are all alone, aren't you?" Logan said, his nut-brown eyes studying me, making me uncomfortable.

"You are just now figuring that out?"

When he gave no response, I continued.

"You do have people here. Are you sure you are willing to abandon them so easily?"

"Abandon is a harsh word. They know where I will be. I can set up some kind of visitation. There are phones and video calling. But I think that sitting here with you right now is evidence that I have nowhere else to be. I told Ronnie the truth and now I am not welcome in my own house. I want to be open about who I am. That is something the people of this town, set in their ways, who made their opinion of me from my father before I was ever born, will never accept."

"I get that." I placed my hand on top of his on the table, near the salt and pepper and ketchup. His skin was warm and nice. "I'm sorry things are how they are for you."

"Same to you," he said, giving me a supportive smile. His smile then faded. "I'll leave you here while I go pack and say goodbye." He stood, began to walk toward the door. Logan stopped and turned. "This could take little while," he said.

"I know," I replied.

He gave me a low wave behind his back and walked away. His low-rise jeans hung off his hips. I remembered how I used to stare at him departing the same way in his high-waisted Guess jeans when I was fourteen. A warm feeling filled my belly as I realized this time he would be coming back, for me. Not in *that* way, but still...

The waitress came and I ordered, wanting to ensure I saved our table until his return. I started by ordering soup, so I could take as many slow sips as possible.

I looked out the window. I studied the four-lane concrete road that had been patched with asphalt as the semis continued their unrelenting assault on the surface, on their way from one major city to another, never stopping in our little Podunk town. I had listened to the sounds of the pounding tires and air brakes moving easily through the night air as I tried to sleep as a teenager. I could see across the road the apartments I had lived in when I was first on my own. Not the same building, of course. Building D had burned several years ago, and the landlord had never bothered to rebuild it. Probably just took a vacation with the insurance money. Hell, there was still a small pile of rubble there that the neighborhood children climbed on. How the city didn't require him to clean it up, I would never know.

After finishing the soup, I ate a cheeseburger. I spent lots of time dipping the thick French fries into the ketchup, long after I was full. Afternoon gave way to evening. I fought off the urge to text Logan as I ordered chocolate cake à la mode. I figured the ice cream would buy me extra time at the table. I might as well eat as much as I could tonight. With the thirteen hour total travel time tomorrow I had no idea when I would catch a snack. I was even more uncertain as to the amount of funds Logan and I would have access to once we touched down on the island.

Logan strutted towards our table as my dessert arrived. He looked more tired now than he had this morning.

"All packed?" I asked, trying to make it sound like a good thing.

A tiny smile, for my benefit, pulled at the corner of his mouth. "Yes. Was I gone long?"

"Days," I replied sarcastically.

"It seemed like weeks."

I had something I needed to address with him. I didn't want to beat around the bush. Ever. About anything. He had already been witness to my worst juncture. If that didn't scare him off, chances are nothing else would.

"How did it go?"

"We actually had a real good talk. She seemed to give up on defending herself by saying she suspected I was gay. But she did intimate that marriage hadn't turned out to be what she thought it would be. I don't know. Maybe everyone thinks that nine years in."

"Was it terrible telling the kids?"

"Yes." His eyes gave me approval that it was alright that I had asked. "Veronica had known our marriage wasn't on the best footing before, but Vaughn and Victoria had no idea. They were baffled why I would move so far away. And I couldn't give them the really-real answer. Not yet anyway—"

"They watch TV. They must know gays and bisexuals exist."

"I know. But one thing I have learned over the years is that knowing something exists and finding out it is lurking in your own house are two different things. Especially to kids, the latter can be far scarier."

The waitress took his order with a noticeable eye roll and frustrated sigh. It was sixty seconds of torture before I could ask him what was nagging my mind. It was an eternity.

"So, we are still on?"

"Yes, of course." He smiled wide now. "You can stop asking me that. I'm one hundred percent in."

"I have always been incredulous that anyone could like me. I don't even like me. And now you want to travel across the country with me? It makes no sense," I whined, stirring the melted ice cream in the bottom of the bowl that I was too full to finish.

"But you have to admit, it does make sense. Because you agreed to it, and so did I. We are being pushed by some force to do this… together."

"This will sound weird, I'm sure, but I have been having dreams that find me walking on a beach in a tropical environment for months now. In one, I even saw my house there. Well, more of a shed, really."

"Well, we can't argue with your prophetic dreams."

"Well, I guess next we should decide where we are going after you finish eating. The restaurant closes in an hour, and I think I have worn out my welcome here."

"Ya," he chuckled. "Usually women are more welcoming when I show up."

"Oh, you've noticed that over the years, have you?"

"Yes. And while I'm not interested, it sure does make life a little easier."

"You have talked a lot about Veronica and the kids, but I haven't heard how your other family members have reacted to your life-changing news."

"My dad died like fifteen years ago."

I knew this.

"My mom has been gone even longer. My step mom lives out in Arizona now. She seemed OK with it. My sister was relieved. She said she always thought I was inclined that way, but then I kept dating women and married one, and then the kids came. She thought her gaydar was on the fritz. She said she thought she was going crazy because what she felt and what she saw didn't match." He sighed as he tipped up his glass and took a drink. Sitting it down, he realized the still-wrapped straw lay next to it on the table. He tore it open and slid it into his iced tea before he drank again. "I wish she would have approached me about it. Maybe I could have gotten this second chance at life sooner."

"See, they were all supportive. Maybe you could have come out sooner while you continued living here. Maybe they would have accepted it."

Our eyes met and we couldn't keep the smiles off our faces. We busted out laughing at the exact same moment. We were so loud everyone around us stared. For the first time since Lexie was gone, heck, since she had gotten married, I was spending time with a kindred spirit.

"Maybe you could be the one to open up this town's view on such things."

"Maybe. But that isn't what I want to put my energy into right now. I would rather spend it discovering the true me, whoever that is," he replied.

"I can understand that."

"While I was gone, I had a guy call about buying my car. He agreed to meet us at the airport tomorrow morning."

"But what will we do until then?" I asked, knowing that Logan's SUV was already filled with all our earthly belongings.

"I'll get us a cheap hotel room tonight."

LEID

I could be good in Hawaii. I would be good in Hawaii.

I never thought I would be able to sleep while staying in the same room as Logan Courtney, let alone in the same bed. But it was a king, we both avoided the center, and we never even knew each other was there. Except I did know he was there, or rather my subconscious did. That is the only way to explain why on the brink of moving my broken life clear across the country and out into the Pacific Ocean I had the best night's sleep of my life. Now I was going to willingly live this way? I should be scared shitless. But I wasn't, possibly for the first time in my entire life.

I came out of the bathroom, my wet hair dampening the shoulders of my T-shirt. Logan was stumbling around in the dim light. I had only turned a small lamp on as he was still sleeping when I got into the shower. He was at the desk and hadn't noticed me. He was busy tearing open a tiny foil coffee packet. Logan's brown hair was standing straight up on the top of his head. His T-shirt was wrinkled but I couldn't say the same about his boxer briefs. They looked just right. Even though Logan had no interest in me, he sure was easy on the eyes. Any woman would love to wake up to this sight in the morning. Even if he wasn't for me, I was glad I got to see him like this. He wasn't putting on his fake charm to woo anyone, not trying to impress. He was simply being his sweet self.

"Oh, hey. I thought I would make some coffee. Want some?" He gave me a half smile. I threw up an iron wall between it and my vulnerable heart.

"No, I don't drink coffee."

"I think there is a tea bag over here."

"I don't drink tea either."

"The faucet?"

"No way."

"I think I saw a Coke machine in the lobby where we came in."

"Bingo."

"I can't believe I am up this early, but we have to get a move on to the airport to meet the guy who is gonna buy the car."

"Ya, I know. Let me gather my things together."

"I love freebies," he said as he pulled the mug up to his lips and took a big, steaming gulp of the hotel room coffee. Logan pulled it away, making a sour lemon kind of face. "OK. Maybe sometimes you get what you pay for. Let me jump in the shower and then we can take off."

* * * * *

The transfer of Logan's car went smoothly and we had a cashier's check for eight thousand more dollars with us. That put my mind a little more at ease. Logan and I had time to kill at the airport so we ate breakfast. I only had some French toast, since it was still early in the morning and, to be honest, I was still full from the dinner I had the night before. I took the opportunity to discuss something with him that kept nagging on my brain.

"Logan, I want to talk to you about something…" My voice came out shakier than necessary.

"Oh my God."

I was surprised by his reaction. How did he even know what I was going to say?

"You aren't pregnant, are you?"

"Oh, no. That would be, well, kind of impossible." It had been over two years since I had had any type of action that could yield such a result.

"Bip-bip. I don't want to know the details. So, what is it?"

"Well, I'm sure you have noticed you already paid for my plane ticket." It was easier to talk about this to him now, since he had actually dreamed up a worse scenario. "I promise I will pay my share, when I can. But I hope that you realize that could be quite some time from now. I don't want you to think I am heading out here with you to be some sneaky free-loader. I want you to know that I am acknowledging now that I will be a free-loader." I looked up at him. He was chuckling at me.

"Yes. I suspected as much. It is probably good if we get it out in the open now. I have some funds to get us established. But if I catch you sitting around eating bon-bons, you will be in trouble."

"Deal. And, to be honest, I'm not even sure what a bon-bon is."

"So, I guess our finances will have to be combined for a while until we can both stand on our feet individually. It feels like I am getting out of one marriage and into another."

"I haven't lived with a man except for my father. That will be new. In fact, I have been living by myself for the past twenty-one years."

"I've never lived openly with my sexuality before. That will be new. I hope you don't mind me bringing men around the house."

I laughed. "I assumed as much. Probably *lots* of them. But we have to get a house first."

"If you are good, maybe I will give you my leftovers."

I just laughed, appreciating the twinkle in his eyes and the ease with which my breaths currently came. The weight on my chest was lifting more and more the closer it came to the time for our flight.

We, meaning Logan, paid for our breakfast and we found our gate. When our seats were called, we joined the line to board the plane. Logan gave the lady at the ticket counter a wink as he handed over his boarding pass. As I approached, she put her hand on my arm, stopping me. My body broke out in a sweat as I instantly worried I had somehow been added to the no-fly list. Could they do that for premeditated mass-murders or unpaid credit cards? She leaned close to me, as I helplessly watched Logan's unaware retreating figure disappear through the door toward the plane.

"One way to Hawaii? And with a stud like that? Enjoy, honey. I wish I was you right now."

Still in shock, I could only return her smile and wobble slightly as she pulled her hand away, removing her flesh gate, the last barrier standing between me and my destination.

In the obvious ways she could plainly see with her own eyes, she was correct. But in others, I was still the same mess I had always been. I was still financially ruined. I was heading into the unknown. I would arrive with no job and no home. I had a faintly sketched out dream and one soul in the world in my corner supporting me. If I stumbled now, there was a good chance I would never be able to recover.

I hurried to the doorway as fast as I could. Logan was up ahead, so I picked up my pace. I tripped and plowed right into the back of him.

"Umph. I wondered what happened to you," he turned, appraising my condition after the crash.

"The universe was just reminding me that I am doing the right thing."

He cocked an eyebrow at me. "Well, I'm so glad, because these are our seats." Logan took the window and I took the middle, even though I wasn't thrilled about it.

We each crammed our carry-on above our seats, then put our smaller bags under the seat in front of us. I grabbed my book I had picked out in the airport bookstore to read on the five hours of the first leg of our flight, along with my bag of gummy bears and laid them in my lap. Logan switched his phone over to airplane mode then stared out the window for a long time. I imagined him saying his goodbyes to his family and home, but he could have simply been watching the luggage carts mill around like bees to a hive. When he pulled his attention away from the window he ripped open my bag of candy, pouring a sloth of bears into his mouth.

When the plane began to taxi, he took my left hand into his right and squeezed. We grinned at each other like idiots. This was *the* beginning of our new life.

* * * * *

"This is a big change for me. I have spent my whole life in the comfortable security of my father's hometown, wrapped within the ease of the lies I created for myself. This is—this is big time."

Logan had been the strong one all along on this adventure, putting up the walls to protect me from any doubt or insecurity. But if he was admitting it now that we were mid-flight on an airplane, well fuck, maybe we were both screwed. But he didn't seem panicked, only honest.

I never wanted to use an airplane bathroom in my life. But some things cannot be avoided. Especially since I have a psychosomatic condition where anytime I believe that I do not have access to a bathroom to urinate then I need to go even more urgently. And this long flight with only one layover totally fit that bill. It was like using a porta potty, but while someone nudged it back and forth. Thank God the pilot didn't hit any real turbulence while I was in there.

After a sub-par inflight meal of a ham and turkey sandwich from a plastic bag that we had to open ourselves, Logan and I drifted off to sleep, leaning against one another. I'm sure the outside world saw us like that and thought we were something else entirely. I'm sure they painted some picture for us involving dating or a honeymoon. But they were vacationers who could only assume everyone was the same.

We were on a one way trip.

For the first time in my life, I didn't give a damn what strangers thought.

* * * * *

We had to wake up for our layover at LAX, Los Angeles International Airport. We walked our stiff legs around in preparation for the next, longer leg of our journey. Logan grabbed some tacos in the airport. They smelled so good and I was tempted to indulge, but I knew my irritable digestive system. I got some French fries and chicken nuggets—good old bland happy tummy food, except for the slight layer of grease that floated on top of it in my stomach. It was still better than having tacos, a notoriously bad choice for me, from the preservative-soaked lettuce to the meat of questionable origins; so much so that they had been banned entirely from my diet after 9:00PM. I wondered if I would have to adjust that rule for a new time zone. Would it now be no tacos after 4:00PM? Or would my stomach irregularities conform to local time? Logan should have followed my lead. He had to visit the airplane bathroom three times and missed out on our next in-flight meal of soup and salad. My salad sat untouched, but I did empty the little bag of croutons.

We arrived in Honolulu at 6:00PM. Logan wanted to go straight to the beach, and so did I, but I talked him into getting a hotel room first. I didn't know if there would be some kind of special events going on that would make them scarce, like the Superbowl or something.

"You are letting your nerves get the best of you again," Logan laughed at me, but not to be mean. It was the same way my insanity used to amuse Lexie. My heart twisted at the thought of her. I would never see her hawk-brown eyes and short, burnt sienna hair again. I was even far away from the same geographic area we had once shared. Her memory was already fading, making her seem like someone in a dream to me now.

We got a cab and loaded our luggage into the back. Logan requested we head toward a more inexpensive hotel. I was fine with that. After all, it was his money that we were spending.

"This street here has some good ones. No ocean view, but only a short walk to the beach. Middle of the road. You don't want those rat-traps down on Pōhaku and Māhoe."

I tried to catch glimpses of the ocean. I couldn't stop staring at the palm trees. Sure I had seen one before in the conservatory at my local botanical gardens. But here they grew wild everywhere, as common as a maple tree in Michigan. I wondered if a resident of Hawaii traveled there if they would be impressed with my boring old maples.

We registered, reminding ourselves that everything just cost more here. Hell, I had known that for years. Frontier Central had the same retail prices for all the stores across the country, except for the six stores on the Hawaiian Islands. They were always a bit more.

We dropped the three suitcases and two carry-ons we had between us into the room, and then took a walk down to the beach. It was a longer walk than the cabby had implied, but we were determined. The sun had fallen below the horizon by the time we reached the beach, but its ethereal glow could still be detected against the clouds.

We were surrounded by bodies of every shade, some born brown, some fried that way under a tropical sun until wrinkled. I assumed everyone we were passing was a tourist. It was a bad habit to assume. Half these people could be employees off work for the night, trying to glimpse a piece of the paradise they lived in before the sun turned its lights off on the beauty for another day.

I had grown up in the white-bread Midwest, where that is what everyone ate and that was their complexion. It was years before I realized the few kids in my grade with a permanent tan were Hispanic. It wasn't until I got to college that I saw a large number of people of color on a daily basis. But by then the college had schooled us on how to be scared of what was different from us. I don't think that was their intention, but that was the result of their diversity teachings all the same.

Here I was surrounded by a delicious, undulating chocolate milkshake of life, streaks of brown and ivory showing separate as they began to mix together. I was an under-stirred lump of vanilla. I was fine with that.

A milkshake actually sounded good right now as I realized sweat had begun to cling to my forehead and back.

"I am actually warm," I spoke aloud, but as much to myself as to Logan.

"It is a nice, balmy night," he added.

"No, I'm not sure that you get it. In Michigan, I was never-ever warm, except for maybe a week in August. I wore a minimum of a T-shirt and hoodie all year long."

"No wonder you were cold. Should have tried pants," he leaned over at me, smiling. He proceeded to kick off his sandals and roll up the bottoms of his jeans. I took his cue, and did the same with my sneakers.

"I am actually in Hawaii with Logan Courtney standing next to me. This is better than any fantasy I had ever dreamed."

"And now you are in the ocean." Logan placed his palm on my back and pushed me forward into the waves at the same pace he was. I was surprised to find that even the water was warm to me, like a bath.

"If I pretend there are no fish in here, I will be just fine," I said, unsure.

"Are you talking about regular fish, or perhaps jelly fish? Oh, I know. I bet you are worried about sharks."

"Stop it!" I screamed at him. "You are ruining a beautiful life-changing moment."

"You are right. I am," he turned and looked at me appreciatively in the fading light. "Oh my God, it's a giant octopus!" he screamed, pointing to the horizon.

I screamed and jumped toward him, which only resulted in spilling us both into the water. We fell in a pile laughing, sitting on the bottom, where the water was only chest deep.

"Did I ever mention that I can't swim?"

"Then I better hold on to you tight, so the surf won't wash you to sea." He wrapped his arms around me and squeezed as another wave slammed, still powerful this close to shore. Logan kept me rooted in place. It felt wonderful.

* * * * *

Logan called a realtor the next morning to show us properties for rent. He picked us up at our hotel in his black car.

Why did he have a black one? Didn't black absorb light or heat or both? It seemed an illogical choice for a tropical island.

First we went to his office to narrow down our possibilities. Mr. Takamoto sat behind his desk, Logan and I side by side across from him, the monitor of his computer turned so that we could all see it, even if not from the clearest angle. Looking at the prices made me nervous. Logan assured me he would get a job soon and we would be fine. I decided the only way I was going to get through this was to only look at the pretty pictures and never the numbers.

Then Mr. Takamoto clicked the mouse, causing a photograph of a tiny salmon-colored house to pop up.

"That's it" slipped from my lips. It was the shack I had dreamed of, the one on the beach. It was the one I knew what the inside looked like based only on instinct.

"What?" Logan asked.

"I mean, I like this one a lot," I tried to quickly cover.

"Oh, you don't want to look at that one. It is small, more for vacationers than a young couple moving here to stay."

A couple of what was the question.

"Add that one to the list of possibilities," Logan said.

"That would make six to look at today, that might not be doable," the realtor reasoned.

"Then take off one of the others," Logan stated authoritatively. Then smiled at me.

"Uh, which one sir?"

"Doesn't matter." And I knew then that he could read my mind. He knew I was only interested in the pink house.

All the houses were on wooden stilts. It was such a different sight than a brick or concrete solid foundation as was found throughout the Midwest.

We went on a big expedition around the Honolulu suburbs and outskirts, looking at apartments and houses that varied greatly in price and amenities. I was still trying to ignore that information. Mr. Takamoto was trying to talk us into going to one of the cities other than Honolulu, so we could get more for our money. But Logan told him we were new here, and wanted to stay in the city, or as close as we could get, at least at first. He was great and took the lead. All the places looked the same: living room, bathroom, kitchen. Usually in our price range they were so small there wasn't much of a bedroom. There was usually past water damage or a suspicious crack that caused me to turn my nose up and not look down it again. Thankfully we had had a break for lunch, but it was now quickly approaching dinnertime.

The next house was three roads up from the beach, where the elevation began to rise. The private road to it was little more than a path through the jungle of low ferns and tall palm trees. It gently wound uphill, until it widened as we approached a row of candy-colored shacks that lay in front of us, the pink one the first. In the middle was a mint green one, with a faded yellow on the end.

I could imagine how once these would have been a tourists' delight, a private dwelling with a beach view, away from the bustle of the city. But the jungle had gotten out of hand in the years since statehood, obscuring the view for all but the most patient observer. The shacks had become weather-beaten. I suspected they offered rustic facilities that today's travelers would rather avoid. The hotels in town had a higher price, but with spacious accommodations and shuttle buses to all major attractions, they were a bigger draw than huts on the edge of the island.

But I was in love.

"I have stayed in cabins at camp that were larger than this," Logan commented sincerely.

"Ugh. My parents wanted me to attend camp with the rest of you lemmings. I was having none of that."

"Roughing it builds character."

"I'm holding you to that," I said, trying to use his words against him to get what I wanted. I wondered if this is what it felt like to be someone's wife.

I had the car door open and was stepping out before it ever came to a stop. It was a little square shack, with steps that led up to a tiny porch and the front door.

Mr. Takamoto seemed baffled by my excitement, but unlocked the weathered white wooden door anyway and stood aside so we could enter first, which was a tight squeeze on the minuscule landing. If I squinted and waited for the sea breeze to part the trees, we actually had an ocean view from here. Thank God it wasn't priced that way.

Inside there wasn't much more room. The door opened into a small kitchen. A little wooden table was already sitting there with two mismatched painted wooden chairs, one pastel green, the other sky blue, as if it was waiting for us to sit down and have toast and orange juice first thing in the morning. There was no counter space to speak of, but several cabinets. We had come out here to unclutter, simplify, and start over, hadn't we?

There was little more than a doorway between the kitchen and the living room, if you could call it that. There was a couch and an older model television with a converter box perched on top of it. The couch folded out into a full-size bed. On the end that we were facing was a twin bed built into the wall, surrounded above and on either side by built-in drawers. They had little pink roses painted on them with pale blue accents. It looked like the work of some little old lady who wanted everything just so. I wondered to myself if we would be allowed to repaint.

"It comes furnished. As I said, I would have to talk to the owner about getting you set up here long term...," he droned on. I tuned him out.

"Um, does this joint have a bathroom," Logan asked worriedly.

"Oh yes, you must have missed it. It is back here off the kitchen."

Logan leaned in. "I only see a sink and a toilet."

"The shower is outside, below."

"An outdoor shower?"

"Sure. They are more common than you would think. It is gravity fed so it doesn't require a pump to pull the water up from the cistern, as the sink and toilet do."

"I gotta see this thing," Logan said, heading out the door with Mr. Takamoto quickly following, wondering how a big fat commission was slipping through his fingers, crumbling into a simple lease agreement for a dump.

I spun around. I wanted this to be *my* dump. I was pretty sure this isn't what Logan had pictured for a Hawaiian beach house. But then again, we had to start somewhere.

"Let me talk to the little woman alone for a second and we will be right down," I overheard Logan tell Mr. Takamoto as he clomped back up the wooden stairs. The sound was already commonplace to my ears.

"So, why this place?" Logan asked.

I smiled back at him. "Remember me telling you about my dream?"

"The Hawaii one? Ya, that is why we are here," he said, meaning the island.

"No, here," I responded, pointing down at the floor.

"What?"

"This. This is the exact same place I dreamed about. It is as if Fate brought us here or something." I paused, trying to gauge his reaction. "I know it isn't what you were looking forward to..."

"If it is your dream, then it is my dream. Let's take it."

"Really?" I squealed, falling into his arms for a hug. The mix of his signature cologne he had worn since high school and his sweat filled my nostrils. It was better than anything I had smelled in my life.

He pulled me to the door. "Mr. Takamoto, where do we sign?" Right then his face sagged like a wet Shar Pei that needed to be rung out. After that, all the friendly gestures were gone. He dropped us off at our hotel. We were to meet him at his office the next morning to do the paperwork.

"C'mon. I have a surprise for you," Logan began, as he headed to a cab waiting at the curb rather than into the hotel lobby as I expected. He pulled me with him and we got in. He handed the man a note and said, "Take us to this address. I'm surprising her."

"Yes, sir," he responded. Without any further words, he pulled away from the curb and started driving us to the outskirts of the city.

"Where are you taking us?" I asked Logan. "You aren't sick of me already, are you? Taking me to a volcano to drop me in..."

"*Joe Versus The Volcano* wasn't a true story," the cabbie threw in. So he thought that he was a funny guy, huh.

"No, I'm not sick of you—yet. You never know what tomorrow will bring."

"Ha-ha. C'mon, tell me. I hate surprises."

"Let's just say it is very Scooby-Doo."

"OK, now I am completely baffled."

"Just as it should be." Logan smiled an impish grin at me.

But a few minutes later I would know because signs surrounded by flaming torches appeared in the fading daylight declaring we had arrived at "Hale's Luaus held nightly."

"Oh my God! You are taking me to a real luau!"

"That's using the term 'real' very loosely," our cabby intoned.

"I called earlier and made our reservation. I was hoping we would be done house-hunting in time."

"Oh my gosh. Thank you." I threw my arms around Logan in a show of gratitude. It was becoming a habit, this ease we had in each other's company. It was comfortable, like when I wore my favorite hoodie, which, coincidentally, I was wearing tonight. I wondered if his effortlessness at touching a woman came from years of being married to one. I wasn't comfortable touching anyone, or at least not before him.

When the cab stopped, he handed his credit card to the driver. As the driver handed it back, Logan was already opening his door. He grabbed my hand and pulled me out his side of the car.

"Let's find our place at the table. The dancers have already started."

A familiar flush of heat covered my skin as I always detested being late for anything. I let him tow me over to where there were long tables surrounding a flat dance floor. Tiki torches burned everywhere, spreading the smell of citronella and making me think of home. Apparently mosquitoes could live anywhere; what a depressing thought. At first I thought the torches and the bowls of floating candles on the tables provided the only light. Then I noticed fixtures mounted to the palm trees, inconspicuously making more illumination to alleviate any potential lawsuits of elderly folks stumbling around in the dark. And we did seem to be the youngest people here.

"Did you use an AARP discount on this or something?" I quipped.

"No. Must be all the families attend the afternoon performance."

"Maybe," I said as we pulled out the chairs at the two spots marked with place cards bearing our names. It was like being at a wedding reception where we were not required to furnish a gift. Logan and I didn't talk, as the drums providing the rhythm for the dancing were too loud. All the dancers right now were male, and shirtless, doing a native dance or one appropriately spruced up for the tourists, I assumed. They ended with a yell, and everyone applauded.

"Thank you all so much for joining us tonight at Hale's Luau. We could not have a celebration without you. We strive to bring you authentic Hawaiian cuisine, history, and entertainment. The first course will be arriving at your table shortly. As you enjoy, our own house band, Bubba and the Pineapples, will delight you with the sounds of the islands featuring Bubba Jr. on ukulele."

Bubba Jr. held his ukulele high in the air from where he stood on the stage. There was more polite applause.

"Whether you come from far away or right next door,—"

"Both," Logan and I whispered to each other and giggled like kids in school, ignoring the teacher.

"—we are glad you are here. You are our Ohana."

"Ahhh, like *Lilo & Stitch*," I cried.

"Maybe we were hasty in moving here. I think our combined knowledge of the whole state amounts to a hundred combined viewings of *Lilo & Stitch*."

I laughed, knowing he was right.

Women with a rolling cart covered in plates stopped at our table. One woman would take the plate of food off the cart, while the other would take it from her and place it in front of the hungry recipient on the table. I wondered if these women helped to prepare the food as well. They were older, probably had grandchildren to play with at home, their faces the color of leather wrinkled with time. Maybe they had worked here their whole lives. The sign out front did say "established 1953," the same year the islands had become a state. Maybe they had started as hula girls and been forced to change job positions when childbearing began to take its toll on their physique and their coconuts began to droop.

The first course was poke salad. It had fish in it, which I don't eat.

The master of ceremonies announced, "For the next course we have what you have all been waiting for. Your first, and possibly last, taste of poi. Enjoy!"

Logan and I laughed as a ceramic bowl was placed in front of us containing a purple yogurt-like substance. I didn't like trying new foods, but I had been curious about this particular regional fare all my life. We raised our spoons, tasting it at the same time. We also opened our mouths at the same time and spit it back out again. It was mostly bland with a shadow of lost sweetness, but with a strange "otherness" to it.

"Oh, did I forget to mention," the emcee joined in again, "Poi can be an acquired taste." He laughed a boisterous laugh. "We eat it here from the time we are babies."

The poi was followed by kalua pig, with sides of lomi salmon, opihi—"the fish of death"—raw on the shell, laulau, and chicken long rice. I tried hard to remember all the names of the dishes because I wanted to avoid them at all costs in the future. The pork was the only thing I planned to eat again. I was familiar with land animals. They seemed safer and still appealed the most to my Midwestern pallet. We wouldn't be able to afford for me to eat pork every night. Hopefully the stores out here sold boxes of macaroni and cheese and pancake mix, as I was accustomed to back home.

I ordered the only "safe" choice of apple pie for dessert. We were still in the great old U.S. of A., after all. During dessert, female dancers in leis and grass skirts emerged to begin a traditional hula dance. I noted the lack of coconuts; colorful bikini tops covered their breasts instead. The music and my full stomach lulled me into a more relaxed state than I had been since I had boarded the plane two days ago. I glanced at the tables around us, and noticed a guy checking me out.

No, wait. Checking *Logan* out. Maybe he did have game. Maybe he merely needed a more diverse pond than where we were from to find gay fish in.

"Logan."

"Ya?"

"Check it out. Twelve o'clock. No, I mean three o'clock. Oh, there is a guy at the table over there," I tilted my head in that general direction, "checking you out."

Logan turned. When he made eye contact, the guy smiled and nodded at him.

To my surprise, Logan didn't return the gesture. He, actually rather nicely, turned his head back to me, with no acknowledgement to the man whatsoever.

"What are you doing?" I hissed. "He's into you."

"And I am into you."

My heart fluttered. I told it to shut up.

"Tonight is about you and me and Hawaii makes three. There will be plenty of time for hooking up later." He took my hand in his, squeezed it, and didn't let go. I also suspected that beyond the excuse he had verbalized, there was also some uneasiness with jumping into his new life. Or maybe finding a new residence was as much as he could handle for one day. I know that is how I felt.

"Let's give it up for the beautiful ladies of Hale's Luau! Next I want to give you a little history lesson about the island..."

As the emcee narrated a rather graphic history of the islands, the back drop on the stage lit up in the appropriate location, orange where the volcano was painted, blue where the sea was represented at the bottom, as the dancers acted out the story in front.

At the conclusion, the men and women danced together to a more upbeat rhythm.

"Alright, now it is your turn. All of our guests please join us on the dance floor, as you are able."

"C'mon," Logan pulled my arm as he got up, our fingers still locked together.

"No way. He said 'as you are able.' I can't dance!"

"I think that was meant for the old folks with the walkers. I'm sure half the people here can't dance," he reasoned, pulling me harder. "It's included in the price."

I shook my head, already knowing fighting him on this point was hopeless. If Logan Courtney told me to jump off a bridge tomorrow, I would. He had always had that much control over me. He had only begun to realize that since the reunion. With one final yank that might leave him sore tomorrow, he pulled me to my feet and towed me to the dance floor, where two of the professional dancers, one male and one female, attempted to teach us a simplified version of the traditional hula dance.

After a few minutes, they gave up on us and moved on to another couple. After that, Logan and I just hung on each other and danced goofily. It felt like this was how the high school reunion should have gone for us if everything hadn't gone off the rails. But I would never have gone to the reunion without the gun. And if Logan hadn't had a gun aimed at his heart, who knows if he would have ever left his routine, but ill-fitting, life with his wife. My guess is, he was pretty close to giving up his charade before I ever walked in there.

All that was set into motion by Lexie's death. My heart constricted at the painful memory.

No. I refused to believe there was anything good to come out of her death. She had been ripped from my life, not to mention that of her husband and two children. How could creating a humongous void in their lives ever be beneficial?

No, I would never understand that. My life is very different without Lexie, but I wasn't ready to say it was better.

* * * * *

We returned to our room for our last night in the hotel.

"Thank you for tonight." I placed a gentle kiss on Logan's cheek, feeling the day's worth of stubble against my lips. I missed that sensation. I silently hoped that I might find someone to date out here. I had given up hope that anyone would ever want to marry me and call me their own forever. But I did yearn to experience the crush, the obsession, the lust, a first kiss again. Logan was wonderful and always fun to look at, but it was only a platonic friendship. At some point, I would need someone to shake my palm tree again.

"You ready to become official residents of Hawaii tomorrow?" Logan asked.

"Yes. It will probably be more official when we get our driver's license changed over."

"Oh, they have cool rainbows on them."

I laughed and shuffled my clothes around in my suitcase, looking for the rotting T-shirt and gray shorts I was using as pajamas.

Logan's phone rang. He glanced at the caller ID, and a pained expression crossed his face before he answered it.

"Hello?... Oh, hi Vaughn. No, you aren't bothering me, but why are up so late, bud?"

I went in the bathroom to brush my teeth and change into my pajamas, taking my time to give him some privacy. The call was over by the time I returned.

"Everything OK at home?"

"Yes. They were just missing me. And this is my home now."

"Home is where the heart is."

"My heart is here," he added, flashing a weak smile.

"Do you think you will go back and visit?"

"Or maybe they could come here. But it is too early to tell about all that. We will see what Ronnie wants. Her and her lawyer, that is. Right now he seems torn whether to say the reason for divorce is I left her for another woman or deceived her all those years about my sexual orientation. I guess it will depend on what will get *him* a bigger payday."

"That kinda sucks."

"Ya, but what am I going to do? I abandoned my life already in progress to begin another. There are bound to be repercussions."

"I feel bad about that."

"Why? It was always my decision to make."

"My life was reaching a logical end."

"Don't say that."

"Or a time to reboot," I added, only for Logan's benefit. That is how things had turned out, but it was something I had never anticipated. "But I feel like I ripped your family apart."

"No. That would have been the case if you had shot me. I never would have had the chance to tell them who I really was. That would have been the real tragedy."

"Weren't you happy with her for a while?" I felt nosy, but I needed to know where he was coming from.

"Yes, at first. By the time I realized I wanted more, the kids started coming. And I love them. I'm glad I have them."

"I guess I feel less bad about pulling you out of there then."

"Pulling me? I pushed you out, girlfriend. You would still be rotting away in your apartment if it wasn't for me."

"No. If it wasn't for you, I would be rotting away in a prison cell right now. You saved my life."

"I could say the same thing."

"You know, if this was a romance novel we'd be together right now," I pondered.

"But it's not."

"And tonight, I am content with that."

I found myself smiling as I pulled back the covers and crawled into bed. The muscles in my face hurt from the exertion of forgotten muscles.

* * * * *

"I got a you a little gift," Logan said, as he shyly handed me a wrapped box.

"Loh-gahn." I drew out his name longer in my shock. "What did you do?"

"Just a little something to get you started out here."

"What is it? A pineapple? A bathing suit?" I asked as I shook the flat rectangular box and could clearly hear the contents rattle within. "When did you have time?"

"Oh, this morning while you were still asleep. I admit, I may have had a little help from the concierge."

"You know, today ends your time living the high life. It will be the old scrimp-n-save routine from now on."

"All the more reason to get you this while I still could."

I stared at him for a long moment, getting lost in the twinkle in his chestnut eyes.

"Open it!" he urged.

"Alright," I relented, tearing the blue ocean with green sea turtles multi-occasion giftwrap that covered my mystery present.

It was a paint set.

"You didn't have to."

"I actually did," his voice sounded mischievous. "This is my way of giving you a push toward your dream."

I tried to blink back my tears. "Standing here with you right now is a dream come true."

"Never stop dreaming," he whispered. He put his arm around me, pulled me close, and kissed the top of my head.

"C'mon, we gotta go," he ordered, walking into the bathroom to check for any hygiene products he may have missed. It allowed me time to pull myself together.

* * * * *

We checked out of our room and took our luggage with us to Mr. Takamoto's office, where we were to sign the lease agreement. As if he hadn't proven enough yesterday that we were small potatoes to him, he didn't even make an appearance today. His secretary more than capably handled all the paperwork for us. Since we had the burden of our bags, key in hand, we paid a taxi to take us to our new abode.

We clumsily dragged our luggage up the white stairs, the paint worn clean off in the center where everyone placed their heavy step. Logan let the keys, one for each of us, dangle teasingly from his finger and jingled them. He frustrated me as I imagined an older brother would. It had the desired effect.

"C'mon! Just open it," I grumbled.

He chuckled and unlocked it, letting the door swing wide open. We both went through the doorway, dropping our belongings in a heap in the kitchen. Then we looked at each other, smiled, and ran into the living room/bedroom, a whole three steps.

"I can't believe we really did it. I can't believe we are actually here," I said.

"I can't believe you actually came."

"Wait... Would you have come without me?"

"Yes. No. Maybe. We can't continue to second guess our past decisions. We are going to drive ourselves crazy," Logan answered.

I raised my hand. "Been there, done that."

He smiled, his brown eyes suddenly twinkling, giving his mischievous intentions away. He moved over to a radio that sat on the shelf. He floundered with the knob for a minute, trying to remember how to awaken such prehistoric technology. Lucky for him it was already tuned to a station. It was playing some strange music that sounded like polka with a Hawaiian influence. I frowned, but he grabbed my hand and we spun around and around, which is all the room provided for space-wise. When we had laughed so hard we lost our breath, he fell onto the couch and I tried to get into my bed in the wall, but I fell and ended up in a heap on the floor. Logan scooped me up rather unceremoniously and threw me onto my mattress. I narrowly avoided hitting my head. All this commotion only made us laugh harder.

Eventually we calmed down. Logan retrieved his luggage and began to unpack. I was suddenly sleepy and decided to stay where I was and see if I could nap. The plastic cover on the mattress stuck to my sweaty skin as I attempted to roll over into a more comfortable position than I had haphazardly landed in. A stack of sheets that I assumed were freshly washed sat next to me, waiting to be placed onto the bed. But I was too tired. We would need to head into town sometime soon for food rations, just the thought of which exhausted me into unconsciousness. It was good to know that I would not have trouble getting to sleep in my new domicile.

* * * * *

"How are you done unpacking already when you brought more stuff out here than I did?" I asked Logan. Our skin was covered in a coating of sweat due to our exertion.

"Because I worked on it while you napped. And I told you to box up more stuff, have it shipped out here."

"It was kind of a spur of the moment thing, me collecting my things off the front lawn and all."

"Ya, I guess you didn't leave under the best circumstances, huh?"

"I do not want reminders from my old life anyway."

But as I said that, I pulled the red reunion dress from my bag. I would not have intentionally brought it, but I was still wearing it when I left my apartment with my belongings that night. It ended up in my car and, by default, ended up included in my luggage when we cleaned the vehicle out for the new owner. The dress was covered with wrinkles and they were set in well. I suppose a dry cleaner could get them out, but I never imagined wearing it again.

Why did Lexie buy me the fancy dress anyway? Why did she push so hard for me to attend the reunion? Was it only that she did not want to go alone? She didn't know that she wouldn't be making it after all. Was she trying to set me up with Logan? She knew he was married. Did she see that maybe we could have some higher connection? Was there a higher force urging her to get us together? Or was it all just a freaky turn of Fate?

And what about all the dreams I had had in the past few months? They felt like a road map to this moment, but how could that be?

"Here, let me help you," Logan said, removing the red dress from my hand where I had been holding it as I tried to sort out the universe.

"Then I won't know where everything is at. What if I accidentally wear your socks one day instead of mine?"

"Uh, I found your socks," he said, hesitantly pulling open an old black tote bag with multi-colored stars on it. "I don't think we will be confused. Mine are all white, black, or gray." He pulled out an unmatched handful of mine. "It looks like a unicorn farted in here. Where do you even buy some of these colors?"

"Any store. You just have to keep your eyes open."

"Why is there garbage in here with it? Did you really leave in that big of a hurry? You know they charge by weight for luggage, right?"

I watched as one colored piece of glossy cardstock fell quickly at his feet. I scrambled to retrieve it, diving onto the floor and getting rug burns on my knees. It felt as though they must be bleeding as another piece of paper fell on my head. I grabbed it and looked up, desperate to find the remaining two pieces. All I was greeted with was a look on Logan's face that told me I was acting insane.

"Want to explain your reaction?" he asked pointedly, holding the third and fourth pieces in his hand.

"No. Give them to me!" I jumped up, snatched them from his grasp, and marched the two steps to the waiting drawer with as much attitude as I could muster.

"OK. If I'm going to live with you, I don't want us to have any secrets. And I don't want to have to worry about you murdering me in my sleep. It scared the shit out of me when you tried to do it while I was awake. Is that like your manifesto or something? Your suicide note?"

"No. It is something I ripped up that I rather wish I hadn't." I couldn't face him. I talked to the wall in front of me. "It is Lexie's birthday card. You have nothing to worry about, except me still mourning my dead friend."

"I'm sorry." He approached me from behind, enveloping his arms around me. "I forgot that is still so fresh. So much has happened in such a short period of time that I forget it was only seven days ago that she left this earth."

I choked back a sob. I had temporarily been able to mask my grief behind palm trees and bruised sunsets, but I was fooling myself. It was still there.

"I'm here, girl. I know it's not the same, but you can't hold it all in. We don't want to have another incident," he paused. "I don't know the cops out here to get you off," he tear-chuckled, and then I did too.

* * * * *

Logan and I sat on our "front porch," which was truthfully nothing more than the small landing where we stood when we unlocked our front door. It was nice to sit out here in the shade and the breeze. Soon enough we would both be working and not have the time for such luxuries. Logan seemed to be controlling the conversation tonight, and I let him. He seemed to have a few things he needed to work out. I was more than happy to be a supportive listener.

"I wish my dad was still alive and I could tell him about myself now. I mean, he would have already been exposed to homosexuality on his television and in his newspaper. They would have prepped him for me."

"How do you think he would take it?"

"I think he would have still loved me, I know that. But he was from an older generation, and I think it would have been difficult, if not damn near impossible, for him to understand."

"Too bad that you will never know."

"I don't know if I am actually bi, or just gay. I feel like if I came out as gay, all those years I spent with Ronnie and the kids would have been a lie. And they weren't; I was happy. There was simply this other side of me I ignored then. I guess I'm afraid. I'm not ready to throw all the small-town traditional crap I was raised on into the garbage quite yet. I want to pick and choose what ideals I want to save first, and pass those down to my kids."

"Didn't you experiment in college?"

"I didn't go to college."

"But, you are a nurse," I clarified, confused.

"I mean, I didn't go away to college. I was already married when the hardware store shut down and I started taking courses at the nearby college."

"I can't believe I never realized it before this, but that cute little high scratch in your voice, that is sort of the gay voice. I can't believe I didn't catch that before."

"You know, that is a myth. That is just what I sound like."

"I didn't mean to offend you."

"No. It's just that— Veronica brought up the same thing," he finished.

"But no one ever said anything before."

"No. I played my part. I don't think anyone suspected."

"Not even in school?"

"You didn't. I had to call other guys 'fags.' It's what we did back then. I imagine the kids still probably do that now. If I used the slur, then no would be pointing at me. I couldn't be one if I accused others, right?"

"I had a lot of friends, none of them close," he continued. "I couldn't let them get to know the real me and find out. You are an outsider with a constant need to be accepted. That is a losing battle, honey. I have been hiding who I actually was for years just to avoid that scenario."

"But I didn't want to be. I tried to play the game, blend in with everyone else."

"But in the end, it was a wasted effort. I can relate to that, to not being yourself. I'm sorry it was like that for you. That shouldn't have been your station in life. You were a perfectly normal human being," Logan said.

"You are perfectly normal too, you know. That wouldn't have made a difference in your case, either," I reasoned.

"Before we left, you kept saying things like 'maybe they could have accepted you if you gave them a chance.' "

"Ya. I wanted to make you feel better. But I doubt they would have."

"Yes, I agree. That is why we find ourselves out here in paradise. We are couple of misfits."

We smiled at each other from our respective lawn chairs that were approximately two inches apart. Christmas music began to play in my head and I wasn't sure why.

* * * * *

There was a low buzz as Logan pulled the door open and held it for me. My mind wandered back to the little bell that used to ring for me regularly at the party store down the street from my apartment. I hoped I would never hear that sound ever again. It symbolized everything I had come to Hawaii to escape: my poverty, where I could not go grocery shopping at an actual store with more than three aisles; my weakness, when I would reach for a bottle to kill all the responsibilities I didn't want to deal with; and my hopelessness, which pushed me to take a gun to try to end other people's lives.

"Logan, I can't," I protested, staring in with what must have been a wide-eyed expression.

"You have to. This is one of your goals," he reasoned.

"I don't know if I would call it a goal. It isn't like saving for retirement or climbing Mt. Everest. An aspiration, maybe."

"Either way, it is a change you want to make. It is one of the things you rattled off to me right after you pointed a gun at my chest. Therefore, it must be very important to you."

"But look at me." I held out my hands in front of me. "I'm shaking."

"No argument. You can't chicken out now. You are the one who talked me into getting one with you."

"That doesn't count. You aren't scared. You already have one," I grumbled.

"If anything, that means I already know how much it will hurt."

"OK, I'm gone."

I turned to bolt, but Logan blocked me with his hard body.

"You *want* a tattoo."

"I do. But maybe today is just not the day."

"Remember, we are going to get them to symbolize our new lives together. But not matching. It's not like we're a couple or anything...." He could see that I was still hesitating. "We already have the appointment. We are already here. The cash is in your pocket. We have already made the decision to spend our grocery money unwisely."

"I know, I know. It is a big decision."

"Not really any bigger than moving across the country."

He had pulled out the big guns. "Are you going to use that against me to get what you want for the rest of your life?"

"Ya, probably."

"Fine."

I turned around and walked in, slightly missing staring into Logan's determined eyes.

We approached the desk. A man looking scary with dreadlocks and more piercings and tattoos than I could count walked up.

"Logan and Macey. We have a six o'clock appointment," Logan told him, taking charge as he always did. I fucking loved it, but it fed into my anxiety. I would have to have a discussion with him about letting me speak for myself soon.

"Oh, ya. It will be just a moment," he said, then disappeared into the back of the store again.

Logan went over and sat on the comfy-looking leather couch while I decided to pace in front of him.

"Why are you so scared of getting a tattoo?"

"The pain, duh."

"Eh, I don't think that is the whole story. You fall down all the time. Your body has to have adapted to some level of pain by now."

"Ha, ha. Very funny. It is scary to think that my body is about to be forever changed, even if it is for the better."

"But change can be good. The last year of your life has been filled with change. But you have survived."

"Not necessarily thrived though."

"Eh, I'd say yes. You can't see it from the inside, but I am on the outside. I can. So, what is the *real* reason?"

I was looking down at the floor, but I still managed to give him a dirty sideways glare. Somedays I was transparent to him. He usually only used it for forces of good and not evil.

"I'm scared of being me," I whispered.

"What?"

"I'm not repeating it."

"I didn't ask you to. But, of all the silly things to be afraid of..."

"It is not silly. This is a big step toward becoming the girl I always kept trapped and secluded in the dark basement of my psyche. What if I don't like her manifestation?"

"FYI, I think I got the first glimpse, and I didn't like her at all. But she has been out a while now. She is less angry, more mellow. I think a tattoo will complete that look well."

"You think so?"

"C'mon back," the gentleman addressed us. We followed him this time.

It was a Saturday. I had wanted to get this over with first thing this morning, but I had learned that tattoo parlors were only open in the evenings. I didn't know if that was due to the fact that they thought someone would only get one after a long night of drinking or the ink jockeys liked to sleep in. The world may never know.

"You are in here," he said to Logan. "And you are in here," he motioned to me.

"We won't be in the same room?" I asked.

"Can be if ya want, I guess," the guy mumbled.

"No way. I don't want to be in the same room with her when she starts screaming," Logan joked.

I hoped it was a joke. So much for his alter ego, Mr. Understanding, who had paid me a visit in the lobby only moments ago.

There was already someone ready for Logan in his room. They shook hands.

"Hey, I'm Brenden. I will be doing your ink today."

I went into the room indicated. Mine was empty. I began to pace. I knew we were a couple minutes early, but I didn't know how long I could bear to wait. My nervous stomach had already made itself known before we left home. The walk here in the heat had exacerbated it once more. I didn't want to have to find the bathroom before we even began.

I decided to sit down on the table that looked like it had been retired from a doctor's office. It even had the same crinkly paper on it. I swung my legs back and forth. Slowly at first, but then faster and higher. I stopped to eavesdrop on Logan. The words were unintelligible. I heard Logan's voice reply, and then laugh. Was he flirting over there? Were there gay tattoo artists? Would he be so bold as to flirt with a straight one? I stared down at my worn canvas shoes. Logan had bought them for me brand new when we arrived. All the walking had done a number on them. And my feet. I would need to get a pair with a better insole next time. I stared at my naked thigh where an awesome tattoo soon would be. My stomach flipped again, but this time with anticipation.

"So, you ready to get some ink?" I was relieved at first that it was a woman, but then I was immediately intimidated by all her piercings and tattoos, as I had been by the desk clerk.

"I think so," I squeaked.

"Macey, right?" She must have read the schedule book. "I'm Manda."

I had expected a much more exotic name, such as 'Ānela. I was surprised at how Midwestern it sounded for someone with dark skin and bleached white hair. A pair of round sunglasses sat on top of her head. I wondered if they were a fashion statement or if she actually used them as protection from the sun's rays. Could she go out in the day, or was she a vampire?

Ah. Now I had a new theory on why tattoo joints were open only in the twilight hours.

"So, what are you getting today?"

"Um, I was thinking of something that symbolizes Hawaii." My voice shook as I spoke. I sounded like a little kid.

"Well, nothing shows that better than an empty wallet."

I laughed in spite of myself. So did she. It was a good joke.

"Some people like to get rainbows. But sometimes rainbows have different connotations these days."

"My friend is getting a rainbow in the next room."

She leaned in to me, as if to share a confidence.

"I knew a guy that gorgeous had to be playing for the other team."

"I know. Bummer."

"There are sea turtles. We could do a shark. Or maybe a cute little hula girl, with a titty hanging out or two."

"I was thinking maybe a flower. Or two."

"Oh, a hibiscus. We could do two different colors. Give you the biggest pop for your pain. Sorry, I kid. I have to haze a newbie."

"Right."

"Where do you want it?"

"I was thinking on my thigh." I don't know why I couldn't make myself sound more confident to her. I had already made up my mind. I would not be swayed.

"Are you sure? That is a pretty common place. You could get it on your rib cage, sort of wrapping around to the side..."

"I want it somewhere that it will show most of the time."

"Your ribs would show when you wear your bathing suit."

I heard the needle starting up in Logan's room, a persistent hum.

"I don't wear one much. The water isn't my thing."

"Wow, OK. I don't hear that from tourists every day."

"We aren't tourists. We just moved here."

"No shit, for real? Well, that does deserve a hibiscus or two. How about one to represent each of you—a blue and a pink." She paused. "The pink will be for him." She smiled and jabbed me with her elbow in my ribs.

She quickly drew up two simple but striking jungle flowers. They were already prettier than my thigh was in its present form. I acknowledged that I liked it, and then she copied it on the copy machine to get the correct size. She traced it with a purple pencil and placed it on my leg. It transferred onto my skin, looking like a temporary one. It was my first glimpse of what it would look like when completed. I could maybe be happy with only that much. There had been no pain so far.

She spent a few more minutes setting things up. She got together little cups of ink. They reminded me of the little plastic strips of paint pots you get in craft kits when you are a kid, the ones you let sit around the house afterward, thinking you will use it again, but they only dry up before that day ever comes. Her colors didn't look like something that would live in my skin permanently for the rest of my days.

"Get in a comfy position with your leg over the side. This is it." Her voice was calm and collected. I am glad she didn't require a reply beyond my action. My voice would have betrayed me. I glanced across the hall, where I could see Logan's feet on the table. The rest of him was blocked by Brenden's body leaning over him. I wished he was here to hold my hand. Although I supposed that negated being big and brave on my own, something I had just been pondering when we arrived.

She touched the needle to my leg and I jumped a little, then relaxed. It wasn't nearly as bad as I had imagined. There was a little pain, but it was tolerable. I had had my ears pierced back in the day. That had been *really* painful. But it was also over before it started. If I remembered it right, I kind of liked that pain. Maybe I could come back here and get something pierced.

Manda tried to make small talk. She asked whereabouts we lived and where we had come from. I'm sure this was boring for her, no more than another day at the office. But I'm afraid I wasn't good at staying engaged in the conversation and she eventually gave up. On the other hand, I could hear Logan's melodic voice chatting it up across the hall. I am sure she wished she had gotten to work on him instead.

The small, scraped sensation I had felt to begin with, like a skinned knee after a tumble from a bicycle, had morphed into something bigger. I glanced down now and then to see if flames were coming off my leg. It was raw, burned. The areas she had started with did not feel better, they actually throbbed worse as a larger area was being included all along. I was glad we had stopped talking, because this was really beginning to hurt. Why did people get this done all the time?

I fought back the urge to cry at the pain.

"Done," she called out. She wiped over it to remove the excess ink. Whatever she used cooled the burning for a moment, and I could appreciate the two beautiful flowers now etched onto my skin for all time. Then the burning started in again.

"Whoa, that looks awesome," Logan said, entering the room, limping slightly.

"Thank you."

"And larger than I would have thought you could stand."

I wanted to stick my tongue out at him, but only gave a weak smile in return. "Let's see yours."

He turned and a beautiful grey and green volcanic island was now displayed on his calf, with a rainbow over the top. It reminded me of the state logo on the license plates of the car we didn't have. This must be part of his declaration that he is actually full-on gay and not just bi. I think bisexual would involve less colors.

"Wow, that looks great. No going back now though."

"Ya, I don't think I would anyway." He smiled, knowing I didn't mean Midwest winters.

We went and paid. We walked out the door, looked at the horizon where the sun had sunk while we were inside, then down the long road.

"I think this qualifies as a day to call a cab," he stated.

"I concur." My leg hurt badly enough. I could not imagine trotting home upon it.

He pulled out his cell phone and clicked the app for the company.

We had agreed that with our limited funds that calling cabs would be off limits except in the most extreme circumstances. His definition of "extreme" was broader than mine. I had not given in yet to calling while I was on my own. That may have had more to do with not wanting to interact with people than actually saving money. But I think Logan was right that we were justified in this circumstance.

* * * * *

Logan and I quickly became accustomed to our new living conditions. The waste water was supposed to go into a cesspool, but it had apparently gotten clogged sometime in the past and the owner had tried to unblock it using dynamite. It caved in. Not wanting to spend the money to fix it, he had put in two tanks, a gray water and a black water, precisely like a camper as a temporary solution. Except, by our estimation, it seemed pretty permanent. It was alright, except we had to hire a truck to come out and empty them periodically. Our road was a private road no one had paved in eons. With all the overgrowth of trees, the fallen leaves rotted and made the dirt thicker over the rock underneath than it would be in other places on the island. It held the water better as well. The truck was heavy, so if the road up was muddy, then we had to wait. We had less issues back in Michigan, which had recently been an entire swamp. If we waited too long or the truck couldn't make it out, then the toilet, source of all black water, would start to stink. Being right by the back door, we could usually prop it open in the evening to help alleviate the stench. Notice I only said "help," not stop or cure.

"Why didn't I move out here and do this when I was twenty?" I said to Logan as I sat backwards on the couch looking out the window behind it. We were getting ready to head to the store, but I was ready before him and killing time appreciating our surroundings while he continued to look for the perfect T-shirt.

"You're not dead yet, Mace. You are here now. The rest of your life begins today." He lifted a shirt to his nose, grimaced, then threw it in the laundry hamper. Boys were so gross.

"I am totally going to put that in one of my paintings."

"Maybe it will become as famous as the cat hanging from the tree limb or Monday monkey. Hey, I want half of all profits."

"Aw, you have that much faith in my art?"

"No. I have that much faith in my witty statements."

"You are going to make some girl very happy."

"Uh, don't you mean boy?" he asked, confused.

"I mean you will make a girl very happy when she realizes she doesn't have to put up with your sarcasm because you aren't into her. Oh wait, that's me."

"No way. You are stuck with me until the end of time."

"Aw. I guess I'll keep you." I threw my arms around him and inhaled the now familiar mix of his cologne, sweat, and hair gel.

* * * * *

Apparently our pre-shopping hug had moved him because he bought me an easel. I resisted, but he insisted. Neither of us was working yet, although he had an interview yesterday that he said was all but a sure thing. I argued we needed to save our money for necessities. Logan argued that having an outlet for my emotions was a necessity.

That is how I found myself here, on the porch, trying to paint.

It had taken me an hour and a half to assemble the thing. If I couldn't figure out how to fold it up again when I was done Logan would be trapped inside the house forever. I was afraid I would push too hard and it would collapse. It had been assembled by me, after all.

To begin is the hardest part. To begin again, harder still. What if I can't create now at the level I did in the past? What if I am not as good as I always imagined I was? What if the joy I once found here is just gone?

I don't know what I was so afraid of. I had made doodles on the plane ride out here. But using my expensive supplies for a purpose was always more intimidating, always had been. It was as though I could never dream up anything special enough to fulfill their potential.

I inhaled, dipped the brush into the sludgy blue, closed my eyes, and exhaled out my nerves onto the canvas, along with that first, innocent stroke.

An hour later, I stood looking at a half-finished picture that appeared to have been done by the hand of a kindergartner. But that didn't matter to me; I was able to reclaim the old feeling of accomplishment.

Creating art was like breathing to me. How had I lived for twenty years without doing it? No wonder I had felt as if a piece of my body had died and decayed and fallen off. It had been starved of oxygen. It had been my art, what had always given me my will to live.

* * * * *

I woke up for the first time in months with no anxiety. There was a peaceful absence of emotion where mental pain and tension had repeatedly been. It didn't last, but it was enough to remind me why I fought so hard to gain it, why I was still here: the promise of peace.

I divided my days into job hunting and painting. One was way more pleasurable than the other.

When I sat down with my paints and canvas, my ears rang with the song of my muse in a language no one could understand but us two. It was overwhelming to the point where I felt nauseous. But I had never been so sure about what to paint before. I smiled, and the image filling my brain became more detailed. I knew I could never paint fast enough to keep up with these hallucinations in my mind. I was worried something else would catch my attention, distracting me and allowing the blueprint to fade away forever. I was overcome with an even weirder sensation then. It could only be described as reassurance. I guess my muse wanted me to know that now that I had the vision, it would stay with me until it was finished.

My life force was emptying onto the canvas, converting itself into colors by brushstrokes. This downloading of energy felt as if it was going to kill me. Or save me. Maybe this is what vibrated inside of me that needed to burst out. Either way, I had reawakened the creative heart inside of me.

Either my painting had improved quickly, or my brain was allowing for my shortcomings, because I knew what the completed picture would look like before I even started. I knew that the lines would be a little crooked in unnatural locations and the writing would go uphill. But I loved the imperfections in my works. It is what proved to the world that a human being had made it, and not a computer or a robot or an alien.

Everything about the landscape here was in constant motion: the sea, the people, the plants, the wildlife. It was hard to capture that in a picture. None of the photographs we had looked at prior to coming here had. Even our shack on stilts swayed when the wind kicked up enough.

I felt guilty for spending so much time crafting worlds, for existing outside of reality. But after I got that creation out of my system I was refreshed, like I had fulfilled my destiny in some way, checked off one more thing on the to-do list Fate had for me. I left a little of my stress and anxiety behind on the canvas. It felt good. But the next day, and the next, it began to build again. I had to begin another work to maintain the outlet. It was healthier than drugs or alcohol, but I couldn't stop cold turkey. Deep down I knew that that would have dire consequences.

"Hey! I know you are in the zone out there, but I am headed into town to do laundry in five minutes. I can't carry all your crap & mine too," Logan light-heartedly complained from inside our home. He had a point. But I truly hated adulting. What if I just bought more clothes to wear instead of taking the time to clean the old ones?

Getting pulled out of working on a picture before I was ready to pause was a jarring experience, especially to complete mundane chores. My soul was a rubber band, being suddenly snapped back inside my body. I loved how the outside world melted away while I created.

TIME TRAVEL

Time has moved forward, my life has not.

Two months later...

I ascended the one lane dirt road, nearing my little pink shack. My tennis shoes squished because I had not been able to avoid all the puddles of the storms the last few days had left behind. The water had absorbed into my memory foam. I hoped it wouldn't ruin the cushioning. I was on my feet all day long at work and I was no spring chicken. The three mile walk to and from wasn't terrible, but once I got home I only wanted to put my feet up until tomorrow morning came around, and it was back down and around the mountain again.

The road became narrower and overgrown the closer to the house I got. After dark it was downright eerie. The giant ferns scared me if I watched them too closely. When the ocean breeze moved them, it was as if they were coming alive. It was like a 1950s monster movie where household ferns had had radioactive sludge dumped on them and suddenly grew ten times their normal size. Then they wouldn't be satisfied any longer with rainwater. They would want human blood. Next thing you know, they would be running for Congress.

It had been an uneventful day at Rainbow Mist Antiques & Gifts where I worked. Also not challenging. I thought I liked doing simple jobs until I had one. Of course, the same could be said for complicated jobs as well. I knew I should look for something that paid a little more, so that Logan didn't have to bear the brunt of the budget. But I had been fortunate to find this one. They paid me under the table there; that had been their suggestion, not mine. I didn't have any garnishments or the IRS cutting into my paycheck. It averaged thirty hours a week, whereas it seemed everyone else was only hiring for twenty to twenty-five.

I had trouble enough remembering how to run the POS terminal at Rainbow Mist. If I added a second establishment, there is no telling what I wouldn't be able to remember. And I couldn't beat the commute. The store was on the edge of town. It was the last store the tourists stopped in before turning around and heading back up the street to their hotels.

I slowly trudged up the stairs, willing my knees to carry me the ten more steps which would get me through the door and onto the loveseat. I stopped to rest at the top of the stairway, turning around to catch the glimpse of the ocean, right where I knew it would be, through a small gap in the palm trees. In the quiet at night we could hear the waves crashing. I turned back to the door as the smell of food coming from my house caused me suspicion. I turned the knob, finding it already unlocked.

"What are you doing home already?"

"I got a ride," Logan replied as he busily cooked at the tiny stove.

"Did this ride happen to come from Michael again?"

"Yes." I saw his ears redden with his blush. "But don't read anything into it."

Logan had snagged a job two weeks after we arrived in Hawaii at Kalama Medical Center. It wasn't especially a surprise. He had been well-liked at his previous employer, Greater Mercy Hospital, and had several good references to refer potential employers to. He enjoyed the duties and his coworkers. What he didn't enjoy was his commute which was longer than mine. He walked to the nearest bus stop, then road it in to the hospital. The bus was often packed and he viewed it as a hassle. It would be a while before we could think about buying a car. While we had both sold our previous ones, we had largely put that money into travel expenses and rent. He generally sucked it up and did it. But if there was any hint of rain, he called a taxi. I didn't think it was the best use of our limited funds, but since seventy percent of them were his, I didn't see fit to make a big deal out of it. Except lately he had been getting rides home from Michael, his coworker. I had never seen him myself, but the way Logan reacted to the mere mention of his name, I knew that he must be attractive.

"What does Michael do there?"

"He's an x-ray tech. He doesn't have to do all the dirty work I do, but he has to work around radiation all day."

I took a long whiff of the air and motioned toward the range. "What are you making us tonight?"

Logan had found a love of the culinary arts since we had arrived. I took it as an insult that he desired broader variety than my grilled cheese and French fried onion baked chicken breasts.

"Mostaccioli with garlic bread."

"I can smell the garlic. Did you finally get the stove and the oven to work at the same time?" We had lived here two months and this had been an ongoing problem that the landlord refused to look at.

"No. But I made the bread first and then left it in there to warm."

"You are so resourceful."

"You better be glad that I am. I have to start paying child support this month. We are going to have to stop going out and hitting the town."

"When have we done that?"

"The grocery store, the laundromat, the video store…"

"Man, I am right back in the same debt-filled situation I was before. I should have never gotten involved with a man who has kids."

"Not exactly the same." He bent down, taking the cookie sheet of garlic bread from the oven. "Now you are surrounded by paradise." He waved his left hand toward the window behind the couch, the largest in the house, and with the right shoved a piece of garlic bread too far into my mouth.

"Ummm," I managed to mumble through the carbohydrates blocking my airway.

A low chuckle escaped him. If I had still let myself be into Logan, it would have melted me into a puddle right here. But having to live with him was doing a pretty good job of discouraging that. I hadn't lived with a man in years. They were fairly disgusting creatures, especially when residing in such close quarters.

* * * * *

Most of the time, we used our tiny porch as extended living space. It worked well to keep us out from under each other's feet, especially if I had my art supplies spread all over the living room or porch. But if it rained we were like men trapped inside a submarine. We couldn't escape surrounded by water on all sides as we were. We couldn't make our space any larger. We were two sardines trapped in the can.

It was one such night when Logan announced out of the blue, "We are going to a movie."

"We are?"

He pulled his cell out of his back pocket. I never understood how the screen managed to stay unharmed while residing there. "From 3 Manō Drive to GTM Cinemas on Nihi Street ." He punched a few keys on his app. "A cab will be here in twenty minutes," he told me.

"What's come over you? We have been out here for two months and haven't gone to the movies once. How did you even know where there was a theater?"

"Because I pass by it every day on my way to work. I always think sometime I will stop in and see something, but of course I never have. So, we are going tonight. I think we are perfect walking examples of the positive effects of not waiting until later." I thought of all the times back in the Midwest I had wanted to go in a store and then it closed before I ever got around to it. Always a bummer.

"What will we see? What is even playing?"

"I don't know. It doesn't matter, does it? Wouldn't anything be better than sitting around here trapped by the rain?"

"You're right. I'm in," I said. I changed out of my pajamas and found my cute, colorful polka-dot rubber boots I had bought for slogging through the mud on days such as this.

A honk outside alerted us to the arrival of our ride. We grabbed our raincoats. The door was old and worn and could probably be removed with one swift kick, but we locked it anyway. We began to clomp down the stairs, but my foot slid off one step unexpectedly and I had to catch myself on the railing, which swayed under the brunt of my full weight.

"Whoa, there. I have never seen another person as clumsy as you are. That is one thing I do remember about you from school. You tripping over chairs and bumping into me and whatnot." Logan laughed as he put his hands on my hips to return me to an upright position.

"Some of that bumping may have been on purpose."

"You need to be more careful. I don't think I could afford your medical bills."

"Hey, I haven't ended up in the emergency room once since we have been out here. You better watch out. Next time I might take you down with me."

"Maybe getting a place with so many stairs was a bad idea."

We were laughing as we practically jumped into the cab to escape from the relentless rain, both of us getting in through the passenger rear door. As Logan pulled the door shut the driver affirmed, "The theater on the corner of Moanalua Road and Nihi Street?" He pronounced all the words without butchering them, as Logan and I would have.

"That's right," he responded.

"Such a pleasure to escort such happy young lovers on a night out on the town."

"We aren't a couple, only friends," I attempted to correct him.

"Oh, I sense not for long."

Dude just wasn't getting it. "We are both looking for a few good men." I didn't know a better way to put it, but I didn't have to. Comprehension dawned on his face.

"Ah, well then may you both have a wonderful evening, and may the possibility of love cross your paths."

"Thank you very much," Logan responded, looking sideways at me and smiling.

With the help of an internal combustion engine and rubber tires, we arrived at the theater in no time. We splurged on candy, soft drinks, and a tub of popcorn larger than my head. Logan wanted to see the latest comic book-inspired multi-super hero movie, but there wasn't a show starting again soon, so I talked him into seeing the new romance based on the young adult novel by Kiley Riley, *Don't Judge a Boy by His Shoes.* She was my favorite author.

Logan and I were early, so we played the cheesy entertainment trivia that occupied the screen pre-previews—and we failed terribly. If you texted in ten correct answers in a row, you could earn a free drink. We had been out of the pop culture loop too long. If we had to rely on our knowledge for beverages, we would both have died of thirst.

"Oh, I have a funny story for you from work," Logan began.

Sometimes his stories were more gross than funny. I couldn't imagine working in the medical industry.

"The other morning, or I think it was actually the tail end of a night of partying for this guy, Michael texts me about this patient he had to x-ray who had been playing truth or dare with his buds. Apparently his friends, and I use that term loosely, had dared him to eat all kinds of shit that they thought would be funny when he pooped it back out again. There were coins, BBs, rubber bouncy balls, God knows what all. Next thing I know, I get a call that this guy is getting admitted because they need to do surgery on him, and he is going to be one of *my* patients. This dude has been at the hospital four hours at least by the time I see him and he is *still drunk*. I can't imagine how much he must have drank to swallow all that shit in the first place and to still be wasted at 7:00AM. You should have seen how pissed his parents were when they showed up."

I cringed. "I thought you couldn't share stories due to privacy acts or something."

"I didn't give you his name or address. Hell, I can't even remember his name, and I wouldn't want to."

"You have a lot of amusing tales from the hospital. You must really like it there?"

"I like my coworkers a lot—"

"Including Michael," I interrupted him again.

Logan took a log sip of beverage before continuing.

"Yes, I do really like my job. How about you?"

"It is a paycheck. When we left Michigan I was hoping to find a job here where I could make money doing what I am passionate about. Don't get me wrong, I like souvenirs, but they are not my passion. I would rather be drawing or painting."

"I thought you were going to ask if they would carry some of your stuff on consignment."

"I did."

"And?" he motioned with his hand indicating he needed more information than that.

"The manager said she liked my stuff, but she would only carry local artists that already had made a name for themselves, that customers came in asking for."

"Huh. Makes it hard to get started."

"Exactly." I echoed his sentiment, resting my head on his hard shoulder.

"Have you checked the job sites at all?"

"Not since I found my job at the Misty Rainbow. Do you think I should still be looking?"

"If you are not happy where you are, you should always be looking to move on to something better. You need to stop taking jobs just for the money."

"You make me sound like a fuckin' prostitute."

"Well, isn't that the definition of one? Will do anything for a buck?"

"Sometimes you are an asshole, you know that?"

"Yes, I do."

"I am out here trying to do my best to earn my share and you are giving me crap for it."

"I want you to. But I don't want you to be miserable because of it."

"Sometimes those two circumstances cannot coexist together. I have had no one to rely on but myself since I was sixteen."

"Well, you can count on me."

"Good."

"Cuz really, I don't have anybody else out here to rely on except you," Logan said.

I had never had anyone say that about me before, ever. Realization dawned inside of me.

"Maybe you can find something in advertising, or maybe some freelance projects," he continued, pulling me out of my emotions.

"Hmmm. I will think about it." The advertising industry seemed too intense and scary. I could imagine all my passion for my art sucked out of me there.

Logan looked at me thoughtfully. "Don't think too hard, alright? I don't want you back in the gun-toting place again."

"Understood." It didn't bother me that Logan could joke about something so serious so freely. It actually helped to talk about it, to remember. I didn't want to turn around one day and realize I had traveled that same road of crazy. I felt alright now.

I was afraid I would wake up one day and all that calm would be gone.

"Life happens. We have to try to find some way to be happy in it."

"Easier said than done."

The first preview flickered up on the screen and the lights dimmed.

* * * * *

I should be working on my painting now, but I was just too tired.

Ah, I remember this now. This was how it all starts. First I paint around the clock, then it is relegated to weekends. Before I know it, I am too exhausted from working a day job to put any time into my passion. Then it falls to the wayside like a cigarette butt out the window of a speeding car.

This was how I had managed to not create anything meaningful in fifteen years. It was so easy to let myself become distracted that I forgot what I was put on this planet to do.

If I don't work, we can't survive. If I don't paint, I can't survive.

There was only one solution. I would need to find a job in the *actual* field I wanted to be in, and soon. I left my thoughts of ineptitude behind to listen to Logan as he made us dinner.

"Michael said that even though it is close, we should stop buying groceries there because they overcharge everyone."

"You sure talk about this Michael a lot," I said as I sat at our kitchen table.

"Ya," Logan said, turning quickly.

"Is that a smile I just saw?"

"No," he said, still trying to hide his face from me as he prepared the food.

"Oh, and a blush!" I surged forward and turned him around. I began to pinch his flushed cheeks as if I was a church lady and he was a newborn baby.

"Shut up. It's nothing."

"You l-i-i-i-ke him."

"I do." He paused. "And I think he likes me too, because he asked me out."

"What? That is huge!" I yelled, shaking him, morphing it into an energetic hug. "I never thought you guys would ever move past the carpool phase." I let him go and backed up to my chair, but did not sit yet.

"Why? Did you think I wasn't cute enough to catch him?"

"No. I merely thought you guys would move from sharing a ride directly to fucking."

His mouth opened wide in shock. He reached out and punched me in the arm. It wasn't far; we were still only two feet away from each other in our tiny kitchen.

"What?! I thought that is how it worked with gay men. Or any man, really."

"I am the same age as you are. That makes me old school."

"Are you calling me old?"

"Are you calling me promiscuous?"

"I'm calling you my roomie who pays most of the bills. I am so happy for you. When is it? Where will you go?"

"We both have Saturday off from the hospital, which I am taking as a sign from the universe that this is the day meant for us." Logan placed a portion of the eggs with diced ham onto each of our plates. We often had breakfast for dinner. Somehow it worked out cheaper that way. "Where are gay men supposed to go on dates together? I have no idea. This will be my first. He mentioned the zoo. The zoo! Am I even allowed to go there without my kids? I feel like I am betraying them. Have I even mentioned Vaughn and Vicky to him? I can't remember! What if he wants me, but not my kids?" He plopped down into his chair in defeat.

I gently patted his hand as it lay next to his untouched silverware on the table. "Now you know how women have felt for...ever. And you are getting way ahead of yourself. I believe living with me has had an adverse effect on you."

"I believe that," he said, shaking his head as if hoping to shake the crazy out of his ears. Now it was my turn to punch him. He only smiled back, his heartbreaker's grin.

* * * * *

My interview with the human resources manager at Island Recollections had gone so well. I didn't want to jinx it by having another on the same day. And with the CEO? I knew it was a small company, but couldn't he simply look over my files and give it a yeah or a nay and save me all this undue stress? I carried my black, fabric covered notebook under my right arm, prepared to fold it open and take notes at a moment's notice. I approached a woman at a desk. I hoped I was in the right place.

"Macey?" she asked.

I nodded.

"He is ready for you. Go right in."

Dammit. Why hadn't the secretary repeated his name for me? I couldn't remember what the last woman had said his name was, and there was no gold metallic nameplate in sight. Heck, I couldn't even remember her name. I attempted to hold my notebook in one hand as I turned the door knob with the other. The door seemed to stick, so I gave it a harder push with one hand when I should have used both of them. Of course that ended with me fumbling my notebook as I burst through the door more quickly than I had intended to. My pen and flash drive bounced out. I scurried to retrieve them.

I could plainly see the silhouette of a man behind a desk, but my attention was drawn to the view out the windows behind him where the sun was streaming in, causing my pupils to slowly narrow. The ocean was an overly-vibrant blue, accentuated by the white waves marching forward toward the shore. The green palm trees framed the corners, helping to provide contrast to the bright, cloudless sky. I loved many things about my home state, but before this moment I thought a view like this could only exist in my imagination. Even my first view of the shore after leaving the airport wasn't this breathtaking. And I was positive I didn't want to work for a guy who would set up his office with his back to such a view.

"Hello?" he asked tentatively, probably deciding by now that I had a mental deficiency.

"Uh, the chick, uh, lady outside said I could come on in." There was my real self slipping through. Fuck it, why not be myself. That had been part of how my former life had gone so horribly wrong. I had always put on a front to maintain everyone else's happiness, at the expense of my own.

"Oh right, the interviews for the vacant greeting card designer position. I'm Davy Kekoa."

His name was Davy? Sounded more like a nickname. But then why wouldn't he use "David" for business if that was his name? Maybe it was similar to guys from the South whose name was just "Jimmy" or "Tommy." As my eyes adjusted to the brightness, I could tell that he was staring at me expectantly before continuing. "And you are?"

"Uh, Macey Reynolds. Nice to meet you." It really wasn't, but it seemed an interview-type thing to say to a man who held my entire life and sanity in his hands.

"Glad you could stop in today, Macey."

He made it sound like this was the drug store. Yes, because I always casually stop in to greeting card and gift companies to talk to the chief executive officer. No biggie. R-i-g-h-t.

"Yes, um, I'm very interested in the greeting card designer position."

"Well, let me see what you have here," he said bringing up my files on his computer. I had dropped off a flash drive with my images when I had left my application at the front desk. I imagined what I experienced as he look at my pictures was akin to standing in front of someone naked. I had put my heart and soul on the canvas to birth these creations. I held my breath as he in turn clicked through the photos I had taken with my cell phone, the only digital camera I owned. From where I sat I could only see the back of his laptop display. His reactions gave nothing away. Maybe he was actually looking at porn and only pretending to be reviewing my work. Maybe he was faking it, like his wife did every night in bed.

I snorted out loud at my own joke. But it wasn't truly mine. I knew it came from Lexie's half of our shared brain: the dirty part.

"Are you alright?" he asked, looking more annoyed than concerned.

I only nodded in response. It was nice to know that a part of Lexie still carried on in the living world. I got a smile on my face then, which I'm sure Mr. Davy could not fathom why it was there.

"All the other candidates have an online presence to display their work. How is it that you do not?"

Damn. I thought I was doing good realizing they needed to be digital and not in an oversized portfolio like the old days. I thought fast.

"Server crash."

"Oh, well. That is unfortunate. Have you been painting long? These show promise but they look," he hesitated, "unfinished."

He looked right at me. I swallowed my saliva with a loud gulp, as a cartoon character would before answering. I wondered what animal I would be as a cartoon character, but decided that had to wait until after the interview. I was anticipating a question such as this. It was akin to answering unwelcome inquiries about a job gap which, to my detriment, I also had.

"I studied art all through high school and college. I got away from it for a while, but recently came back to it."

"Oh, that explains it."

Explains what?!

Wait, I don't want to know.

"You are aware that we are looking for someone to create Hawaiian images, primarily landscapes, aren't you?"

"Yes. There are some in there."

"A few, but many of these look mid-western. This one has cattle and snow. Around here we only paint snow if it is on top of a volcano."

"I only started drawing Hawaii when I moved here, obviously. That is why I haven't built up as many images yet. But I will."

He flipped back to what I assumed was the first page of my file, my resume, mostly consisting of my time at Frontier Central. "You are from Michigan?"

"Yes. Is that a problem?"

"No," he seemed flustered now. "It is simply that this position requires someone who knows the landscape and stories of Hawai'i as well as the back of their hand." He paused, quickly flipping to the end of my scant portfolio. "I only see paintings. I don't see any examples of your digital work in here."

"Because I don't have much," I lied. I didn't have any. "But I'm willing to learn."

"That's the thing. We need someone who can jump in right away. Would you say you are proficient in Image Tunnel 6.0? Are you familiar with Brushtip Deluxe? We only use that for converting images, but it can take a little time to learn."

I didn't want to say no, but anything else would have been lying.

"No. But in past positions I have proven myself to be a quick learner on new systems."

He made a weird deep grumble under his breath. "Didn't they cover that in college?" He squinted at my resume, as if trying to make the qualifications appear out of thin air. "There is no graduation date on here. Did you finish?"

"I did, that is why it lists my degree." I hated divulging when I graduated. I didn't feel like it was anyone's business. And more often than not, it disqualified me due to my advanced age. I wasn't eligible for Social Security, but I definitely didn't qualify as a fresh-faced co-ed.

"But when?"

Ugh. I had to divulge it. By the look of his line-free brown skin, he could well be younger than me, and he definitely was multiple times more successful.

"2002."

"Oh, well that's why. They weren't around then. And you haven't taken any classes since then? To keep your degree up-to-date?"

Ew. Did people actually do that? Like, continue the torture that is school when they already have the piece of paper that says you are done? That is the proof of four years' worth of suffering. And I may have only attended for four years but it already seemed longer because it took me ten years to pay it off. I must have made a disgusted face right then because his look shifted to puzzled. I knew then that I stood no chance.

I stood, trying to think of something polite to say before I ran right out of there. But I didn't have to. He took the hint, standing as well. He hesitated, as if he wanted to thank me or shake my hand or something. But I only turned and beat it out of there. I avoided eye contact with all the other employees on my way to the exit.

I didn't expect to hear from that man ever again. And it was a shame, because in time I knew I could do a good job at that position. And I would maybe enjoy it. But I was not delusional enough to realize that there weren't at least ten other candidates who could walk in tomorrow and already know how to perform the duties required. Hell, the guy probably had his brother or cousin lined up and I was just a formality. I was a minority to interview for government reporting.

* * * * *

My phone rang. I glanced at the screen, expecting Logan's contact picture with the tall red and white stripy hat I had won him at a carnival to be there. Instead, there was no picture or ID for the number, but I had an inkling who or what it may be.

"This is Davy Kekoa from Island Recollections calling. Am I speaking to Macey?"

"This is," I answered hesitantly. Had I actually gotten the job after all? I let myself momentarily get my hopes up.

"I called to let you know that we have gone with another candidate," he said confidently.

"Oh," my voice instantly dropped, "you could have saved yourself the time then." He was the CEO making calls to people who were not hired. He was *way* too involved in the finer points of his business.

"I wanted you to know that I think you are very talented, but you simply couldn't provide that authentic island feel we needed for our business." Davy's disappointment floated from the phone.

"I get it. I understand," I practically mumbled.

"I mean, if you are still interested in this line of work, I could give you some pointers." He sounded nervous. He had no reason to be nervous.

"That's fine, you don't—," I tried to interrupt. But he kept on talking.

"Like taking some classes in computer design for instance. We could maybe discuss it over dinner."

I was going to hang up on him, right this instant— Wha?

"Are you asking me out?" I was incredulous.

"Yes, I suppose I am," he replied hesitantly.

"Like a date?" I squeaked.

"Look, this was a bad idea. I'm sorry to bother you—" His tone was standoffish.

"No, I, uh," I hesitated. I had kept him on the line, but now I was clueless as to how to respond. "I'm not good enough for the job, but I'm good enough to date?" Maybe it came off as critical, but I was trying to wrap my mind around something he had had a week to plan.

"Just because you didn't meet the qualifications of the job doesn't mean— You just seemed nice in the interview alright. I thought maybe we could see if there was something more there." He was back to sounding like Mr. Businessman again. Maybe I had already lost him.

"Nice? That is what you look for in a woman?"

"Well, interesting, alright. You seemed interesting."

"I guess I can't argue with that judgement. I don't hide it well…"

"And you shouldn't. How about I pick you up for dinner tomorrow night? Since I didn't give you a job, it will be my treat."

"I have to work the evening shift tomorrow night, since you didn't give me the job." I smiled an impish grin. Now I was teasing him. It probably didn't even register in the sound of my voice. I probably just lost him. And I didn't even know yet if I wanted him.

"How about Saturday, then? 6:00PM. Unless your work schedule still prevents it, of course."

He had picked up on my teasing tone. He was giving it right back to me while providing a way out if I wanted it. I should probably take it. This would end badly, I was positive.

"Sounds good. Let me give you my address."

"But I already have it. On your resume." He sounded as if this was not the first time he had picked up women this way. I didn't know how I felt about that. It made me feel less special. But on the other hand, it worked *really* well.

"It can be tricky to find."

"Oh really?"

"Ya. When you think you have reached the end of the road, keep going." I sounded like I was coaching a child on how to do a maze.

"Keep going. Got it."

"And if it's muddy, your car might get stuck."

"I've got a Jeep Rubicon, so it will be fine."

Oh. I had always wanted to own a Jeep. I couldn't say no now.

"Then it's a date, I guess."

"You seem unsure."

"I am skepitcal why you would go to all this trouble for me." It slipped out. It was the truth, but I hadn't meant for it to sneak through my lips.

"Huh. Well. That's an unusual reaction."

"Hey, you said you found me interesting."

"Yes. In my experience, most women want you to make lots of effort."

"Maybe you are dating the wrong kind of women."

"Maybe. See you Saturday"

"OK. Bye."

A date? I hadn't been on a proper date in nearly a decade. What was I thinking? I pictured the job interview in my head and wondered if it would be like that, but with food in front of us. I shuddered. I was already sorry that I had agreed to go.

* * * * *

I really needed things to work out with Davy. I knew that. While Logan was the greatest best friend (aside from Lexie, R.I.P.) that a girl like me could have, it was lonely only having him. Sure, the clerks at the grocery store and the laundromat had started to offer a friendly "aloha" when they saw me, but they didn't chat beyond that. Logan and I were still outsiders in paradise. He was quickly making friends at work. I only had three other coworkers, and most customers were tourists, so the opportunity for repeat customers was slim. I knew better than to hope for romance and love with Davy. I was so broken that I was pretty sure I wasn't even capable of those emotions anymore. But if I could at least acquire a local friend out of it, then this dinner would be totally worth it.

I was watching out the window when I heard a vehicle approaching. I looked at myself in the mirror on the back of the bathroom door one more time. I had gone with the same black pants I had worn to the interview (I only had the one pair) and a billowy shirt whose color in the salmon family I adored, but it actually made me look fat. I knew a dress would be more appropriate for this occasion, but I hated them and couldn't bear to put one on. Besides, the only one I presently owned was the red one Lexie had purchased for me for the reunion. It sat in a random drawer, unwashed and crumpled into a ball. Davy would have to accept me as I was or shun me forever.

I didn't really care.

Which was a lie.

I totally did care. Logan wasn't home. I was thankful that he was gone so that I didn't have to hear his brotherly jokes. I was disappointed he was not here because he would have provided me the support and encouragement I so desperately craved.

I pulled the door shut behind me and locked it. It wasn't like there was much of value to steal, but as with anywhere else sometimes troublesome youth were known to come in and trash the place if given an opportunity. I walked down the stairs slowly and methodically in my sandals trying not to trip. Looking at the steps as long as possible also gave me an excuse to avoid looking at Davy sitting in his Jeep, top down. When I did, he was smiling at me. It made me uncomfortable. Instead of smiling back, I fought back the bile rising in my throat and walked around the front of the hood to get in. This was a bad idea. My stomach churned as I sat down next to him, eating tonight seeming like a total impossibility.

"Hi."

"Hey." It wasn't warm. My voice sounded hollow.

"You ready for this?"

"No," I responded truthfully.

He laughed and backed up, steering us onto the road headed in the direction of the city.

"You aren't actually going to give me job pointers, are you?"

"Not unless you want me to," he replied. "I didn't get a chance to ask you what kind of food you enjoy on the phone."

Ugh. A sticky subject for me. A bad one to start with.

"Burgers, fries, pizza."

"Ah, good old American food."

"Yup, that's me. A corn-fed Midwestern gal... Wait, that's cattle."

Davy let out a big belly laugh this time, so big he temporarily drove us off the private dirt road. We were almost up to the pineapple farm entrance, where it began to be paved.

"I'm just here for your amusement." I shrugged in my seat.

"Are all girls from Michigan like you?"

"No, not a one. There used to be two of us, but not anymore."

"A sister?"

I laughed at him this time. "No, a best friend, but she died three months ago."

"Ah, so is that why you moved out here? To get away from those bad memories?"

"Yes, that would be the short explanation." I didn't want to get into mental breakdowns, alcoholism, and attempted shootings on our first date, especially before we even arrived at the restaurant.

"Oh."

"Is that not OK with you?" I accused.

"No, I well. I didn't mean to offend you. It's only that if that's the reason you came, it sounds as if this could be some sort of extended vacation until you head back."

I gave a low, dark chuckle. "No. You don't have to worry about that. I have nothing to go back to."

Luckily, we rolled into the city limits right then. He pointed out a few restaurants as we passed, but ultimately he took me to a glorified shack down by the beach. It didn't turn me off. I wasn't scared of shacks. After all, I called one home.

"Are you sure they are up-to-date on their health license around here?"

"I know that it doesn't look like much," he began as we both slid into opposite sides of a red vinyl booth, "but they have excellent all-beef hamburgers with a local twist. The bacon double cheeseburger comes with pineapple on it. The smoky vs. sweet vs. fat is a taste sensation not to be missed.

"Ugh. I hate pineapple."

A loud laugh broke out from him again. "You live in Hawai'i, pineapples are our number one fruit crop, you literally live down the road from one of the plantations, and you don't like them? That is kind of absurd, if you don't mind me saying so."

"I bet not everyone in Idaho likes potatoes. I lead an absurd life, I guess. You didn't find me this hilarious in the interview."

"Oh, I did, but I had my professional face on. I tried not to let my amusement escape."

"It may have been a more pleasurable experience if you had."

"You still wouldn't have been qualified for the job."

"I knew that going in. But nothing ventured, nothing gained. I just... it would be nice to make a living at what I love to do for once in my life."

"That should be everyone's dream."

"But dreams don't pay the bills."

There was a beautiful view out the window of the beach and the ocean. No wonder they didn't have extra money to improve the exterior. All their money probably went into location, location, location.

The waiter came and took our orders. I ended up getting chicken tenders and fries because that seemed the safest choice, for many reasons, the biggest of which was my stomach could combat the greasy chicken better than some other fried animals.

Mmm... fried animals.

When my basket was set in front of me, Davy grimaced at my choice. Apparently I had offended him by not being a risk-taker and trying an American-Hawaiiana hybrid sandwich. Boo-hoo. If he was going to go sour about such a thing it was good that he was not in fact my boss at this time.

I tried to secretly study him as he took a big mouthful of medium-rare cow, some mixture of BBQ sauce and grease running down from the corner of his mouth. He had big brown eyes. I was always a sucker for those. Logan was evidence of that. The texture of his black hair looked very fine. I wouldn't mind touching it sometime to find out how it felt between my fingers. When he looked up at me, I quickly ripped a chicken tender in half and started swirling it in my honey mustard sauce. The hot juices that seeped from the chicken burned my fingers. I wished this place served hard liquor so that I could ease my nerves. Beer and wine weren't my thing and that is all that was served here. I hadn't even been interested enough to touch a drop of alcohol since Logan and I had gotten onto the plane. But this was an exceptionally stressful situation. I may be able to handle it better if I was appropriately intoxicated.

When I looked up, he was engrossed in his meal again. He had nice lips. The dark T-shirt he had on showcased the muscles underneath. Looking at him, I decided that even though he was the head of the company, he may be younger than me.

"How old are you?" I blurted.

Breaking the silence apparently startled him as he coughed on the current mouthful that he was masticating. He swallowed and wiped his face with the napkin in his lap. As uncouth as I was, mine still lay next to my plate.

"Um, thirty-four. Why, is that a problem?"

"No. It's just that I'm thirty-seven. Wouldn't want you to regret getting involved with an older woman or anything."

"Macey, are you *trying* to scare me off with this date? It's not working, but it sure feels that way."

"I'm not sure I'm ready to date."

"Then why waste my time agreeing to go out?"

"Because I hoped I was."

"And when do you think you will be ready?"

"When I'm dead."

"Well, that changes everything then."

"It does?"

"There is a difference between not being ready and never being ready. I wouldn't push a woman if she wasn't ready. But someone as pretty as you saying they will never be ready is truly a shame. It needs to be rectified."

"Ugh, I think we need to get you glasses."

"Problem with my compliment?"

"Look, I have a lot of problems, but none of them have anything to do with you. I didn't want to get into this on a first date, but if you want a nice, normal woman, I ain't it. I'm depressed, anxious, have low self-esteem, anger management issues. And that is only the tip of the iceberg. So if you want to run now, feel free to." I stopped and then thought of something to add. "Just please leave enough money to cover the bill because I don't want to spend all night washing dishes."

He shook his head from side to side and I didn't know what that meant. I decided to wipe my hands. When I started to get up, he placed his hand over mine.

"Sit down. I'm sorry, but I've never met a creature like you."

"Now I'm a creature? As in a monster in a horror flick?"

"A woman who is open and honest. That is a rare creature to find."

"Oh, I am hiding all sorts of things from you. At this rate, you probably will never find out what. And stop calling me 'a woman.' It makes me feel as though I am in a maxi pad commercial. I consider myself 'a chick.' "

"As in a baby chicken?"

"Like I might be old and square on the outside, but I still feel young and cool on the inside. There is no good way to express that outwardly though. The best way I have found is Hello Kitty jewelry."

He cocked his head sideways. I couldn't read his eyes. His hand on mine was warm and reassuring as I stood there staring down at him.

"Let's see if we can make it through one date. I think I've already gotten my money's worth, but let's see what else happens, shall we?" He flashed me a shy smile.

What else happened was we took a walk on the beach after dinner. I was too full, but the cool, wet sand between my toes felt nice. You know what else felt nice? Davy holding my hand as the sun sank out of sight in a mess of orange and purple.

He offered up information about himself. I was glad to be removed from the hot seat. I found out he had been married and divorced in his twenties. He had watched all his friends begin to have kids, but he had none. This created a rift in his friendships as he didn't have as much in common. They didn't want to bore him by inviting him to their children's birthday parties.

He had taken care of his mother who was in poor health for several years in his home, as his only brother had moved to the mainland. But she had passed away the previous spring. As a result, he had spent Thanksgiving and Christmas alone. I offered that I had always been welcome for holidays at Lexie's, but she had gone to be with family out of town last Christmas, so I had been alone as well. We looked at each other in understanding, recognizing the extreme loneliness that you only know if you have experienced it firsthand.

After all the light was gone, we walked back to the car, put our shoes on, and he drove me home.

As we sat in the car talking, another pulled up next to us. I recognized it as Michael's. Logan got out of the passenger side and looked over at us in Davy's Jeep. The only light came from Michael's headlights.

"You comin' in sometime tonight, Mace?" Logan yelled and winked at me. He banged on the hood of Michael's car, then headed up our stairs. We all watched him unlock the door and flick the lights on, all three of them. Michael's car backed up and left, the engine sounds echoing in the night before fading into the distance.

"Uh, who was that?" Davy asked. His voice sounded higher than usual.

"That's just Logan."

"Uh, you didn't tell me you were living with an Eddie Bauer model."

"Funny. I can see why you would think that."

"Macey, I don't want to get in a relationship with an involved woman—"

"No, it's not like that. Logan is my roommate. We moved here from Michigan together."

"And in all the time we were together tonight you didn't think to mention him?"

"No, I didn't. Logan and how I came to live in your lovely state are kind of fused together. And that's not something I am ready to attempt to explain to you yet. I'm sorry if you are mad that I didn't remember to tell you my male roommate was also out on a date tonight... with his boyfriend. And look, if you have a problem with that, then we are going to be done right here and now because love is love, no matter how many penises and vaginas are involved."

Davy sat quietly for a minute, letting my rant sink in. Then a smile crept across his face. "No, I don't have a problem with him being gay. My biggest problem is the jealously I felt when I realized you lived with him."

"Jealousy?"

"Yes. It is truly amazing how quickly a male can form an attachment with a female. Scientists should study it or something. I hope you aren't sore at me."

"No. Surprised, I guess."

"You shouldn't be. But before I send you in for the night to sleep near that guy," he motioned toward our residence. "Wait, you guys don't sleep in the same bed, do you? That place is pretty small."

"No," I laughed. "Same room though."

"Oh, Lord have mercy. You are sleeping adjacent to the Adonis?"

"Are you sure that you are not gay?"

"No, and I'll leave you tonight with this to prove it."

And he put his hand on my cheek so that I wouldn't move and leaned in to kiss me. I felt a spark as his lips touched mine. I tried to remember how long it had been since I had been kissed, then quickly pushed that thought from my head in order to enjoy the present. He pulled away just a few inches, opening his eyes to meet mine. I tried to give him an approving look that said I was up for more. He closed his eyes, as did I, and our lips met again. This time they parted. First our rapid breaths passed between us, then his tongue tangled with mine. There was excitement deep in my abdomen and I chose to ignore it. I wanted only this for tonight. This was nice. I could taste a hint of onions, and I didn't even mind. He pulled back, removing his hand. My cheek was cool where it had been, even though the night was still warm and humid.

"Can I take you out again sometime?"

"Yes, I'd like that." I wasn't sure if I seemed too eager. Mostly I wanted to get out of the car now and inside my safe little house.

"Aloha, then."

"Goodnight."

I hopped out and ran up the steps into the house, tripping twice. I didn't know if he was watching me or not. As I walked in the door, I heard his Jeep start up and pull away.

"Well, well. How was the big date?" Logan asked, munching on an ice cream novelty cone. He handed me one as I slipped out of my sandals.

"I could ask you the same thing."

"Yes, but you won't, because I'm not a girl and I won't blabber about it all night, as I'm sure you are dying to do."

"He asked me out again," I summed up.

"Awesome." We high-fived. "Must be you put on a good act," he surmised.

"Actually no. I kind of let my freak flag fly and I couldn't scare him off. Maybe next time."

I threw away the paper wrapper and bit into the chocolate and nuts on top. It was sweet and cold and had just enough frostbitten taste to it. I knew it didn't matter to Logan whether we had sweets in the house or not. I knew he bought them for me. I hoped they wouldn't adversely affect his physique.

"Yes, you keep up that determination that you can run off what appears to be a totally decent guy." He shook his head. "It is things like this that prove to men that women are crazy."

"But remember, I am not a woman, I am a chick."

"Oh yes, I forgot your preference. Hello Kitty and all."

* * * * *

I stood on my tiny porch, the air heavy with moisture. There were always candles called things such as "ocean breeze," but the reality was the wind off the ocean slapped my face. Sometimes even now it hit my skin and I flinched, expecting the icy sting that the winds of winter brought back home. All the trees and ferns in the thick rainforest moved behind me. The noises of nature—the leaves rustling, the birds chirping, the insects calling—it overwhelmed me when I had first arrived. And it still did, sometimes. I stared out in front of me, waiting for it. I was waiting for that brief moment, it occurred around every sixty seconds or so, when the wind parted the palms in front of me, revealing the green-blue ocean hiding beyond those obstacles. The scents of the forest composting itself mixing with the ocean saltiness filled my senses. As the porch creaked under my bare feet I thought of how unexpected an experience this all was. A few months ago in Michigan this was a dream I had. I stood there wondering if this was indeed real, or just another dream and I was due to wake up soon. I never wanted to awaken from this.

* * * * *

"Sorry to have to make an unscheduled stop. I know I told you I was taking the whole day off and we would spend it together, but Toni, my secretary, brought this discrepancy over the printing cost to my attention a few minutes ago."

"It's fine. I don't mind."

"I mean, I guess it could wait until tomorrow. But I would be thinking about it all day."

"That is alright. You said it would only take a few minutes, right?"

We were traveling in Davy's Jeep down a one-lane paved road with a rocky cliff on our left side, and a beach and ocean on the right. Davy had the top off even though a light mist was falling, but I didn't mind.

"Yes. And you can hang out while you wait. You can help yourself to a snack, but I usually don't keep a lot of food in the house."

Sometimes listening to Davy talk could be so intimidating. I would choose totally different words from him, and usually did, making me sound uneducated, even though I wasn't. I was just me, and the words didn't get edited for accuracy or grammatical correctness before they fell out of my mouth. I learned a long time ago that if I spent too much time coming up with the perfect thing to say, I would never get around to saying anything at all. That is why I liked painting. I could keep working on it until I got it right, or until my patience ran out.

When I didn't respond, he chimed in with, "My house isn't such a bad place to wait for a few minutes."

As he said this we came to a giant white house with lots of different angles. It looked fancier and bigger than the other houses we had passed on this private road. Of course the whole side that faced the Pacific was made of glass. As I was about to make a wisecrack about its opulence, I realized we had reached the end of the road and Davy stopped the Jeep, killing the engine's rumble.

"Uh, *this* is your house?"

"Not what you were expecting?"

"Wow, I feel like an ass."

"Why?" he inquired, puzzled.

"You have seen where I live a bunch of times. You must think I am such poor scum."

"What?" he asked, confused. I wondered when he would get to "who, when, and where."

"You come pick me up from my little shack for a month and you live in this—castle?"

"It's not a castle," he laughed at me.

"It is right on the friggin' beach," I exclaimed, throwing my hands up in the air.

"This is Hawai'i. Lots of people live on the friggin' beach," he said, echoing my pseudo-swear word.

"You know what I mean." I glowered at him. "It is like you are Prince Charming coming to pick up Cinderella the maid to attend the ball."

"I am not Prince Charming. I don't think I could get you to attend a ball if I tried, and you are certainly not Cinderella."

"You are right. *She* had better shoes and a fairy godmother."

He got out of the car and headed to my side, but I was too quick. I jumped out before he could reach me.

He shook his head at my tiny attempt at independence. We walked up a long stairway towards his door.

"I bet these steps are a bitch in the wintertime... Wait, what am I saying!"

Davy laughed so hard he doubled over.

"I'm sorry. I was picturing all these steps covered in ice and trying to salt them... See, Logan and I say this stupid shit all the time, but we understand where we are both coming from. This is why we should not be allowed to socialize with the locals."

"You can take the girl out of the Midwest, but you can't take the Midwest out of the girl. See, it is things like this why I could not have you as a Hawaiian artist."

"You know, I have never understood how they can call Michigan 'the Midwest.' It is not west and it is not in the middle of the country," I prattled on as he got out his keys to unlock the door. "I could see eastern Midwest or even western East."

Suddenly there was a sharp sound and something furry jumping on me.

"Down, Buddah!" Davy shouted, grabbing a collar. The behavior didn't seem threatening, only startling. "I'm sorry about that. He gets excited about strangers. And I didn't warn him that you were coming."

"Oh, you wanted it to be a surprise," I joked. I leaned over to study the beige colored ball of fur, which only took that as an invitation to jump on me again.

"I'm sure he recognizes your smell. I've come home with it on me enough times."

I blushed picturing our make out sessions in the car that were getting hotter and heavier with each date. What if this "business call" was all a ruse to get me to his house to do the deed? I wasn't sure I was ready for that yet, but I wouldn't turn him down either. It had been way too long since I had been with a man, in that way. Not that I had forgotten. Wait, was it possible to forget things like that? I was sure Buddha could smell my armpits getting sweaty as I worried about that possibility longer than I probably should have. I began to scratch his ears and he quickly settled down, holding still now that he had my attention.

"Ah, it looks like you have made a new friend. Dog person?"

"Yes."

"You've had a few?"

"No, actually. Not since I was a kid. I've always wanted one though." I stopped scratching and Buddha began to lick my hand voraciously.

"Well, it looks like Buddha says you can come by and visit him anytime." I wondered idly if Davy meant the same held true for me to visit him. It was a safe bet to say, whether he meant it *that way* or not, as I had no wheels and it was way too far for me to walk from my place. So it would be doubtful I would ever take him up on it.

We walked into the living room that had all light-colored furniture and a gorgeous view of the waves rolling in against some off-shore rocks.

"Make yourself at home," he gestured to the couch. The dog jumped up, almost nose to nose with me now, tail wagging frantically.

"Buddha! You know you aren't allowed on the furniture," he scolded. The dog hopped down, still in good spirits, as if this was just a little game they regularly played together. "I shouldn't be long," Davy apologized again, escaping down a hallway to where I presumed there was an office. I sat down on the couch and petted Buddha, already feeling more relaxed. There were some military veterans that had service dogs to help manage PTSD. "Maybe I wouldn't have tried to shoot up my classmates if I had had a dog to take the edge off, huh?" I whispered to him. He responded by licking me in the nose. "Maybe I just need a puppy. A witto, itty-bitty puppy-wuppy," I baby-talked to him. He sat down and cocked his head at me. He had crazy, wavy white fur that stuck out every which way. I pushed it back from his eyes so that I could look into them. That is when I noticed that one was blue and one was brown. It was a little freaky to look at.

I decided then it would be a better use of my few unsupervised minutes of being in Davy's house to poke around.

I went through his kitchen cabinets. He truthfully did have nothing to eat in his house. Why everyone at the local restaurants knew him by name was now making more sense.

I went through the end table drawers in the living room. They contained a large quantity of comic books. They weren't in plastic sleeves as a collector would store them. They were in a haphazard stack with creases, as if the stuffy businessman actually enjoyed reading about super heroes in his free time. It was a new side to him I didn't know about, but I liked it.

On the mantle in what looked to be some sort of rec room was a picture with someone I assumed was his father. They were shaking hands in front of a big Island Recollections logo. I wondered if that is when Davy took over the company. I wondered what the story behind that was. I would have to ask him sometime.

He came back to find me staring out his big, panoramic window at the ocean beyond. He put his hands on my shoulders and gave a little squeeze.

"Feel better now?" I inquired.

"Not really. It's all settled, but we are going to have to pay up more than what was in the contract," he exhaled loudly.

"I hate that," I deadpanned.

Davy chuckled. We had spent four weeks going out and I still felt uneasy when he laughed. I was never sure if it was with me or at me. It shouldn't matter one bit as long as he wanted to spend time with me. But, well, it did.

"Ready to head out on the boat?"

"Yes." I turned around in his arms and gave him a quick kiss. "I can't believe you have a boat."

"It's actually my family's boat. And why is that so surprising; we live on an island."

"Only rich people have boats."

"You grew up on the Great Lakes," he continued, choosing to ignore my previous rude comment. "Why didn't you have a boat?" he asked, trying to stereotype me.

"It's not like that. The state is very wide. Not everyone lives close to one of the lakes."

"But you did."

"And I never knew anyone who had a boat to take me out on, so I have high expectations for today."

"Well, I hope I can fulfill them all." He kissed me long and deep, like in the movies. Except we didn't have a soundtrack playing, which was a shame.

I thought he would drive us into Honolulu—there were many marinas filled with big, fancy boats that I never paid attention to because they had no involvement in my life. But instead we continued to move away from the city, to a smaller marina, next to a quaint little bait shop rather than attached to a yacht club. We went in and bought some sandwiches, chips, and drinks, throwing them into a cooler Davy had brought with us. We left the bait there. We had no plans to fish.

Since we'd had to stop at home, Buddha got to come with us. He was a good little passenger while the Jeep was in motion but when it was stopped, he trampled us both.

Davy carried the cooler toward the boat, as Buddha and I obediently followed.

"Wow. Is this a yacht?"

"We never thought of it that way. I guess it could be considered a weekender."

"Ooo-K."

"I don't get to take it out as much as I would like."

"Not enough girlfriends?" I teased. Then I hoped I hadn't crossed a line. I had no idea what I was to him.

"No. Not enough time away from work."

He helped me climb up the ladder to get aboard. He spent some time starting it and checking the gas gauge. He systematically removed the ropes that secured it to the dock, then he backed it out before shifting it into forward. He went slow through the boat lane, then kicked it up to an unbelievably fast speed. He turned around to see if I was having fun. I sat clutching my seat, afraid I would be bounced or blown off, or both. He laughed when he saw me.

We jetted across the water like that for a long while. I watched Davy at the controls, our wake forming behind the boat. Now and then I thought I could see the other islands, but it was hard to tell with the saturated clouds that still hung low, making a haze. Eventually he slowed the boat down. I thought he might be able to hear me over the wind and the engine now, so I yelled, "How far out are we going?"

"As far as you want," he answered.

"This is good. I wouldn't want to get lost in the middle of the Pacific or anything."

He laughed. "We aren't anywhere near the middle. O'ahu is still plainly visible behind us."

I turned to look. To me it seemed to be blending into the watery horizon. But he slowed down to a crawl anyway to ease my mind, cutting the engine.

"I wanted to get out where no one would bother us."

"Mission accomplished. Are you planning to murder me out here?"

"No. But why does your mind always go there, to the dark place? I am thinking of when we were in the appliance department at Savings City. You had to yell across the store and tell me the freezer was so big you could put three bodies into it."

"Well, you *could*. I was just stating facts."

"It is not a scenario everyone would think of."

"You said you liked me because I was interesting."

He shook his head, fighting a smile.

"Can I ask you something? When did you become head of the company?"

"My father started it. He wanted to pass it on to my older brother, but he was not interested. My father handed it over to me when he retired. He planned to travel the world, but he assured me he would be available anytime to answer my questions. He dropped dead of a heart attack three days later, before he ever got to book a flight off the island."

"I'm sorry. That's terrible."

"He had a good life. But he should have taken more time to enjoy it when he was young."

"Kind of like you are today?"

"Maybe so. I was planning on satisfying my hunger out here," he winked at me, changing the subject.

He picked up the red plastic cooler and my stomach did a weird flip as I wondered if maybe he meant more than just the food. We had been going out for weeks, and I was still so terrible at this dating stuff. Every time he texted to ask me out again I was shocked that he hadn't written me off as a lost cause. And why would he want to hang out with me anyway? I had no money and he was the CEO of a small but profitable company with a gorgeous house, a dog, and access to a pretty fancy boat. If anything he should dump me as I was a textbook gold-digger, except I was too unstable to ever be able to fool him if that had been my motive. Although now I did want to dognap Buddha. But it made no sense for Davy to like me, or for me to like him, for that matter. But this was a beautiful day, with the sun shining for the moment. We were rolling with the sea, and I had a turkey sub in my hand with the sodium equivalent of the body of water surrounding us. I had a handsome man who worked out every day by the look of his abs as he shed his ironed gray T-shirt.

Buddha studied me, watching for a crumb to fall, but I woofed down the sandwich. I chalked it up to the sea air making me hungry. Davy put Buddha below deck. Finding a CD player down there, we played the only three CDs that were on board. Davy tried to dance with me, but I was achingly bad. I hadn't tried to dance in the presence of another human being since the luau, and before that it had been a middle school dance. In some ways I truly was only the sum of my parts, which meant the awkward fourteen-year-old girl who resided inside of me, still looking for love and approval.

He laid out a blanket on the deck. We sat there and watched the sun glinting off the big waves. I couldn't resist touching his chest. It was a hairless wonder. I pondered if it was like that naturally, or if he groomed it that way. I didn't ask. He lifted a hand to my cheek, gently tucking a lock of my hair that had escaped my ponytail long ago behind my ear. A jolt went directly from his touch to my loins. I don't know if it showed on my face, but he leaned in and kissed me.

If I wasn't genuinely into it, the thought of someone else's tongue in my mouth seemed kind of gross. But at moments such as this, I wanted to be as close to Davy in every way that I could. His hand went up the back of my shirt, touching the bare skin. I assumed more cultured girls would know to wear a bathing suit onto a boat, but I had no intention of going swimming and had given up on fashion consciousness in this life before I began. All he found up my shirt was my bra closure, which he promptly released. I got lost in the dance of our lips and lost track of where his hand was until it began kneading my left breast. I may have let out a little moan, but you couldn't prove it. As if possessed by some other-worldly force (The one the ancient Greeks referred to as horniness), I put my hand in his lap and stroked him through his khaki shorts. I could feel the bulge in his pants. He broke our kiss, nuzzling his nose into the side of my neck. I heard him moan as clear as day. Which, as I mention it, the day had actually temporarily clouded up again. As he slipped my shirt and bra off, I fumbled with his belt and zipper. He stripped me down and lay on top of me and we made love as a misty rain fell on us to cool our skin. I felt like I was on fire everywhere.

* * * * *

And by the next morning I was. I was sunburned head to toe. Logan tried to treat me at home, but it hurt too bad to even sit down, let alone for him to touch my skin. When I started vomiting he decided it was so severe that he gave up and took me to the hospital where he worked. They hooked me up to an IV and slathered me with some ointment with a numbing agent in it. I had access to a television with cable. I was in heaven.

Logan was so mad. He told me what an idiot I was for being so pale, even after cultivating a minor tan while on the island,

and thinking I could spend the day on a boat with no sunblock. How was I supposed to know that the water reflected the sun's rays and intensified them? I was from Michigan. The most sun I got back there was going to the county fair for the day.

And I hadn't done that in a decade or more.

"You haven't been to a fair in over ten years?" Logan asked, dumbfounded.

Had I been talking out loud? Maybe I did need to be in the hospital.

"Yes, you do. You know I am always right. And I bet I am right about how you got a sunburn on your ass."

"Shut up." I made sure I *did* intentionally say that out loud.

"You and the Hawaiian card king finally went all the way."

That is how Logan had taken to referring to Davy, mostly to torture me.

"You guys got your greeting on," he said with a Cajun accent and some sort of hand spanking motion.

"Ugh. Guys are so disgusting. I can't believe I got with one of you yesterday."

"And see where it landed you?"

When Davy found out where I was, he visited and sent flowers to my room. He seemed torn between whether to laugh at my unnative paleness or sympathize with my pain. He faked the latter plausibly.

Michael was working, so he stopped up. This was my first chance to get a good look at him. Usually he was always pulling away in his car or standing at the bottom of the stairs at night. He had a faintly Asian look about him. With bleached white teeth and polished good looks, he could easily be a model. Even while wearing his baggy scrubs, I could tell Michael worked out. He brought me a stuffed animal. I appreciated the gesture but expected it would hurt too much to touch it for a few more days, and then I would be shedding skin onto it for weeks.

They sent me home the next morning, with strict instructions not to leave the house for a week. Logan was to apply the special cream to me twice a day to aid in healing and prevent infection. It was possible this would scar me for life, and in more ways than one. My rat bastard boss fired me, despite the hospital visit and the doctor's note. To makeup some of the difference, Logan started taking extra shifts at the hospital. I was trapped in the house, bored with no company. The solar flares were jacking up the pixels in our TV reception—another contributing factor to why my sunburn had been so grand mal bad. Davy would drop by with popsicles or gelatin for me in the evenings, but he was bored at my house too. We couldn't snuggle. We couldn't even play board games because I had to bend my body too much to move the pieces around the spaces on the board. I had already lost my job due to this stupid burn. I wouldn't lose my man too. That would really be a burn.

As much as I had disliked my job, I did miss having somewhere to go every day, a purpose. It was beyond silly, but

I also missed Buddha. I had only met him the one day, but just the thought that there was a dog that could be in my life on a regular basis had me jonesing to pet his furry little head again and smell his nasty dog breath. Maybe I could steal him sometime and bring him to my house.

Logan took me to the doctor for a checkup a week later. It still hurt to move, but the pain was tolerable. The medicated cream had helped speed the recovery. I now looked more like a molting lizard than a red lobster. Thank God for small miracles.

I worried I was slacking on Logan by not looking for a job, but I still wasn't looking normal enough yet that I could even go on an interview, let alone stand for extended periods of time or walk to travel. Our financial situation would only hold out for a month or so. That is what made it so surprising when Logan came home one night in a simple black car, proclaiming it as ours.

"What the fuck—" I stood staring at the car.

"Is there more coming with that statement," he glared at me queerly.

"What the fuck are you talking about?"

"A car. Four tires, seats. Absolutely essential where we come from. Not as essential here, but will sure be convenient. Now, I realize that with the two of us working different places and different hours, we will have to juggle it or whatever, but, well, isn't it awesome! We are drivers again."

"Wow. I'm not even sure that I remember how."

"We aren't talking about your love life."

I gave him a dirty look and continued. "Um, how did you afford this?"

"I got it super cheap off a guy at work. His sixteen-year-old son got a DUI and he really wanted to punish him. So he sold his car—to me! Bad for the kid, but good for us. Even better news, car insurance rates here are almost a third of what they are back in Michigan. But, we lose out with the higher cost of gas."

"Great, but where did you get the money?"

"Oh. It is a little bit of savings from when we came out here. I have a little more, but I am going to use that to fly back and see my kids in a month or so. Still trying to get people to cover for me at work before I book the tickets."

"I thought you were thinking of bringing them out here?"

"Well, I was, and I still want to. But two tickets are more expensive than one, and I'm hoping to get some of the divorce stuff taken care of while I am back. That will also affect the date I go."

"Oh."

I knew I should be happy. I had access to a car now. One for which I hadn't had to contribute. And my roommate would leave me and I would have a shack in Hawaii all to myself for days.

But, Logan had a hidden stash of money he hadn't disclosed. His, but still. He had bought a car without consulting me. He was going to abandon me to go back to Michigan. One ticket is cheaper than two? What if I wanted to go back to visit? Even as I thought it, I realized how ridiculous it was. I had no one to go back for.

Later Logan found me on our porch. I had my easel set up with my paints and brushes next to it, but I was sitting in the folding lawn chair, staring off toward our postage-stamp view of the ocean.

"Ah, are you all right out here?"

"Ya, I'm fine."

"Why aren't you painting?"

"Setting up all the stuff made my skin hurt too much to continue."

"Want me to put it away?"

"No. Just leave it."

"Mace, it feels like since I brought that car home you are mad at me. I thought you would be happy about it."

"I am. I mean, it's nice to have a car again."

"So what's eating you?"

"You have a secret stash of cash you can buy cars and plane tickets with."

"Ya, so? It's my money. We're not married. And I am not letting you starve or even asking you to pay your half of the rent. So what's the problem?"

"You are so much more of a grown up than me. I used to be like that."

"And you hated it and you came out here to escape it."

"I don't know. I am sad I guess. Being reminded that you have more people who care about you back there doesn't help matters. All I've got is you. If you decided to not come back—" Tears clouded my vision against my will.

"First of all, you have Davy, so I am not the only one who cares for you. Second, I live in the middle of paradise. It is very difficult to pull myself away from that. The only things that can are my kids, which third, I told you I would always stay involved with before we left. Four, I have to come back for Michael. Wait, what was I counting again?"

"I don't remember."

"C'mon. Let's go for a drive. I would take you for a walk down to the beach; it would be cheaper. But you still seem wrecked with that sunburn. I could only put ten dollars in the tank today."

"So we are going for a short drive, then?"

"Maybe only to the beach." He winked at me. It was a very Logan thing to do. I stood up and hugged him. I thanked the powers that be for sending him to me in the first place.

ERUPTION

You can't handle my brand of crazy.

Davy and I had plans to hang out Saturday morning. I don't know why I had agreed to get up so early. I still didn't have a job which had me accustomed to sleeping in late every day. My sunburn had healed, but I hadn't had any luck finding anything that I would like. Soon I would have to settle for the ones I wouldn't like.

Davy burst in through my front (and only) door. Logan was in the kitchen, shirtless, cooking breakfast for us. I was putting on my clothes in our combined living room/bedroom. Davy caught me topless.

"I had a great idea last night! Oh, sorry," he covered his eyes as a true gentleman would, and then seemed to remember that we were dating. "Ooo baby, can I have some of that?" He made a move toward me, but Logan stepped in front of him.

"Sure you can," Logan replied, then grabbed Davy and dipped him as if they were dancing. "You can have some... breakfast."

I hurried and put on my bra and T-shirt, a gray number worn soft from many washings with an orange sunset on the front—a logo that looked straight out of the 70s, as they were laughing it up. It was nice how they had become good friends, like brothers from another mother. But if Logan was like a brother to me and Davy was like a brother to him, where did that leave me and Davy?

"So, what's this big idea of yours?" I asked, knowing that curiosity killed the cat.

"I told you I wanted to take you down to the markets this morning—"

The markets were similar to a farmers market where we came from, except they were open six days a week out here instead of only Saturday mornings. People set up tables under a carport-type roof and sold their handmade wears. The tourists loved it. Logan and I had taken to walking through every few weeks or so. It was like shopping at the mall, but outdoors and with better bargains. We usually came home with items such as knickknacks or pocketknives or throw pillows that we didn't need that only filled up our tiny bungalow.

"Yes, but they aren't even open for another hour."

"I know! That is why we have got to get a move on."

"You do realize you are making no sense, right?"

"You guys can't leave till someone eats this food," Logan chimed in, sounding all domestic. He needed a little pink frilly flowered apron to go with his tanned, naked chest. Maybe I could find one to buy him at the markets today.

"Ah, I'm not making myself clear," Davy groaned, as he ran his hand through his usually orderly black hair, leaving it a mess. This was very out of character for him. I was starting to get worried. Logan threw me a sideways glance as well.

"Grab an armful of your paintings and let's go. We are going to get you a booth today," Davy said, slipping into his managerial voice as he composed himself.

"What? No way. We can't do that."

"Sure we can. C'mon. Let's go."

"We haven't reserved a space."

"You know they always have a few extra for drop-ins."

"I don't have a table."

"I have one in the car. Island Recollections on occasion has booths at greeting card shows and such. You can use it until you get your own. C'mon!"

"God, I wouldn't even know what paintings to take..."

"Ones that you think will sell. C'mon. I'll help you load them up into the car."

"I guess I will make this breakfast to go. I gotta come see this. Macey putting herself out there for the public? This should be good."

I stuck my tongue out at Logan as I began to flip through the canvases that had begun to take over our small space.

"But I haven't catalogued all these yet." I was good at coming up with excuses.

Davy sighed in exasperation. "We can get photos of them when we put them out. The colors will pop more in the natural light anyway."

Damn boyfriend who was so knowledgeable about light and color. "Well, it might rain today. I wouldn't want them to get wet."

"That's what the roof is for," he replied.

"I'll grab some garbage bags, just in case," Logan said, with a devious grin. He knew what I was trying to do and he was making it even more difficult for me.

"But, I don't have—"

"Don't worry, I've thought of everything," Davy said as he took the three canvases I held from me and headed for the door.

"Change?"

"I got some. Plus, I picked up a reader and downloaded the app so that you can accept credit and debit cards."

"Greaaat... But what about a spontaneous volcano eruption?" I yelled. He was already on the steps. I didn't think he could hear me any longer.

"Pele is always a risk when one lives on the islands," he called back. I flicked him off even though he couldn't see me. I turned to Logan. He was dumping the Spam, hash browns, and eggs into tortillas and wrapping them in foil.

"You gotta help me, Logan. You gotta get me out of this." As I became more desperate, my airway constricted, causing my voice to get higher.

"No way!"

"What? You aren't on my side?"

"Not this time. I think this will be an interesting experiment. And aren't you always trying to find a way to make money from your art?"

"You really think I will make enough money to help us at the markets with my crappy artwork?" I scoffed. "Hell, I couldn't even get a job with Davy and he was into me."

"But that led you to a relationship with him. And what if displaying your work leads to something more? Something unexpected?"

My mouth hung open as I tried to think of a comeback that wouldn't sound like a whiny child. I had none.

The door swung open as Davy barged in. In four quick strides he was back to my painting pile. He flipped through, selecting three more.

"Oh, this looks good," he remarked, picking up my plastic box of smaller 5" X 7" and 2-1/2" X 3-1/2" canvases.

"Hey, I like the one with the rainbow too much! You can't sell that one!" I chased after him.

"We'll see," said the know-it-all.

Logan put on his flip-flops, picked up all the little aluminum foil logs of delicious-smelling food, and pulled the door shut behind us all. My stomach grumbled in protest. I looked at my clothes. I hadn't even had time to get dressed properly for my date, and now I was going to be representing myself in a half-rotted T-shirt and Daisy Dukes with yellow paint on them?

I stopped at the bottom of the stairs to have a mini-panic attack. Logan slammed into me, dropping one of the wrapped breakfast burritos. I barely noticed. I hadn't had an attack in so long that the suddenness of it hurt and terrified me. I willed it to go away with my mind, but it was no use. It was a familiar feeling and my body welcomed it openly, like a favorite pair of old jeans. I used to feel like this every single second of every day. Since I had been here, the ocean breeze had, for the most part, blown it away anytime it tried to creep back into my life. But now I couldn't even remember how to make it go away. Maybe it never really had, just lied dormant like a cancer on my soul, waiting for a weak moment to return and strike.

But in a sick way, it was also like a hug from an old friend. One who always told you what you wanted to hear.

You can't do this.

You are crazy.

You are a loser.

You are a hack.

Go back to bed, Loser.

"I-I—," I stammered.

I turned to Logan whose face instantly went pale when he saw my expression. It must have been crazy, something reminding him of that night at the reunion. He reached out for me, but even though he was closer, Davy was quicker.

"Come on, let's go."

He pulled me toward his Jeep and I didn't physically resist. But I dug my fingernails into his leather seats as we rode the short distance. By the time we arrived, my fingernails had made half-moon-shaped holes in his seats. Logan had offered me a burrito on the ride, knowing food sometimes helped to equalize my crazy. I had declined. Now I was very glad, because as soon as we got to the parking lot and I saw the other artisans setting up, I walked a few steps from the car and ralphed all over the ground.

"Are you OK?" Davy ran to my side, taking notice for the first time of my condition.

"This is too much for her. We should head back."

I turned and looked at a genuinely terrified Logan. He knew how far my crazy could take me. He had been the one behind the barrel of my gun. Seeing his reaction only intensified my attack.

"She just needs a minute. Baby,—"

"NO!"

I had never heard Logan raise his voice like that before.

"What did you say to me?" Davy walked up to Logan, chest puffed out. They were essentially the same height.

"I said 'no.' This is too much for her."

"I think I know better than you do about what she needs!"

"Really? You have only known her for a few weeks."

My pile of puke lay forgotten on the asphalt as I watched them argue over me, hypnotized.

"From what I hear, you haven't known her much longer," Davy spat back.

"I understand where she came from. I was there for what happened, for why she came out here."

"And what exactly happened?" Davy stared at me now with harsh, black eyes.

"She hasn't told you because she wasn't ready," Logan defended.

"She can talk for herself, can't she?"

Both their faces went red. I was afraid someone would actually throw a punch. I stepped in between them, putting one of my hands on each of their chests, trying to ignore how hot this all was.

"What happened, huh? I've slept next to you at night. Should I fear for my life?" he yelled even though I was standing directly in front of him. I noticed we had drawn a crowd of other vendors and early bargain hunters hovering nearby. I looked at Logan, who seemed to apologize with only his eyes for bringing up this topic. I met Davy's eyes and responded only loud enough for the three of us to hear.

"Yes, you probably should." My whole body was shaking as I tried to think of the best way to break it to him. But the words spilled out in a rush of panic before I could stop them. I braced myself between the two men, pushing as hard as I could to try to stop the shaking. "I took a hand gun to my twentieth high school reunion, intending to kill as many as I could. But the only one I pointed it as was Logan." I turned to Logan again and barely above a whisper finished, "He stopped me."

"What?" Davy breathed. His eyes changed. I saw him go from looking at me with love to repulsion. My heart broke. "You, you had a gun? You were going to kill people? Murder them in cold blood?"

"Davy." I wanted to explain to him why that had seemed like my only option at that time. But he already knew the ending, that I had planned to actually carry it out. All the steps I took on the road to get there would be irrelevant to him.

"What? Like some kind of sick, middle-aged school shooting? Except you weren't brave or smart enough to do it back in the day when you should have."

"Please," I begged. I had no idea why.

"Or to actually deal with your problems the way everyone else has to, without resorting to violence."

"You don't understand," I whimpered.

"What? Did somebody call you a horrible name? Make you feel bad?"

"It was more than that. I was there!" Logan broke in.

"Really. Was it bad enough to shoot people? Must not have been if you stopped her."

"That's just it. I didn't stop her; she stopped herself," Logan defended me.

"It all sounds so pathetic."

"I—I guess it does," I stammered.

"You aren't the woman I thought you were."

"I am the same person that you met at the interview," I tried to explain through the lump in my throat and the rolling sobs.

"I was a fool to believe that your past was not important."

"You were never a fool."

"If this came out, it could hurt my career: Island Recollections CEO Dates Insane Murderer."

Logan made a disgusted noise. I felt it rumble through his chest against the palm of my left hand.

"There were never any charges filled," I squeaked.

"Like that makes a difference. The intent was there."

"I was desperate."

"What else would you do if you were desperate enough?"

A fresh batch of tears flushed from my eyes. The "s-word" was on the tip of my tongue. It had been a viable option after the murders would have been completed. I could feel the closeness of that feeling again. It was here, in this moment. I wanted nothing more than to plunge a knife into myself and bleed out all this pain. But I didn't say it. He would only hear it as another excuse. He didn't know. He would never know.

"She was mentally unstable," Logan piped in.

Maybe *he* could sense how close I was to that same despair.

"How could you defend her? You were her first target."

"But she didn't fire. *That* is what counts."

I pulled my hand off Davy as he backed away. He held up both his hands. "I gotta process this for a minute," he said, retreating off to the cover of the palms and ferns that bordered the lot.

I crumpled into Logan's chest, his arms quickly encircling me as I cried. If he said anything, I didn't hear him. But I was glad the truth was out there. I wanted Davy to be repulsed by me and leave. That is the way things have always been and were supposed to be.

I also wanted him to come back and tell me that it didn't matter. That the past didn't matter, only this new life I was trying to build out here in the middle of the Pacific Ocean, about as far away from flat fields and tractors as I could get.

My brain was tearing itself apart. The anxiety was so loud, but the other voice that was my weirdness, also my true self, pulled on the string in my heart. I couldn't stop breaking apart into pieces. It was the first time I had since we got here. Maybe what I needed was a good cry.

And a straitjacket.

Shut up, anxiety. I wish I had a gun to shoot you with.

* * * * *

Logan and I had gotten back into Davy's car to wait. The booth had been all his idea, so it didn't seem right to set up without him. We could have started walking home, but I would have had to leave my paintings behind. Plus, we wanted to give him a chance to come back which, after fifteen minutes, he did. He was an expert negotiator. In the business world he never let his emotions get the best of him. But I knew even he wouldn't have gotten himself under control in that amount of time. He walked back slowly, his complexion looking gray. I didn't even know that was possible for a person with dark skin.

He looked up and met my eyes. They didn't seem angry, only sad.

"Let's get set up. We'll talk about this later," he said, his voice hollow.

I nodded. Logan and I climbed out and started carrying items into the markets. All the other vendors were now fully set up with nothing else to do but follow our movements with curious eyes.

We followed Davy to the info booth, where he purchased a space for me. I didn't pay attention to how much. I should have asked so that I could reimburse him later, but I didn't. I followed Davy to an empty booth. He and Logan got busy setting up. I flashed fake smiles at the shoppers already walking by, praying they would pass by again on their way out.

In the rush no one had thought to bring chairs, so the three of us stood behind the table.

It seemed I was a new curiosity among the reoccurring booths the locals were used to seeing. When people slowed and showed interest in a painting, I tried to think of something to tell them about it. An elderly couple laughed when I told them the yellow stains on my shorts came from the canvas they were looking at. At least I was amusing, if nothing else. A couple from Nicaragua stopped by and picked out a painting they fancied— a sunset where the water was too green in my opinion. Davy handled it because he was trilingual. Actually, he spoke a touch of Mandarin along with Hawaiian, English, and Spanish. He was so intelligent and well-educated I didn't deserve him. My heart echoed what I had known all along as he swiped their credit card and handed over my work. We hadn't priced anything. I figured he would know better than I would what to price it at. I trusted him with that much, though I had never trusted him with my heart. In retrospect, it seemed as if that had been a wise choice.

Davy turned and looked at me.

"Thank you," I managed.

"Your first sale." He stated the obvious. Then, meeting my eyes, "Let's talk."

"OK." I knew it had to be done. I just didn't want to be the person to bring it up. I was sort of hoping we could finish this horrible day in endless silence.

Logan motioned for us to go, that he had it under control.

We walked behind the booth and out of earshot of everyone else. Davy took both my hands in his, which were warm and comforting. It felt too nice. I knew I didn't deserve him.

"I loved when you told that couple about the paint stain on your pants. Classic Macey," he chuckled, but his eyes kept staring at the ground. I was shorter than him You would think they would have to meet my eyes on the way down, but no.

"Do you see? I am the same girl I was yesterday. Or when you took me out on the boat. Or when you interviewed me. I'm just not the girl I was on the mainland." I tried using local slang to speak his language. He noticed because he finally raised his eyes to mine. He gave me a smirk.

"I realize. It is simply a lot to take in so suddenly."

"I know." I took a deep breath. "That's why I am letting you off the hook."

"What?"

"Yes. You are such a great guy Davy." Now I was the one who couldn't make eye contact with him. "But it has always been obvious to me that we don't run in the same circles. Heck, we know I don't run at all." He could not help but chuckle at this. "I am so thankful for our time together, but I think it's time you pursue other women. I can't thank you enough for today and the booth. It opened my eyes to new ways to get exposure, new ways to measure success. It was a great idea." I was worried he would instantly want to take his table back before the day was out. And what if he drove off and left Logan and I here without a vehicle? Crap, I should have thought this through and broke up with him later.

Here I am, thinking only about myself again. No wonder no one wants to date me, I thought as I pushed a perfectly good suitor away.

"If that's how you feel," he responded. A chunk of my heart broke off as I realized he wasn't going to fight for this. I would think he was delusional if he did, because we really had no future together. But it hurt all the same. I didn't want to be right.

Our eyes met and he leaned in to give me a final kiss.

Wow.

There was tongue and heat and passion. When we parted, I almost begged him on the spot to take me back. It was that good. Instead, we walked back to the booth and a waiting Logan, who instantly sensed what had transpired and asked no questions.

"I sold another one. What is my cut?" he said jovially, trying to lighten the mood.

All three of us stayed all day until closing time at 4:00PM. Davy had often left the booth to shop or grab us food. Or he had stayed there while Logan and I had browsed. Those two paintings in the morning turned out to be the only ones we sold all day. But I thought it was a promising start.

Davy drove us back home and helped us unload with few words. When he left, Logan and I made mixed drinks with whatever was in the house and walked down to the beach and sat in the sand. Despite my severe panic attack and breaking up with Davy, it wasn't as bad a day as it could have been. And I didn't even want to think about tomorrow yet. I would deal with that when it came. I laid my head on Logan's shoulder and squeezed my eyes shut tightly against the setting tropical sun.

"Look at your life now. It's not so bad, is it? If you had committed murder-suicide, you couldn't be enjoying all this now."

"Ya, I guess so."

"I am just making the point that you never know what is ahead for you. You can't judge tomorrow by today."

"You sound like a fortune cookie."

"I'll take that as a compliment."

"But how Davy reacted. It felt like I went through with it."

"Only you and I know your real intentions. Well, and now Davy. It is shocking. It will take him a moment to get past it."

"You know, I'm not even sure I want him to. We didn't have a big spark or anything."

Logan bumped his shoulder into mine. "Then why are you sitting here pouting about it?"

"Because I guess I just wanted it all."

"A functioning life in paradise isn't enough for you?"

"I guess it should be."

* * * * *

So, ya.

No job. No boyfriend.

But I did have a stockpile of canvases and paints and a booth space paid up for three months. I made it down almost every day to display my wares. Sales were slim, some days zero. But any coin was more than I would earn sitting at home. And I found that customers enjoyed it when I painted inside my booth. I found it terribly hard to concentrate as strangers ogled me, commenting loudly, but it was multi-tasking at its finest. Logan would help me set-up or take down when his schedule allowed. I was finally starting to look as though I lived in Hawaii. I was getting a nice tan, in all but the worst areas scarred from my heinous sunburn.

The weather had been especially hot today and the heat had worn me out. I tried to properly rehydrate when I got home, but I never truly recovered, so I gave up and went to bed early.

I was sound asleep when I heard loud footfalls on the stairs. It didn't sound like Logan's measured, athletic gate. It sounded like a cow trying to make it up.

I lay silent, waiting for the visitor to approach the door to see what would happen. It was still for a long moment. Then the sound of two keys on a metal keychain hitting the wooden porch. Then loud, uproarious laughter. I had been wrong. It was not a cow climbing the stairs, but four drunken feet.

After more jingling, the key slipped into the lock and the door opened. There was a loud thump, as if someone had thrown down a dead body. More laughing ensued; it lasted a full sixty seconds.

Then lots of shushing, Logan's voice floating through the darkness.

"Shhh. You'll wake Macey", he scolded.

"Dude, ya need a place with two bedrooms. Or, like, one at least," Michael yell-whispered.

"Dude, we are lucky to be able to afford a living room."

I was fully awake now, with nothing to do but listen to their drunken conversation.

"Dude, you could get a one bedroom. You are the one paying all the bills anyway."

My mouth dropped open. I had always been for Logan's relationship with Michael, but he had offended me. He was right, but it still hurt. Maybe I would chalk it up to drunken truth.

"Naw, Macey's good. She opened my eyes, man."

"Ya. I still don't understand that. You will have to 'xplain it all to me sometime."

"Ya. Sometime, man."

There was a lack of conversation then, but they were not quiet. The sounds of lips pressing together and heavy breathing could be detected by my resistant ears.

They had come back here once or twice before, but I was asleep then and only marginally aware of their presence. Usually they went back to Michael's. He had a roommate as well, but he had his own bedroom. My best guess tonight was that they had both gotten too crocked to drive, and it was closer to walk to our place than Michael's from the evening's bar of choice. I couldn't blame Logan. He was experiencing his experimental twenties over again. I could be jealous though, and I was. I was looking forward to experiencing such carefree times myself... sometime.

Logan and Michael were seriously dating. I'm concerned that Logan fell right from one serious relationship into another. It seemed to me he should take some time to play the gay field first before settling on just one boy toy. But maybe he was one of those guys who liked to always be in a relationship. I was more worried that at the rate they going, they would want to consider moving in together. Michael already had an apartment closer to the hospital. Without Logan, I would be sunk financially. We had come out here to take on the world together. I didn't realize that that could change sooner rather than later.

I peeked out from under the light quilt I covered up with nights. I had gotten used to sleeping with the weight of a mountain of covers on me from my decades of chills back in Michigan. Even in this tropical paradise, I still needed that force to hold me down, so I used the thinnest one I could find. Logan only ever slept with a sheet over him, and I believed that was mostly to cover up his morning wood when it burst forth from his boxer briefs. It didn't always work for full concealment.

I could see their bodies intertwined in the moonglow spilling forth through the screen door. The inside door had been left unlocked, open. I felt secure anyway, as I had two strapping men at arm's reach if I should need them. Right now their arms were all over each other. Logan whispered something into Michael's ear and he laughed loudly again, which was echoed by Logan's shush. I smiled despite my guilt at spying on them, which I had no right to do, no matter how miniscule our home was. I was so happy to see Logan speaking up for himself with Michael. A new role could be hard to play, even if it was the one you were born to be. I was still struggling with my own. I saw the silhouette of a piece of clothing flying across the room. I could see the silver beams glinting off the muscles of Logan's chest.

I heard a zipper, then saw Michael go down to his knees in front of Logan. Even if I had been dead asleep I would not have been able to miss the volume of the sigh that escaped Logan's throat as he threw his head back in the moonlight. I drew the blanket over my head again. I could block out the sights, but not the sounds. Not that I wanted to, because they were fabulous.

Damn, Michael was one lucky man to get to feast at the buffet of Logan.

I heard them unfolding the couch, then the springs protesting their combined weight. Among the panting I swore I heard an "I love you" slip out. Despite the open windows, testosterone filled the room, making my head dizzy and causing me to sweat. I didn't want to be turned on by my best friend's sexual escapades, but it was hard not to. They were really hot.

When they quieted, I did drift off to sleep for a few more hours. When I awoke, the sun was giving the sky the faintest glow. I tried to remember how the light looked for a time later when I would have the opportunity to paint it. The boys were still sleeping off their hangover. That is exactly what their satisfied faces looked like as they lay all tangled up in the sheets, like peaceful little boys. I silently slipped on a clean T-shirt, my shorts, and my sneakers, heading out for a walk. When I returned an hour later, Michael was gone. Logan stood in only a pair of khaki shorts in the kitchen. By how low they hung on his hips, I knew he had nothing on underneath.

"Hey," he said, nodding at me as the screen door's screech announced my arrival. He bowed his head before a smile could break out across his greasy face.

"Good morning," I said. Then coaxed, "It was, wasn't it?"

Now his smile was so big I could see it from his profile before he turned to face me.

"We were at it as soon as you stepped out the door," he admitted.

"Darn, you mean I missed the morning show? But I so enjoyed the late one."

"Sorry about that. We were so blotto I don't remember much. I probably wasn't a very considerate roommate."

"It's fine. Nothing you haven't had to endure when Davy was here."

"That boy had some moves. Not that I ever noticed."

"Ah!" I yelled, throwing a dish towel at him. "You know, the difference is, I get to enjoy both sides of the show when you bring Michael over."

"It's so unfair."

"I love seeing you so happy."

"You know what?" He laid down the spatula and turned away from the still sizzling pan full of eggs in front of him. He bent forward towards me.

"I enjoy being happy," he whispered to me, as if it was our secret. I couldn't resist taking two steps around the table so that I could hug him. Unfortunately, my nose came in close proximity to his armpit.

"Aw, man. You have got to shower. You smell like booze and sex."

"I bet if I cooked up some bacon, you would not even notice."

"Try me," I replied, smiling mischievously at him.

* * * * *

Logan and I both had the day off so we took a walk to remind ourselves of the beauty that we were surrounded by. This was my second non-destination walk of the day. It appeared I had acquired some sort of sick new fitness habit. We ended up in the city, down by the marina. We splurged on ice cream. We picked up where our conversation of this morning had left off.

"I wish we could both be happy at the same time," Logan mused.

"Well, we almost were, for a few weeks," I added.

I licked my chocolate chip cookie dough ice cream cone as I walked. I looked down and noticed for the first time since moving here the cracks in the sidewalks, something I had spent an accumulation of endless hours staring at back where I came from. My head had always been heavy and troubled and only looking down. Here there were so many beautiful sights. I only noticed the ground today by accident, even as I was reminded what I lacked while rejoicing in my friend's happiness.

"Have you heard from Davy?"

"No. Well, he stopped by my booth. He said my painting was coming along well. A compliment is good, I guess. But it is over between us. I think I scared him pretty badly."

"Well, you can't scare me off."

"That has been proven." I purposely bumped his shoulder, but he glared at me as if I was just being my clumsy self again. The waves crashed against the beach across the street from us. I had been so impressed by its power and swells when I had first arrived. It was all so foreign to me. I had trouble sleeping to the endless roar at night.

Now I hardly noticed it. I slept to its rhythms, finding it a comfort. I didn't know how I would ever sleep without that sound again. I hoped I never would have to find out.

"If you guys are over, then you should keep your eye out for new prospects."

"Prospects?"

"You know, boyfriend material."

"Ya know, if Davy taught me anything it might be that I am not ready for all of that yet."

"Well, I hope you are sometime. Because it is a great feeling."

Logan smiled widely, all his perfectly straight teeth glinting in the sun.

* * * * *

I was sitting on the couch reading when Logan came in the door, replacing his phone into his pocket. I gauged his expression slowly and pulled out one ear bud.

"How did the call with the wife go?"

"About as well as could be expected."

"Has she come to terms with all this yet?"

"Not yet. I don't regret marrying her. I love my kids. It is hard to be so far away from them. I hope soon she can realize I freed her to go find someone who can fully love her for who she is. I would have never been that man. I want her to find happiness like I have with Michael.

"She wants to sell the house," he continued. "Well, her divorce attorney does. He says there is $180,000 to be made off of it."

"You are not going to let her, are you? It was your dad's house, your house."

"If my sister has no objections, I will let her. As much as I will hate to let it go, I am out here now. I am a different person. But I would like to be able to take Michael there once, show him how I grew up." Logan laughs. "Can you imagine how he will laugh when he sees all the cornfields, the old, muddy river? He will think I am such a hick."

"No he won't. He will realize that is the place that shaped you into the person he loves today. How did you even meet Veronica anyway? She didn't go to school with us."

"She is from Washington state. She was attending college here. We met through mutual friends. It was just easier to be with her than other girls. I thought that meant I was in love with her. Now I know different."

"So you were not in love with her, you only had a deep connection? Now I am even more jealous."

Logan laughed at me as I stuck my tongue out at him.

* * * * *

I finally got a part-time job working nights, which still allowed me to take my paintings to the markets during the day. I was a night auditor at a hotel for one of the smaller chains. Carrying the two jobs was exhausting and I got to where I didn't know if I was coming or going. That could be why it didn't seem to faze me to chat it up with Davy when he passed by my booth, casually enough. Or when we went out for a drink and he ended up naked in my bed. Apparently we would keep it casual. That is really all we had before, we were merely calling it something different now, which would mean less pressure and a more realistic view of our end game.

Logan shook his head in the morning, but fed us both breakfast anyway.

And so it went until I met Beverly.

It was just a normal Saturday for us: my live-in gay, my friend with benefits, my foster dog, and I hanging out in a booth as the morning sun began to bounce off my completed canvases. We talked and joked, caught up on the events of our week with one another. After I had met Buddha I knew that for my life to feel complete, it needed to have a dog in it. And not just any dog—*that dog.*

A few weeks ago Davy went to the mainland on business. Of course I offered to dogsit while he was away. I think Davy thought I would stay in his cushy house while it was empty, but instead I had brought Buddha home with me. It was a completely illogical move. Our shack didn't have enough square footage for the two humans who already inhabited it to live comfortably. Adding a medium-sized dog to the mix? Insane. But it was weeks later and Buddha had yet to return home, even though Davy had.

"You know I only come by to visit my dog," Davy would always joke. At least I thought it was a joke.

Buddha found places to fit in. On someone's lap, on the empty bed of whoever was working the night shift, under the tiny kitchen table. Logan wasn't crazy about it, but Michael was a big fan, and hung around more than ever before to play with our new addition. Buddha charmed everyone. Logan couldn't toss out a dog that his boyfriend was so fond of.

"Who's a good boy? Yes, who's a good boy?" I cooed as I scratched Buddha's ears. His rump dropped to the ground in pure delight as his rear left leg began to wildly convulse in a reflexive motion.

"Well, I thought I was last night. You seemed happy enough," Davy chimed in.

I gave him a non-committal smirk.

"Ugh, I don't want to hear about it. I'm glad it was through by the time I got home. I wish Michael wasn't working this morning. Then we could gross you out with our innuendo," Logan protested.

"Two good-looking guys getting sweaty together? I don't think I would mind picturing that."

"Girl, I think you have a gay man inside of you," Davy laughed at me.

"No, it doesn't work that way," Logan deadpanned, going back to work making price tags. "What do you think on this one?" he asked me.

"Ugh. You know I never have any idea... Take our rent and divide it by ten."

"Ya, no one is going to hand over that much coin for this one. It looks like you used it to clean your brushes off," Logan said.

"Hey," I yelled defensively, grabbing my painting from the table display easel and clutching it to my chest as if it were a child that he had insulted that needed consoling.

"I think that one shows the most promise."

I turned to see a woman with rich burnt sienna skin and long black hair tied into a ponytail and draped over one shoulder. Her voice gave away that she was older, but her skin was well-preserved. This is how people looked when they didn't have to grocery shop in negative fifteen degree temperatures. People held up better and had less rust in warm locales, just as cars did.

"Thank you."

"Are you the artist?"

"Yes." I suddenly felt silly standing there clutching a canvas, especially if that was the piece this woman was interested in buying. "Name your price. No reasonable offer refused. Bear in mind I do need to recoup my investment in paints, brushes, and canvases. And it comes pre-hugged by the artist!" I cringed at my own words. I had never been a salesman and experience wasn't helping. Sure, I was getting more comfortable talking to strangers, but that only made it easier to have diarrhea of the mouth. I liked paintings where mistakes could be covered until they were perfect. Conversations weren't like that. You only had one shot to get it right.

"Oh, you are a special spirit, aren't you?" she stated, flashing me a smile.

"That is what I keep saying," Davy said, opening his arms out in front of him. I tried to slap him, but he was too fast and I only got air. Buddha jumped up onto Davy to defend my honor, almost toppling him into a metal support. We were so unprofessional; we were the definition of a comedy of errors. Other vendors near us probably hated us. And here we were thinking we could make sales. I might as well just pack up and stay home from now on.

The woman smiled at us, then carefully studied each piece. She looked long enough that I was certain she was just being kind and we would get absolutely no sale from her. But it turned out she had something better to offer than money.

"Have you ever talked to someone about merchandising your images?"

"Haaa," I chortled, and quickly covered my mouth to hold it in.

"That's amusing? Not the reaction that I was expecting."

"I, um, tried to sell my images to this guy, but he didn't want them."

Davy shrugged.

"And you still keep him around?" she raised one thick, black eyebrow flecked with white at me.

"For comic relief," I deadpanned. Davy, being his usual self, doubled over in laughter at that one.

"An artist and a comedian. You really are the total package. Do you have an online presence?"

"Social media and stuff? No. We," I gestured toward Logan, "don't a computer."

"All businesses must be on social media these days."

"I know that I probably should have a website with pictures of my work on it. I mean, I don't know who would find it and buy anything..."

"It may be hard for people to find you with the glutton of messages in the world, but not putting yourself out there guarantees that no one will."

"I guess... What? Do you have a gallery or something?"

"Oh, nothing that fancy. I have a couple of shops where I try to showcase good art in tourist-friendly ways."

"You mean souvenirs?"

"Yes, unless that is unappealing to you."

"No, actually I would rather have my stuff on a T-shirt or a postcard than in some stuffy gallery. But I used to work at a store like that. The owner said my stuff wasn't Hawaiian enough."

"What did he say?" she nodded to Davy.

"He said the same thing," I answered.

"I am noticing the same thing about these two paintings. I see a single maple tree within the jungle on both of these. I think you are doing it subconsciously. The casual observer would never even notice it within the sea of green. I actually don't think of it as an inaccuracy as your Davy might. I see it as a trademark, an Easter egg as the younger generation might say. I take it you are not from here?"

"No, I'm from Michigan."

"How did you find yourself out here then?"

"Oh, I just washed up on the beach one day." It was actually accurate. I had come here kind of lost, killing time trying to earn a living. Parts of that were still true, would probably always be true.

"I'm thinking people come from all over to visit out here. Many of them love the beauty here, but I feel as though they are overwhelmed by it. What if they looked at your paintings and this fusion of style you have going on is just what they are looking for? An object to remind them of home while on vacation and vacation when they are at home."

"That is, uh, beautiful. Can I quote you on that? Put it on the website I have no idea how to create yet."

"Sure can. And adding testimonials to your site is the kind of marketing idea that doesn't come naturally to everyone. If I helped you get set-up, I bet you could go gangbusters. How are your sales here?"

Ugh. This whole conversation had seemed too good to be true. I didn't want to jeopardize where I felt this discussion was headed. But I didn't want to lie to her either.

"Abysmal." It leaked out of my mouth like a green pepper belch before I could sensor it. This is exactly why I wanted an audio do-over option for conversations.

"Oh, slow but steady." Davy jumped in to save me with his industry jargon. I glanced at him appreciatively.

"I'm Beverly. Here's my card. I don't want to get ahead of myself. Why don't you bring a few pieces by next week? We can do a trial period with them in the store, see how they do." She shook my hand. I thought she would walk away once she released my grasp, but instead she used that hand to point at the previously hugged painting that Logan have been mocking only minutes before. "And bring that one." Her voice seemed to echo with those last four words as she walked away, even though I knew that it was impossible to echo outside with no hard surfaces to bounce off of.

"Whoa. You might, like, make money off this now or something," Logan sounded like a stoner.

"No. She probably says that to every vendor here, trying to get more people to visit her shop," I reasoned. I hung my head, settling back into the anxious doubter I felt comfortable being.

"You sure are quiet Mr. Regional Leader in cards and gifts. What do you think about this?"

"I texted Toni. She says we supply them with some items," Davy answered Logan, looking up from his phone.

"What does that tell us?"

"That she has good taste. And they keep their accounts current."

I threw a palette still holding red paint at him. It splattered onto his ugly Hawaiian shirt.

"You know, you would be in big trouble if you weren't so stinkin' cute."

"Michael! Where is Michael!" Logan bellowed to no one in particular, but it made the people passing by look our way out of curiosity.

"No, seriously now," my laughter faded. "What do you think?"

"I think you should go next week and talk to her."

"Maybe you should come with me. You are the expert."

"No way. She might be intimidated by that or think you are trying to pull one over on her. You don't have anything to lose by participating in a trial period with her and you have everything to gain. I assume you know not to pay her to exhibit. It doesn't sound as though it is a consignment situation."

"No, I won't. Thank you." I threw my arms around him and hugged him. I backed up only to find that now my T-shirt had a streak of red paint across it. Davy laughed so hard I thought that he was going to stop breathing.

"You got what you deserved," Logan scolded, looking down his nose at me piously even though he was sitting and I was standing.

"Oh, no you don't."

He made a move to run, but that was his mistake because then I had an open shot at hugging him. The paint streak wasn't as pronounced on him and it was mostly under his arm on the side of his shirt, but he pouted anyway. Davy wheezed. Buddha barked.

EMBRACE

I may actually be on the cusp of embracing my weirdness.

"I used to pray and pray and didn't think God or whatever was listening. But now I think maybe you are the answer to all those prayers."

Logan and I sat next to each other on the couch as rain poured down outside. He was reading a sports magazine while I was sorting my brushes.

"Wait. You think that God sent you a hot, gay man who you have lusted after for years and can never have as an answer to your prayers? I think the crazy church protestors would disagree with you."

"You are the best friend I have ever had, may Lexie rest in peace. I think you may even be better than her in some ways. She tended to be too easy on me, too gentle with her words which I guess woman sort of have to be with each other, otherwise it comes across as catty or bitchy. But you are a guy, so you can tell it like it is, because that is expected of you."

Lexie tried to be a good friend. She was sympathetic, but how much could she truly understand? She had not been popular, but she didn't seem to receive the same pariah status I had been awarded either. Logan shared my outcast experiences, in his own way. It made us feel more kindred. "But it would be nice if you would stop reminding me how unattractive I am. You mention it at least once a day."

"Now, that is not what I said! I said, *I* would never be interested in you. You will do just fine for someone else."

"Gee thanks, I think."

I let my brush handles clank to the bottom of the coffee can before I spoke again.

"Logan, remember how I told you about the dreams I had of a mystery man on a tropical beach? I think maybe that man was you."

"What? That makes no sense. Maybe it was Davy."

"No, that's the thing. There weren't any romantic connotations in the dream. Plus, it was a white guy, not a brown one."

"I thought you couldn't see him."

"I couldn't see the face. I could see arms and stuff. I knew it was a man and not a woman."

"So, you are trying to tell me that the universe, for some unknown reason, fated us to be out here together all along?"

"I do."

"That's fucked up."

"It comforts me."

"How?"

"Otherwise I would keep second-guessing my decision to be here. But if the universe wants it for some reason unknown to me, who am I to argue with the universe?"

"Strange," Logan replied.

"I have come to think if you have to look back on a decision and wonder if it is the right one, it wasn't. Right choices flow into your life so smoothly that you never think twice."

"Once in a while, you actually make sense."

"Why, thank you."

"Ya. I didn't mean this was one of those times," he snickered.

I promptly stuck my tongue out at him.

Logan only laughed in response. He didn't even pretend to be offended. I guess it was good he was so easy-going. If we truly got angry at one another, there was nowhere to escape to.

* * * * *

Logan was packing to head back to Michigan. Trouble was, he had no winter clothes. It was still only fall back there, but he hadn't brought any of them with him. The likelihood that his P.O.'d wife had actually held on to any of them for him seemed implausible.

I felt a combination of sadness to see him go and also a jolt of excitement at living by myself for a week.

"Is it weird, being with Michael? Do you walk down the street holding hands?" I asked.

"Sometimes. I guess it just feels different. Being with him feels completely natural. It felt weird when I was with Veronica. I never minded holding her hand, but any more than that in public was unsettling, like I was playing a part."

"Do you think you will be with Michael for a long time?"

"I just feel safe with Michael. He doesn't expect too much too soon. He knows I am new at all this: living my true self, showing affection in public with a man, wondering what people are thinking. What a date looks like or feels like. What that should be now that I'm out, what it should look like with Michael and I as a couple. I asked him if it's frustrating for him. He admits it is a little. But he told me 'It is better than if you had never came out of the closet and came out here to Oahu, and you were not in my life.' Why would I ever be tempted to leave that and play the field?"

"I can't believe your wife is actually dating her divorce lawyer!"

"I know, right?"

"Do the kids like him?"

"It sounds as though he buys them expensive gifts to bribe them. I don't approve, but whatever gets them through. I know video chats with me aren't filling the hole in their lives that I left," he said. "You know, I heard that he already got her finger sized."

"Wow, he moves fast."

"I think she has figured out not to waste any time before moving on with her life. The divorce really is the best thing for her."

"I'm glad this move was a good one for you, too."

"It has been very good."

"Good. Then I won't worry about dragging you out here."

"You didn't 'drag' me, as I paid for both of our airline tickets."

"I know," I replied.

"But old habits are hard to break?"

"Something like that. More like it is almost impossible to rewire my synapses."

"Stop trying to use big words to sound funnier."

"But it is my trademark, my go-to."

"I know. Covering your insecurities with humor."

"And buying Hello Kitty items."

"What is the deal with that? My wife used to waste money on that crap. Why do all 40-year-old women love a cartoon cat?"

"Hey! I am not forty. Yet. And it makes us feel like little girls: happy. What do you cover yours with?"

"I don't know. Platonic female friendships?"

"Ha-ha. I love you, Logan Courtney. Even if you did turn out to be as gay as the day is long." I was truly happy in that moment. There were no further words to describe it. I continued, "I still blame Veronica for turning you against our entire gender."

"Hey, I told you not to speak badly of her. She is the mother of my children, after all."

"There is still something about that woman I just don't like."

"That she got to screw me for ten years and you didn't?"

"Bingo."

* * * * *

Beverly took five of my works that she liked best. She made a handful of postcards and tote bags with the images. They sold well. We worked it out so that she paid me a commission off each sale of my images, based on the product line. I didn't make much money, but it worked out to be more than I made at the markets, and without the fee for the booth or a large time commitment on my part.

Logan went back to visit his kids for a week. It happened to be the same week that Lexie's birthday occurred. If I had mentioned it to Logan, I am sure he would have rescheduled, fearing for my safety here all alone. But I kept my mouth shut. I was left alone to contemplate: did dead people continue to have birthdays?

I went for a long walk along the shore until I happened upon a large rock in the ocean that spoke to me. I clumsily crawled out onto it using other nearby rocky outcroppings.

I needed to have a heart-to-heart with Lexie's spirit and I need a special, other-worldly place for it to happen. This seemed to fit the bill.

"I know you aren't even around to hear me. You had no unfinished business to keep you behind. But I need to imagine you are not merely getting eaten by worms or busy playing Yahtzee in heaven with George Michael and Prince. I need you to still be with me, still be guiding me. I'm still not strong enough to live life on my own. I may never be." I paused, an image of Logan entering my mind.

"Logan is great, but he can't take your place completely. And even if he could, I wouldn't want him too.

"I-I met a guy. Well, I'm seeing a guy. His name is Davy. He is Hawaiian with skin the color of milk chocolate. It's strange; I've never dated a guy who was a different color than me before. Not that that makes him weird or anything. We both know that I'm the weird one. Always have been, always will be.

"With Logan back in Michigan, it got me thinking about your kids. I miss them, I really do. Oh, but probably not as much as you do. I bet they have grown so much. I sent them some gifts. Not much because I ain't a Rockfeller. I made them each an 8" X 10" canvas for their bedrooms, so that they would get a sense of what I see out my windows every day. I also sent some kitschy souvenirs I thought they would like, including toys and postcards. I hope they enjoy them. I would have loved that as a kid.

"Remember how everyone always knew to bring me back postcards from a vacation? Well, just you. I don't have my collection anymore. It got lost in the eviction. Oh wait, you weren't around for that, were you? I guess you won't be around for anything from now on.

"I'm trying to spend time with the people who I love and who have grown to be my family.

"Logan. I owe him my life. And he is thankful I didn't take his.

"Logan is always telling me I need to grow a thicker skin. I'm not sure that I ever will. But it is comforting to know that he is there for me if I need him. And Davy. Davy, who didn't give me the chance I first wanted, but has given me so many more in the time since. And I have Beverly as a mentor. And my dog Buddha, that I stole form Davy.

"Buddha. Everyone needs some wet dog smell in their life. Unconditional loyalty and a two-year-old who never grows up.

"My life is so full, where once there was only emptiness. I never could have dreamed of a time in my life such as this. I guess I have built a little safety net for myself, should I ever be about to fall again.

"Believe in yourself. Self-confidence. Not in all things, but I gotta start somewhere. I believe my paintings are good. And even if they aren't, I love them too much when they are done to notice. They are each like my babies. Actually, I probably like them better than I would actual children because they can't talk back. Even if people make rude comments, it doesn't defeat me like it would have years ago. Maybe I had to be older to make my best art? Does that make any sense to you? Granted, I'm sure having twenty years more practice could have helped. I missed out on that. I missed out on that joy of making art babies all this time.

"I keep getting up and pushing forward every day, so I guess deep down I must have faith that I won't lose it and kill me or anyone else anytime soon. It has to stay buried deep because if I was conscious of it, I'm positive my anxiety would try to combat it.

"Ha! I'm positive about something for a change. Ah, I'm sure that isn't how you meant for me to use it.

"I can't believe it has been eleven months since I quit Cutter's. You told me I would be alright and I didn't believe you. I reached the lowest point of my life: losing you, planning a massacre, facing jail time, homelessness. And it all turned around somehow, just because I kept going. Even when giving up would have brought me sweet peace and life made my every thought ache. I kept going, somehow. I have to think you had something to do with that Lexie. Your influence all those years we were friends or your spirit reaching out and touching me from the beyond.

"What's crazy is it feels like my dreams pushed me here, as if by some divine force. But why would a divine force set me up to kill people? What if Logan hadn't stood between me and everyone else? It could have been a real bloodbath. I like to think maybe the divine force values my life more than theirs. Isn't that a sweet thought? Or what if my feelings for him had diminished over the years and I had blown him away without hesitation? That seems to be a mighty big gamble for some deity who jacked up my life by making me crazy with bad parents in the first place.

"I finally realized I needed to fight back against all those old feelings and situations, but the action I chose was misdirected and lost. I didn't know the right way to go about it. I had anger, but no goal to strive for. I may have realized that the best revenge is my own successful, happy life. I won't beat them by thinking of them every day, but by never thinking of them at all. That will be the real victory. I could not have had that victory had I killed them. That event would have never left my mind.

"I hope I can avoid being that low ever again. Even if I was, the only place to go seems to be back up.

"Ha. I'm saying that as I sit on the side of a volcano in fuckin' Hawaii. I *never* could have guessed eleven months ago when I quit Cutter's that I would be here right now. Of course, I would trade it all to have you back again. But since that seems impossible, I will enjoy the view from here.

"Can you believe that my painting is more than a hobby? I am trying to make creations that people actually want to buy. Isn't that crazy? Now, when I am not at work, I am painting. Can you believe you can market art? In my spare moments, when I'm at work, I am scribbling sketches of new picture ideas. In the in-between moments, I am trying to come up with new marketing ideas. All my works don't come out good enough to sell, but most do. And those that don't I haven't the heart to discard, so mine and Logan's place is starting to run out of empty wall space. It is driving Logan nuts. But he is off at Michael's a lot, so it is almost as if I have the place to myself. Which, is actually kind of uncomfortable. It makes me think of Michigan. I don't want to get into a situation like I was there ever again. Stuck in a rut, fighting my gut instinct for safety and responsibility, being too far down to pull myself back out. I came out here to find happy. I don't think I'm there yet, but I think I may be getting closer...

"I may have saved the best for last. There is a girl who messaged me. Beverly had had me interviewed for a tiny little local magazine, the kind loaded with advertising that is free at the grocery store. I figured it was a whole lot of nothing, even though it made me feel kind of famous.

"Anyway, this young girl, Sarah, still in high school, said she read my story, where I talked about the bullying I experienced growing up and my recent boughts of anxiety and depression and how I made the big life change of moving out here to pursue my dreams. Sarah then looked up my paintings online. It sounded as if she is struggling with many of the same things I have over the years. Apparently I showed her that her life may be crappy now with school stuff and classmates, but that she could move on from it. She sounded as though she was in a really bad way previously. I sure hope she sticks it out. I asked her what painting on my site she liked best. I sent it to her. I mailed it yesterday, so I anticipate hearing back from her again, hopefully positive things.

"I feel as though there is an aching emptiness in all our hearts. It stays there until we learn how to love ourselves. Some people grow up from a baby with that ability. Others struggle with it all their lives.

"What if everything I have been through, leading me to this moment, was to help Sarah? Just a thought..."

I opened my hand and let the pieces of Lexie's birthday card that I had been clutching be carried off by the wind into the currents.

I would begin looking for next year's card tomorrow.

I'm all alone again.

I'm alone again. But this time it's alright.

If you are having thoughts of harming yourself or others, please call the National Suicide Prevention Lifeline at:

1-800-273-8255

There are people out there who care. The haze around you might make them hard to recognize, but they are there.

JENNIFER FRIESS is an author, blogger, and editor who lives in Lenawee County, Michigan, with her husband, son, and dog. She loves entertainment trivia. She doesn't match her socks. She is a picky eater and likes it that way. Jennifer is the author of The Riley Sisters series, available now in paperback or on your favorite device.

Follow Jennifer here:

BLOG: ImNotStalkingYou.com
My mildly entertaining random thoughts

TWITTER: @jenf2

FACEBOOK: www.facebook.com/imnotstalkingyou2

www.ingramcontent.com/pod-product-compliance
Lightning Source LLC
Chambersburg PA
CBHW020249200626
46816CB00001BA/201